I0778317

THIEVES OF JOY

THIEVES OF JOY

JEN GUBERMAN

UGM Publications

ISBN: 979-8-9851781-0-4

Edited by Amy Guberman, Alexandra Corbett,
Kylie McGee, & Seth Perry
Book Cover by Jen Guberman
Layout by UGM Publications
Author Photo by Alexandra Corbett
First printing edition 2021.

www.UberGuberman.com

For Seth.

"Comparison is the
thief of joy,"

Theodore Roosevelt

"She's up there!" a man with a camera pointed up at the top of a nearby skyscraper, just as a figure in a bright green spandex bodysuit launched itself over the edge.

The man sprinted toward the base of the building, another man with a camera taking off down the street.

Had the second man not bumped into Tallis, he likely wouldn't have noticed the commotion on his walk to work—after all, none of the other passersby seemed concerned.

Tallis watched the man for a second, following his gaze over to the figure in the spandex bodysuit as it was plummeting to the ground.

"What the hell!" Tallis yelled at the man, who was steadying his camera on the airborne figure. The man simply grumbled and shot him a sharp look before quickly returning his attention to his camera.

The figure was getting dangerously close to colliding with asphalt, and Tallis couldn't understand why nobody around him seemed concerned. If anything, most people still didn't seem to notice.

"Somebody help them!" he yelled, pointing at the blur of green.

He stared in horror, his paralyzing dread only beginning to dissipate when the figure's fall gradually slowed until it was at a complete halt, hovering about ten feet off the ground. He ran over just as the first cameraman stood from his post. When he stepped closer to them, he could hear giggling.

"Did you get it?" a woman's voice asked, as the person in the green bodysuit pulled back her face covering to reveal her smiling face. Upon closer inspection, Tallis could see an expensive-looking bottle of perfume attached to her green chest.

"*How?*" Tallis muttered aloud. He kept staring, taking a moment to realize the thin, clear cables keeping the figure suspended safely.

"I think so. We'll have to see how it looks in post, but I think we finally did it this time!"

"Excuse me," Tallis pried, keeping his voice soft.

The cameraman from across the street returned to his buddies, shouting something about a badass lens flare. When he realized Tallis was talking to them, he stopped mid-sentence.

"Sorry for bothering you," Tallis said, "but I was just wondering… you're Creative Anchors… right? What exactly are you guys working on?"

"We're not allowed to disclose that information at the moment," the CA in the bodysuit answered promptly.

"It's okay. I work for Ms. Iris, too. I'll probably be logging data for this footage later in the week anyways. Just wanted to get the inside scoop."

The CAs processed for a moment, clearly not recognizing

him from the office. It didn't really surprise Tallis that they had no clue who he was, after all, he usually stayed hidden behind his computer, just doing data entry.

"It's just a perfume ad for Lorenzi Co." The CA in the bodysuit pointed to the perfume attached to her. "We're trying something new to see if we can make it look like it's falling from heaven."

Tallis's face lit up. He wanted to ask a million more questions, but he bit his tongue. The last thing he wanted was for Ms. Iris to find out he was distracting her precious CAs.

"That's awesome!" Tallis said, nearly vibrating with excitement. "Man, you guys literally have the coolest job. Just saying."

"Hell yeah, we do," she said. "I wanted to be a CA ever since I was little. I can't imagine sitting on my ass all day every day at a desk."

When she looked back over at Tallis, she threw in a quick "no offense."

"None taken," he said. "I better let you guys get back to it. Good luck. Can't wait to see the final ad."

"Thanks, man," one of the cameramen said with a nod, turning his attention to the woman, showing her the camera screen.

Tallis continued on his way, struggling more than usual to stay focused. It wasn't every day he saw someone jump off the side of a building. He was relieved the woman was okay, but he wondered what it would be like to have a job like that—a job that makes you truly feel alive.

His focus kept bouncing between thoughts of his morning and expectations for his day, his mind only silencing when he stopped along his usual route to gaze at a reflection in a puddle. It had just rained the night before, as it often did in the city of Neuvale. While he was on his way to Bru—the local café—the colorful pool caught his attention. A pink neon light reflected in its mirrored surface. Water droplets tumbled from the overhang of a nearby shop, landing in the puddle with little splishes, rippling the reflection into brilliant pink waves.

Something about the reflection of lights on the surface was hypnotic to him. Tallis appreciated everything life had to offer—the natural and the manmade. There was just something extra stunning about the combination of the two.

Tallis stood for a moment longer until the droplets seemed to stop, pulling him from his trance. He looked up at the source of the light—a simple sign for a tech repair shop called Buzz's Electrosuite. Reminding himself of the task at hand, his attention snapped back into focus and he hurried on his way.

The pat-pat of his flat soles grew louder in his ears with every step as he began to walk to the beat of a song in his head. Eventually, the concrete sidewalk turned to steppingstones in soft grass as he neared the entrance of Bru.

Contrasting sharply with the glass, neon lights, and cement of the city, the café was an unremarkable building of stone and wood.

As he tugged on the solid wood door, a wave of warm coffee-scented air hit him like heat from an open oven. He got in line behind some strangers in a short line to place his order.

"Next!"

A few steps forward.

Outside, the sun was beginning to rise, but inside, you could never quite tell what time it was. The coffee shop's thick, amber-tinted windows reminded Tallis of honey. As he stared at the long menu, he wondered how honey would taste in coffee.

"Next!"

Of course, Tallis already knew what he was going to order. Ms. Iris always ordered the same thing. He knew better than to forget her order.

"Next!"

Tallis shuffled forward in line. He looked over toward a small table with the milk, sugar, and straws, watching as a man in a wool coat poured a little purple vial into his coffee, giving it a stir.

"Next!"

A petite blonde woman ordered some soy-mocha-mega-something.

He reached into his pocket to fish out his card in advance. He hated holding up lines. Pulling his hand back out, he felt a hangnail tug. He held his finger up in the dim light to get a better look. Picking at the tiny piece of skin, a shudder rippled over him as he imagined how horrific it would be if he pulled a hangnail and it just kept going, unraveling him like a fleshy mummy.

"Sir!" a woman behind the counter crowed.

Tallis peered past his finger at her.

People were glaring at him, looks of dismay and disgust painted on their faces. When he realized which finger was up, he shot his hand down into his pocket, as if the finger's itself was embarrassed for him.

"Whaddya want?" she asked, eyebrow cocked.

"Medium iced coffee. Two pumps of lavender with a splash of cream," Tallis said, almost robotically.

She huffed, turning her attention to the register.

"Please," Tallis added.

The barista rang up his order and shooed him aside from where he stood, hands in his pockets. Several of the tables in Bru were low to the ground with cushions on the floor as seats. A group of students sat clustered around a corner table. Several of the students were leaning over the tables while they talked, and everyone seemed to be chattering at once. Tallis began to wonder how many people there were in the world. He realized how each person out there was uniquely different, each one made up of thousands of little life moments—no two the same. He wondered what variable made some people cling together while rejecting others. In fact, it must have been a miracle that everything in the universe lined up for these students to have even met each other.

While Tallis wondered about the students, the barista was shouting his order, glaring directly at Tallis in his daze.

"Sir, I think that's your drink," a young woman said, tapping his shoulder.

Tallis turned to the woman and back to the counter with a clumsy smile, picking up his order from the counter before making his way to work.

Opulence Incorporated was one of the largest industries in Neuvale. Every successful news piece, advertisement, or song to hit the public came through Opulence first. Tallis saw the company as a complicated circuit board. Each component had an important role, even if some of those roles may not seem as exciting. At least, that's what he told himself.

Junior Assistant. Tallis thought his title seemed rather vague, but he appreciated the amount of variety in his day-to-day routine. Sometimes, Ms. Iris would have him clean the breakroom, and other times, she'd have him watch commercials and take notes about the footage for the company's historical log. More often than not, she made him compile information into the databases for the CAs. He loved seeing what the CAs were up to—those were his favorite days. The only thing he could think of that could be better would be living life as a CA himself.

Tallis held his palm to the security scanner outside the towering office building shaped like a huge glass shard. The scanner hummed and let out a sharp chirp as a digital image of Tallis looked back at him. Dark lashes surrounded the grey eyes that stared blankly on the screen as the door slid open, welcoming him with stale air that smelled of pleather and perfumes.

On the fourth floor, Tallis scurried to his supervisor's office with her coffee.

"Ma'am," Tallis said as soon as he stepped into the room. "I was thinking… I'd like to talk to you about applying for that open Creative Anchor position."

His boss held out her hand for the coffee, not even looking up from her computer as she stood. Tallis handed her the cup. She removed the lid and took a swig, letting coffee tumble from her open mouth down her double chin and back into the cup almost as soon as it touched her tongue. "Pebbermint?" her voice garbled through the liquid.

"Ma'am?" Tallis asked.

Ms. Iris held out her cup, the lip of it tickling Tallis's nose. Tallis stared back over the cup at her, eyebrow cocked.

"Sniff," she said.

An awkward pause, then an audible sniff.

"I'm sorry," Tallis said. "I can run and get a new one."

"You've already wasted enough time. You were late today; did you know that?"

Tallis looked at his watch. 7:03.

"Of course you didn't."

"Three min—"

"Jorden's people turned in another batch of holos. I need you to process the paperwork for me."

Tallis opened his mouth to speak but was met with Ms. Iris's hand as she hushed him, waddling around him in her stubby patent leather heels and out the door into the communal office space.

"Yes, ma'am," he muttered, taking a purposeful inhale through his nose. A cool exhale. He turned and scooped up the weighty folder on Ms. Iris's desk, making his way to his workstation.

Tallis rationalized that perhaps she's had a rough morning. She always looked forward to her coffee, and for all he knew, she might have been having the kind of morning where everything seemed to go wrong. To him, it wasn't her fault.

Tallis's cubicle was as antiquated as they came. Opulence loved to provide employees with the latest and greatest, but why would the Junior Assistant need a chroma screen, right? Instead, Tallis sat around waiting for his desktop to wake with a hum. His desk phone was practically an ancient relic, with its raised plastic buttons and its spiraled cord. "You don't get phone calls," Ms. Iris had said when he asked for a cheap earpiece instead.

Tallis explained away the issue, assuming perhaps the department just didn't have the budget for it at the moment.

Even though Tallis had to be at work before everyone else in order to get Ms. Iris her coffee on time, he didn't mind the quiet time at the beginning of his day. Because her office was far away on the other side of his department, he felt like he had the entire area to himself. Technically, many of the desks in the area belonged to the CAs, but they rarely— if ever—did desk work. So, like most days, the office was rather lifeless.

Thumbing through the pages while he waited for his computer to boot up, Tallis reached for the day-old cup of water on his desk, taking a sip and accidentally swallowing a gnat.

His desk phone started ringing like a shrill alarm, breaking the silence of the empty office.

Tallis picked up the phone and hit the speaker button before setting the phone back on the receiver and leaning back in his chair.

"Hey, Big Daddy," a deep, velvet voice oozed over the speaker. "You looking for some fun?"

Tallis went cold and nearly flew from his seat as he turned the speaker off and snatched the phone up.

"Wrong number," Tallis said, projecting his voice in case Ms. Iris could hear the call from her office.

"Dude," the voice over the phone dropped several octaves. "It's just Chris."

"Why'd you call my work phone?"

"You don't usually check your personal at work. I know

better than that. Anyways, I'm thinking about doing Xavier's bachelor party this Friday. You down?"

"Sure," Tallis said, keeping his voice low. "You decide where to host it yet?"

"Yup!"

"Where?"

"We'll pick you up. Just be downstairs and ready to go at nine."

"Alright."

"And bring something kinky," Chris said, as if it were a common request.

"What?"

"A sex toy, Tal, bring something for sex."

"What the hell kind of party do you have planned?"

"A *bachelor* party. We're not going for teatime and a ballet."

"Is it like… a present?" Tallis managed.

"No, I thought we'd all go back to my place and—YES, you dipshit. It's for Xavier and Vanessa. Get 'em something fun. Not that complicated, bro. Just be ready by nine. B—"

"Wait," Tallis stopped him. "What do I wear?"

The workday went as Tallis expected. He made his way through the folder of papers from Ms. Iris, he spent a while reading through new articles from Opulence News, and he watched and sorted footage from the Creative Anchors. While he was going through footage, he saw a piece from one of the CAs for a new music video. The singers were on top of one of the thousands of skyscrapers in Neuvale, and the camera hovered over them, drifting up and away through the course of the video until the band looked like nothing but a small cluster of pixels on Tallis's monitor.

"Go home," Ms. Iris said, flopping her coat over her arm and locking up her office door. "Everyone else is gone, and I'm not paying you overtime."

"Yes, ma'am," he said, closing out of the video and shutting down his computer.

Ms. Iris was halfway down the hall when Tallis scurried after her clumsily. He marveled at how fast she booked it down the hall. The fact that she walked at all was a miracle with how pigeon toed she stood in heels.

"I'm sorry again about your coffee this morning," Tallis said, his toe catching on the carpet, causing him to lurch, tripping and catching himself before falling.

"It's fine," Ms. Iris said flatly, reaching the end of the hall and summoning the elevator. "It was admittedly nice to break out of routine. The lavender gets a little old. I just think peppermint tastes like I'm drinking toothpaste. Get me a caramel latte tomorrow."

"Of course," he said as the elevator doors encapsulated them in the moving glass pod.

Outside the doors of Opulence, Ms. Iris and Tallis parted ways without a word. Ms. Iris lived in a nearby complex, so she was able to return to work at a moment's notice. Tallis, on the other hand, lived in Sector 8, but Opulence was in Sector 12. Walking four sectors back and forth every day would take far too long, especially with how crowded the walkways in the city got. Fortunately, each sector of Neuvale had its own subway terminal, and Opulence paid for Tallis's subway pass. He almost never took one of the overpriced taxis, and he felt like it was unnecessary to spend money on a car when the subway was never far—and always free.

Just like every other day, Tallis took the lower walkway from Opulence to the Sector 12 terminal—about a 10-minute walk for a normal person, at least 15 minutes for someone like Tallis.

Along the way, he brushed shoulders with endless strangers. He could have noticed the striking facial tattoo of the gentleman who bumped into him, or perhaps the woman who looked him up and down hungrily with her brown baby doll eyes. Instead, Tallis was standing curbside, watching a particularly mangey pigeon picking at a smooshed french fry. A nearby crow fixated its beady eyes on the starchy mess. It swooped down, snatching the fry in its beak and disappearing, leaving the daft pigeon confused.

He trotted down the slick tile steps of the station, the echoic rumbles of the subway drowning out the sounds of the people and digital advertisements around him. A holographic advertisement for hotdogs and grilled brats flickered and rotated in place across from the bathrooms. Mindlessly, he stepped through the lights of the hologram on his way toward the approaching subway.

The ride to Sector 8 was packed. Tallis stood with bodies plastered to every bit of him. Gripping the handhold hanging from the ceiling, he watched the blurred stonework and zipping lights pass through the windows of the racing subway. With each stop, a hoard of people would scramble off, only to be replaced by another. When the screen above the sliding doors displayed a vivid "8," Tallis wormed his way through the masses, wiggling until he got off the subway and could make his way out of the station and aboveground.

As he walked toward the entrance of his apartment building, Tallis was busy daydreaming about what it would be like to put wheels on a subway and drive it around like a streetcar. He smiled to himself as he imagined the ridiculousness, but his glee dissipated as soon as he heard his phone chime. He rotated his wrist, checking the message on his watch.

He realized he forgot to get Xavier's gift, even though he was hoping to do it today while he was in Sector 12. Tomorrow would have to be the day. He wasn't even sure what kind of thing to look for, but he knew there was an adult store a couple blocks away from Opulence. He'd seen it on his way to the cleaner to pick up Ms. Iris's clothes once.

In his apartment, Tallis took off his shoes and dropped them near his front door. His TV chirped a catchy tune as it turned on and immediately pulled up his favorite show, which he disregarded on his way to the bathroom. He ran the sink for a moment so it could warm up before running his hands under the water and then his wet hands over his face. He looked up at the vanity, the dark circles under his eyes slightly masked by his faint freckles coating his entire face. Hands still wet, he ran his fingers through his dark hair, a section of longer hair that hung in his face moments ago now slicked back.

Tallis grabbed a slice of leftover pizza from his fridge and flopped back on his cushy black sofa. His mind began to wander to all the possibilities for the weekend and where Chris might be hosting the bachelor party. This string of thoughts eventually brought him back to his upcoming task: find a present for Xavier.

Tallis wondered what kind of things adult stores even sold. He didn't want to buy lingerie for his best friend's fiancée— something about that felt strange to him. He didn't even know what size Vanessa was, and he didn't want to get in trouble for misjudging.

Tallis tapped the screen of his watch. "I wanna shop," he announced. His TV changed the display from his favorite show to the shopping menu.

"What are you shopping for?" a soft, feminine voice asked through the speakers.

"Umm," Tallis hesitated. "Sex toys."

The screen changed again, this time displaying a screen with a list of products. He sat, skimming through the list of categories and filters, not even knowing where to start. He thought it was an odd request for presents, but he didn't want to be the only one at the party who didn't follow instructions.

"Can I help you?" The shopping assistant bot appeared on the screen.

"Yes," Tallis said, prompting the bot.

"How can I help?"

"What's a penis ring?"

The next morning, Tallis got Ms. Iris her caramel latte and made sure it smelled like caramel before he left Bru. When he got to the office, Ms. Iris tasted the coffee, keeping her eyes locked on Tallis while she processed. She gave him a nod of thanks that was so subtle it could have been mistaken for a twitch had Tallis not known her better.

A couple hours into his day, some of the CAs barged into the office, their bellowing laughs and energetic banter ripping Tallis from his spreadsheets. Their entire presence was absolutely intoxicating. They could strike up a conversation with anyone, and they oozed confidence. Even the way they walked seemed superhuman to Tallis, strutting with their shoulders back and heads held high, as if all the cares of the world were beneath them.

Tallis's desk was near a lounge room that typically remained empty, except when the CAs were in the office. The group—four of them, this time—sat around the table in the lounge room, leaning back in their plush chairs like a group of college kids in a dorm room.

"Did you see that shot Lexi got yesterday?" Tallis heard one of the CAs ask.

Tallis had seen the shot. After all, he had to process the paperwork for the ad. He was a big fan of Lexi's photography style. She seemed to have a way of capturing deeper meaning in her pictures, even when it was just for a simple product advertisement. In that particular low angle shot, she captured some puffy white clouds in the sky above the model. When Tallis first saw it, he found himself down a rabbit hole of researching the symbolism behind clouds. According to one article he read, they can be symbolic of secrets, and he loved the idea of making the viewer feel like buying the product would reveal some sort of elite secret. It gave a sense of exclusivity and luxury. Of course, he had no way of knowing for sure if that was Lexi's intention at all, but it certainly made *him* want to buy the shoes from the ad.

"My picture beats the hell out of yours, Marcus!" Lexi bit back.

"Not true! No offense, Lexi, but your shot was way overexposed. You completely missed out on making that model look like the badass he is. You turned it all light and airy!"

"That's my style though! Talk to me when you've learned the basics of photography." Lexi let out a dainty giggle.

"Lexi, you know I'm all for your dreamy aesthetic in your pics, truly, but how is that supposed to go with the ad? It's for glowing shoes, and you can't see… ya know… the *glow*! Because everything in the picture is too bright," the fourth said.

"I'll be the judge of that," Ms. Iris said, joining the crew in the lounge room. Her typically rigid posture melted into some sort of awkward slump, as if she felt it would make her seem "hip," when in reality it just made her look as if she had a bad hip.

One of the CAs tapped their watch, casting Lexi's pictures on the screen. They were stunning. Tallis wondered how they could even capture a picture like that. He knew photo editing programs were common at Opulence, but he couldn't get over how much it looked like the model was actually hovering over the ground, ascending into the clouds.

Ms. Iris spotted him gawking and shut the door, the glass walls frosting over with the privacy shield.

Tallis felt embarrassed but redirected his thoughts back to his spreadsheets. He had to process the paperwork for the same ad campaign the CAs were working on. They often went on adventures across the city—capturing and creating everything beautiful from videos, to photos, to stories and more—all while Tallis experienced nothing but blips of it through his paperwork. Whenever he felt envy creeping in, he'd remind himself that someone has to do his job. If it weren't for him, no one would get to see the things the CAs do.

The CAs and Ms. Iris were in their meeting through most of the morning. Tallis was waiting on Ms. Iris to approve some of the documents he had to submit, but since it was getting late in the afternoon, Tallis decided to take his lunch break and leave the documents on her desk instead.

He took a sandwich he had packed the night before and made his way to the elevator. Once outside, he tried to remember how to get to the adult store. He knew it was somewhere along the way to the dry cleaner, so he just pretended he was on his way to deliver Ms. Iris's clothes.

Sector 12 was the main business and shopping hub of Neuvale. There were 15 sectors, and the higher the number, the more expensive and fancy the district. Even though Tallis had lived in Sector 8 most of his life, he had always been especially enamored by the energy in Sector 12. The streets were packed with glass—skyscrapers, advertisements on glassy screens, even the upper walkways that bridged between the buildings were black glass.

Usually, Tallis would stay on the sidewalks at the base of the buildings. He rarely had a reason to go anywhere but the subway and the office. On the rare occasion that Ms. Iris sent him on a task outside the confines of the office, he'd take the upper walkways. These were simply pedestrian bridges connecting shops and businesses located a few stories up. There were glass elevator pods throughout the streets to take you up to the walkways, and they were easy to spot, with their orange neon halos.

Tallis trotted over to the nearest elevator, stepping aside to let a few people out of the pod before cramming himself in with the other four people waiting. It zipped upward toward the first landing. Every four floors had another walkway, crisscrossing over the city street below. Once the pod stopped and the doors opened, Tallis continued on his way, but at a notably slower pace—he couldn't help himself. He could see so many people and so much life buzzing above and below. The first walkway—the one he was on—stood at the fourth floor of the surrounding buildings. He looked down over the railing to observe for a moment. The people below rushed around, but it all looked so fluid, like bees in a hive. He checked his watch, realizing he needed to pick up the pace in order to make it back to his desk on time.

He could see the dry cleaners up ahead, with their animated neon sign depicting floating bubbles. Just a couple storefronts ahead of it, he could see the adult store, with its far less innocent neon display—handcuffs and a winking woman.

For a moment, Tallis stood outside the store, wondering why they call it an adult store instead of a sex toy store when most of the time, stores are named after the things you buy inside. By his logic, grocery stores, jewelry stores, and office supply stores should all be considered adult stores too.

Tallis stopped stalling and tried to shake off the awkward feeling creeping through his mind like it was a coat he could shed. He reached for the door, pushing it in and felt a rush of fragrance and warm air. A bass-heavy song with a steady beat pulsed through the black walls. It wasn't the display of electronic toys that caught Tallis's attention so much as the expressionless mannequins in bondage suits, masks, and chains seated on swings hanging below the high mirrored ceiling.

Picking at his nails uncomfortably, he pressed further into the expansive store. An employee picked up on his obvious cluelessness and strutted over to him.

"Can I help ya, honey?" she asked, pulling Tallis from his thoughts.

"I—" he couldn't help but notice she was practically spilling from her corset. He forced his eyes back up to meet hers. "I'm looking for a friend."

"Well…" She giggled. "I mean, you can certainly meet all kinds of *friends* here." She smiled sweetly, biting her lip.

"No, not that," he said. "Sorry. I meant… I'm looking for a present for a friend. He's getting married, and the best man wants us all getting him… sex stuff. For the bachelor party."

"How fun!"

"Yeah."

"Do you know what your friend is into?"

"We don't really talk about that, no."

"No worries. Let me show you some of our most popular products and see what you think," she beckoned with a finger for him to follow.

Tallis followed her through tight shelving full of explicit images on boxes.

"These are really popular!" the lady chimed, thrusting a small package toward Tallis.

He turned it over in his hands, looking over a picture of a strand of different sized beads.

"What are you supposed to do with these?" he asked, just before reading the title of the product. "Oh. Never mind."

"How about something like this?" she asked, holding out a fleshy dildo and wiggling it with a peppy smile.

"I think he's got a real one of those."

She put it back on the shelf and held up a finger for Tallis to wait one moment while she scurried off to another shelf. Tallis let his eyes wander across the rows and rows of products. Sex seemed pretty straight forward; he wondered why there were so many different toys.

She returned with black fuzzy handcuffs, dangling them in front of her.

"How about these?"

"Perfect," Tallis said plainly, checking his watch.

"I'll check you out," she said, carrying the cuffs toward the register. "Will this be all for you today?"

"Yes ma'am." He held out his card to pay.

Her scanner beeped and she put the furry cuffs in a little black bag.

"Actually," he said, as he was about to reach for the bag, "do you have any penis rings?"

Back at the office, Ms. Iris was still in the conference room with the CAs until it was almost time to leave. Tallis didn't mind his job, but it wasn't as exciting as that of a CA. Even for someone who can find the beauty and joy in anything, Tallis still watched the clock at the end of every Friday. He never even did anything out of the ordinary on weekends. He was just grateful for some variety.

When the end of the day hit, Tallis was just beginning to shut off his computer and grab his belongings as Ms. Iris scuttled out of the conference room and toward her office. The CAs laughed and chatted like a bunch of friends kicked out of the bar at the end of the night as they exited the office.

Tallis was a few paces behind them, headed toward the elevator when Ms. Iris flagged him down.

"Tallis," she nearly growled at him before he stopped in his tracks, his heart beginning to flutter sickeningly.

"Yes, Ms. Iris?"

"You're not cut out for life as a CA," she said bluntly, squinting at him as if he asked a confusing question. "I know that sounds harsh, but someone needed to tell you."

Tallis was speechless.

"Besides, what talent do you think you'd bring to the team?" she asked.

"I..." his armpits were soaked already. " I take pictures."

"You 'take pictures?'"

"Yes, ma'am."

"Would you call yourself a photographer?"

"I mean—"

"If you wouldn't consider yourself a photographer, you're not talented enough, quite frankly."

"I also write," he defended softly.

"But are you a writer?"

He hesitated.

"You're not the right fit for the position, Tallis."

"Yes, ma'am. I'm sorry."

"Do you know what you're even apologizing for?"

"Umm…"

"You were being nosey and not focusing on work—" she began to lecture, but Tallis unintentionally tuned her out as he noticed the empty elevator pod sitting down the hall. He just wanted to leave.

"I'm sorry," he said again.

"Boy, I'm gonna need you to stop mindlessly apologizing! You screw up, yes. You're not focusing on *your* job. You're good at what you do, Tallis. I'm glad I have your help in the office, I hope you know that—"

"—I do."

"But you're just not cut out to be a CA." The second time stung just as much as the first, as if it confirmed he indeed heard her correctly. "You have to be interesting. That's all it boils down to. An eye for what will wow the public and the ability to capture that. Each of our CAs is uniquely captivating and fascinating. Quite simply, dear, you're boring."

Tallis forced down the lead lump in his throat, staring straight ahead at the elevator pod. He clenched his teeth and nodded.

"Dear, I don't mean that in a bad way. None of them would be able to do the things you do. And as I've told you before—the public would never even see their work if it weren't for the work you do! You're just as important as they are. Just promise me you'll stop daydreaming every time they come into the office."

Tallis's jaw shifted side to side as he forced himself to look at her. "Yes… ma'am."

"Come on," she said, her tone softening. "Let's get out of here."

They walked together to the elevator, but at this point, Tallis was moving almost twice as fast as her until he tripped on the same spot on the floor as the day before, sending his black shopping bag out of his hand as he tried to catch himself. The furry handcuffs and penis ring skidded across the floor, and Ms. Iris's eyes followed them like magnets. She took a few steps forward and collected the toys before Tallis could swipe them up. She held them in her hand as her focused expression melted into an amused grin.

"Maybe you're more interesting than I thought," she said with a chuckle, dropping the toys in the black bag as Tallis held it out like a trick-or-treater.

Tallis grumbled, his heart sinking as he felt his face grow hot.

Without another word, the two stepped into the elevator, never meeting eyes. As always, they parted ways outside the building and Tallis made his way to the subway. This time, Tallis was so absorbed in his own thoughts that he only stopped to watch the pigeons once, and he only lost a few minutes to an intriguing reflection in a window.

By the time he arrived at his station, he had already created a list of four possible places the bachelor party could be, and none of them were likely to be accurate. He never really went out on the town, aside from the occasional late-night restaurant or bar visit. He knew there was an adults-only arcade in Sector 10, but that was unlikely.

After a lengthy nap at home, Tallis realized it was dangerously close to nine o'clock, and Chris would be there to pick him up in a little while. He took a quick shower, threw some gel in his hair, and moseyed into his bedroom in his towel.

He debated calling Chris to ask about the dress code again. Chris gave him a wishy-washy answer the last time, and Tallis didn't want to show up over or underdressed. He decided against calling, not wanting to sound needy.

He walked over to his closet, tapping the tablet hanging next to the door. The screen illuminated with a 3D image of Tallis in nothing but boxer briefs. He tapped the small button labeled "pants" and scrolled through the options, settling on a pair of slim fitting black slacks. The slacks appeared over his image on the screen. Next, he browsed the shirts.

He tapped a burgundy shirt with black trim, and it materialized on his 3D figure. Using his finger, he moved his figure around on the screen to check out all angles of his outfit. Satisfied, he hit the check mark in the corner of the screen.

Please wait appeared on the screen as he heard the soft whirring of his closet. After he heard the click, he opened his closet doors, revealing a shallow space with his pants and shirt neatly hung before him.

Tallis got dressed and inhaled a cold slice of pizza on his way out the door at precisely 8:58pm. He stepped out the doors of his apartment building just as a limo rolled up. Lounging halfway out the back window, Chris met Tallis's stunned reaction with a jack-o-lantern grin.

"You got a limo?" Tallis asked, processing the sleek black vehicle with its blue under lights.

"No, I got a horse-drawn carriage," Chris said as the limo slowed and stopped, the driver getting out and walking around to the back door.

As the driver opened the door, music poured out and darkness gave way to neon lights, leather seats, and a lit display of mini liquor bottles.

Tallis stood there, entranced by the crystalline reflections on the spotless black finish.

"Get in!" Xavier called from within.

Tallis wedged himself through the door, expecting a cramped back seat, only to find the back of the limo far more spacious than he imagined. Five other guys sprawled out across the seats, each with a drink in hand. Before he could get comfortable, Chris shoved a crystal shot glass in his hand and filled it.

"Thanks," Tallis said uneasily, sloshing part of his shot as the limo lurched, taking off down the road.

He tossed back the rest of the shot before he could spill more. Chris hardly waited for him to bring the glass from his lips before he filled it again.

"Hey, man! Glad you could make it!" Xavier's warm voice called from across the limo.

Xavier's brilliant white teeth gleamed. His pompadour gelled precisely without a single hair out of place—even if there had been, Xavier would have sooner plucked the hair entirely than let it be singled out.

"You guys are gonna love this place," Chris said, holding up his drink before gulping it. "Come on, Xav, get one last look at freedom!"

Chris opened the large sunroof, and the men in the limo began whooping like fools for Xavier, who passed off his drink to a friend as he worked his way forward through the back of the limo. He stood, sticking out the top of the sunroof from the torso up. Chris cranked up the music, and the energy of the group seemed to buzz violently with each bass note. A few moments later, Xavier sunk down into the rest of the party and Chris pushed his way toward the new opening.

Even through the loud music, Chris's muffled cheers could be heard by the entire group, who followed him with even more celebratory sounds. When he pulled back down, he called to Tallis.

"Dude! You next!"

"Sweet," Tallis said, bumping Chris's fist as he wiggled his way over. He stood, lifting his top half through the sunroof.

Cool night air whipped around him, knocking the breath from his lungs for a moment as he adjusted. The sky was black, but the city painted it in every color. Vibrant digital signs flickered past him in a glowing blur. Artistic lighting on buildings filled the background while holographic ads seemed to zoom past the limo. Tallis was particularly dazed by the lights, each reflecting off the glossy top of the limo, racing by like colorful lines and squiggles. It was as if the world around him was pure electricity.

He felt a tug at the back of his shirt, so he tucked back into the limo.

"Time's up, Jeff's turn," Chris said.

Tallis nodded, taking his seat and pouring another shot.

After a while, the limo began to slow until it stopped entirely. The men all squirmed in their seats, knowing their curiosity was finally about to be satisfied—where was Chris taking them?

The driver opened the back door, standing aside and motioning for the guys to exit. Chris fell over several of the other men trying to be the first out the door.

"I wanna see your reaction!" he said as he stumbled out and brushed off his slacks. "This is my little brother's bachelor party and I'm sentimental—don't laugh at me!"

Xavier stepped out, followed by several of the others before Tallis. As Tallis stepped out, he realized he didn't recognize anything. A nearby streetlamp with a simple sign indicated this was Sector 3. He looked up and down the street, which was comparably darker than the sectors he was familiar with. The buildings were brick instead of glass and metal, and the signs and lights were mostly all red and pink, instead of the vibrant rainbow of the other sectors.

"Dude, where'd you take us?" Tallis called up to Chris as he continued looking down the street, spotting a few people in hoodies sitting beside piles of garbage in front of a boarded-up business.

"Stop paying attention to that stuff," one of the guys

said, drawing Tallis's eyes forward, where the guys were disappearing into a huge display.

The front of their building had a black curtain instead of a door. On both sides of the curtain, there were huge domes protruding from the sides of the walls. One bubble was glowing pink, the other teal, but they both were full of live, vibrant tropical fish.

At first, Tallis thought perhaps this was an aquarium. That is, until he saw the hologram. Directly beside the entrance was a hologram of a woman in a skimpy black bodysuit. She struck a suggestive pose before putting her finger to her lips in a sly hush, the hologram disk below her sending up smoke as she faded, only for her to return and repeat the same motions a moment later.

Tallis looked up toward the top of the building, which flaunted a grand marquee sign: *Illusion*.

"Dude!" Xavier poked his head through the curtain. "Come on! We're waiting on you."

Tallis followed him through the curtain and the heaviness of intoxicating perfume filled him. The first illusion of Illusion was simply the size of the space. Outside, the building seemed like it would hardly be larger than a sit-down restaurant. Once inside, the tall ceilings were already enough to make one feel as if they'd been transported somewhere else.

Xavier worked his way through the crowd, which Tallis nearly got lost in while taking in the sights. Spread throughout the room were catwalks surrounded by booths. The walls of the building were all covered with TV panels that turned the walls into one continuous screen portraying dancing women. Below the panels along all the walls was the longest bar counter Tallis had ever seen.

He wondered why they weren't getting drinks, but he continued to follow Xavier forward, toward a huge fish tank in the center of the club. There was a staircase along the edge of the tank, which Xavier climbed, two steps at a time. Tallis followed, growing even more confused. As he reached the top, he realized the fish tank was simply the base for an entirely separate platform with its own catwalk and private tables surrounding it, each with high-backed booth seating. Xavier's party sat at the table right near the end of the catwalk stage.

Xavier's friends all urged him over, eyes and smiles wide.

"It's about to start!" Chris said, sliding over and making room for Xavier and Tallis, who ended up with half a buttcheek hanging over the edge of the packed pleather seat.

Tallis scanned the faces of each guy in the group, trying to figure out what was about to start when suddenly, the music in the club faded and people grew quiet. Everything was already dark to begin with, but it was as if all the neon lights in the club were dimmed, even the individual lights at each of the VIP tables.

A couple spotlights flipped on, focused on the catwalk. A thumping beat rumbled low in the ground, vibrating through the seats as it floated upward, filling the room in rhythmic music. A woman's voice thanked everyone for being there tonight.

"Let's go ahead and get the show started!" she shouted, followed by the cheers of everyone on the platform above the fish tank. "First up is Misti!"

A woman with dramatic curves and slick black hair down to her waist strutted out in a skimpy bodysuit and dangerous heels. As she strutted across the stage, nearing their table, a shiny metal pole rose from a hole in the stage floor. Misti grabbed the pole and gave a few graceful spins, her hair whipping behind her, mesmerizing Tallis.

According to the MC, Misti loved adventure, fast cars, and milkshakes. With every move she made, golden coins flashed across a screen at the back of the stage, displaying a growing number. The guys at Tallis's table tapped on their watches as they watched.

"What are you doing?" Tallis finally asked Xavier.

"Cheering her on," Chris interjected for Xavier. "You can download the app and just tap the coin to tip the dancer. Do you have your DigitPay account set up yet?"

"My what?"

"DigitPay, bro!" Xavier chimed. "We've been over this! Cards are gonna be obsolete in another year or two. Stop using that thing and set your account up so you can pay with your watch. I didn't get you that thing just to wear as a piece of jewelry! You could be using it for so many things!"

Tallis reluctantly set up his DigitPay account on his watch, which only took a moment. When he was done, he looked at Xavier again. "Now what?"

"See that?" He pointed at the number on the stage screen. "That's how much she's raised in tip money. The girl who makes the most by the end of the show has to do another dance. Download the Illusion Club app and just tap the coin however many times you want, whenever you want. It goes to whichever girl is on stage."

Satisfied with the answer, Tallis turned as Misti was making her exit.

"Let's give a warm welcome to Cherry!"

Again, the crowd cheered. This time, a petite redhead waltzed out. Her features looked surgically enhanced and clearly not proportionate for her body, as her dense curls weren't the only thing bouncing.

"Dude! Download the app already!" one of the guys in the group nudged Tallis.

Tallis pretended not to hear him as he kept watching the show.

Cherry did a few moves, shaking every part of her that could possibly jiggle or bounce before walking, one foot in front of the other, toward the back of the stage, giving a twirl, blowing a kiss, and stepping backstage.

A couple more girls gave their performances and the group of men kept tapping on their watches, sometimes more than others if they found a girl that struck their fancy—but none of them seemed overly picky. At some point during the show, a waitress dropped off a huge platter of wings, cheese sticks, and pretzels, with enough beer for each man to have his fill.

As the next girl exited the stage, the song changed over to another fun beat. There was a pause, and the MC spoke up again.

"Last but not least, give it up for Big O!"

A young woman with porcelain skin, bold brows, and big blue eyes stepped onto the stage. Her ash hair framed her face, which was alight with a bright smile—the first Tallis had seen the entire show.

She practically skipped to the pole, the silver tassels garnishing her bodysuit bouncing with every step and catching the light. When she reached the end of the stage, she bit her bottom lip and smiled again, reaching far up on the pole and throwing her weight, spinning and moving her legs every which way. She let out a warm giggle and Tallis felt his entire body grow warm.

He poked around at his watch frantically, throwing his gaze back up to Big O every few seconds, afraid he'd miss her.

"You good, man?" Xavier asked.

"How do I get that app?"

"Here," he said, reaching over and pressing around on Tallis's watch. When the coin symbol popped up, Tallis tapped on it as if he had to make up for not tipping any of the other girls.

Big O did a slow strut around the pole, and Tallis couldn't help but notice her intricate back tattoo of ivy and flowers. While the other guys hooted and hollered at her as she dropped into a low squat, knees wide, Tallis watched and wondered if there was any meaning behind her tattoo choice.

The number on the screen kept increasing with every tap until she reached the back of the stage, gave a little "bye-bye" wave and disappeared behind the curtain.

"How do we know who's winning?" Tallis asked no one in particular.

"They'll announce it in a minute," one of the guys answered, munching mindlessly on a cheese stick.

After a few agonizing moments of anticipation, the MC called all the girls back onto the stage.

"Let's see which one of our lovely ladies was most popular with the crowd tonight! As you all know, the winner has to give a special show to thank everyone for their help. Not only that, but a little birdy told me we're celebrating a special someone today!"

Some of the guys started elbowing Xavier, and a bashful grin crept across his face.

"Someone here is getting married!" the MC let the last syllable ring out in a sing-songy voice. The dancers clapped and smiled for Xavier as the MC announced him by name.

"I bet Misti's the winner," one of the guys at the table said to another as the MC redirected everyone's attention to the women on stage. "There's a reason she's been doing this so long. She's damn good at what she does."

"The results are in…" the MC said, leaving a pause. "Let's give it up for Amber!"

All the dancers except one with thick golden curls and legs like towers left the stage. Amber proceeded with her dance, and Tallis felt the foreign warmth melt from his body as he turned his attention to his beer and a pretzel.

The pretzel tasted like freezer burn, and at this point, the dip had a layer of cold cheese skin on top. Tallis mindlessly munched on his gourmet dinner while his friends gawked at Amber, who was making her way to their table. When she reached the end of the platform, she took a step down, wobbling in her heels until she balanced herself and smiled like that was her biggest accomplishment.

"Who's the lucky man?" Amber asked, her voice nasally.

Xavier's face reddened as he winked at Amber.

"Come on over!" she said, beckoning him after her as she strutted to a lone chair one of the other girls had pulled over in front of the stage.

Xavier looked at his friends as if he needed approval, and when he was met with boisterous urgings, he scrambled out of the booth and over to the chair, taking a seat.

Tallis glanced over just as Amber started her dance for Xavier, but he turned his eyes back to the remaining chunk of sad pretzel in his hand.

When the dance was done, Xavier gave Amber a generous tip before going back to the booth, returning fist-bumps with the other men.

The rest of the night, the friends drank, ordered more food, and talked about whatever came to mind when they weren't watching the performers strutting by or the models on the giant TV screens covering the walls.

"I'm gonna grab another drink," Tallis said to Xavier. "You want anything?"

"We've got beer up here," Xavier reminded him, motioning to the mess on the table. "Don't go mixing beer and liquor!"

"I only had one. It's not my favorite. Just want to get something different."

"Grab me a rum and coke."

"You sure?"

"Yeah, man," Xavier replied. "You're right—this beer is shit. Thought I was the only one not really drinking it."

"You got it."

Tallis walked down the stairs along the fish tank platform and made his way to the bar.

"Two rum and cokes," he told the woman behind the bar. "Please."

He took a seat on a little barstool with a glittery pleather cushion. It let out a crude noise and Tallis bit his lip, suppressing a snicker.

"You can laugh," a warm voice said. "It was funny."

Tallis looked up, locking eyes with Big O. His throat went dry, and he could feel the nervous sweats practically smack him in the face.

"It's okay! I know it was the chair." She giggled. "It happens all the time. There's a reason we don't fix or replace it."

All Tallis was able to manage was a choked "oh."

"You're at the booth with the guy getting married soon, right?"

His heart fluttered as he realized she must have noticed him individually in the crowd. Whether or not it truly meant anything, it made him feel special for a moment. "Yeah. He's an old friend of mine." He cringed at how awkward he felt trying to play cool.

"That's exciting! Congrats to your friend!" She tucked her hair behind her ear, revealing a dainty golden chain woven through several piercings along her ear.

Tallis gave a flat-lipped smile and a nod as the bartender passed him his drinks.

"I hope you boys have fun," she said, waving her fingers at him as she turned to leave.

"Wait--" Tallis said through a cough. "I'm Tallis. I didn't catch your name."

"Big O," she said, her smile subtle and her eyes expressionless.

"I hate to sound inappropriate, but that seems like an odd nickname for someone with your figure."

She let out a deeper, genuine laugh.

"Sweetie, it's not a size thing."

"That's what she said," the bartender chirped, eliciting laughter from several eavesdroppers.

"I don't--" Tallis drifted off.

"It's a sex joke, love," Big O said.

"Ahh," he said, reluctantly welcoming back the nervous sweats, which had only just started to fade. "But, if I may ask, what's your real name?"

She looked from Tallis to the bartender and batted her thick eyelashes a few times before turning back.

"My name's--"

"Big O, you're needed in the private rooms," the bartender said, holding up a cellphone and pointing to the screen in her palm.

"I have to go! It was great meeting you, Thomas!"

"It's--"

She was already halfway across the club floor.

"Tallis," he muttered to himself.

Back up in the bachelor party booth, the guys were talking about some new movie when Tallis returned with his and Xavier's drinks.

When the party ended, most of the men were staggering back out the club doors to the limo. The driver stood outside the back door, holding it open and staring off into space while he waited for the drunken men to fall back into their seats.

"Dude," Chris said, looking at Tallis with unfocused eyes. "How are you still standing? I swear I saw you drink like ten drinks."

"Most of those were waters," Tallis said. "Last time I got drunk, I puked on my neighbor's door before I could make it to my own place. She literally left a bag of her dog's shit in my mailbox after that. Lesson learned."

"Dude," Xavier said as he leaned forward, his stomach lurching as he grabbed for his mouth. As if vomit was optional.

"If you make a mess in my vehicle, there are fines!" the limo driver said from outside, never peering in as he slammed the door shut, trapping the foul scent inside.

The driver brought the boys back to each of their homes and each time, everyone wished each other a slurred goodbye. Tallis, the last to be picked up, was the first dropped off.

"Thanks for coming, man!" Xavier slurred, leaning out the window as Tallis walked up to his apartment building door.

"Thanks for inviting me," he said, turning and smiling at his drunken friend. "Guess you'll open the presents when you're sober?"

"Aww, shit, dude! I forgot about the presents! Yeah, man. I'll open them in the morning or something. Thanks!"

He waved goodbye and moseyed back up to his apartment, stumbling a few times and steadying himself with a hand on the wall. Once inside, he kicked off his shoes and waddled to his bed, flopping backward into it, falling asleep moments later.

The next morning, Tallis's mouth tasted like hangover— old beer, onion rings, and the sugary syrup of soda. While

Tallis felt wholly disgusting in the moment, his stomach didn't care. It was time for food.

He made his way to his fridge, spotting nothing but some random condiments, a questionable package of deli meat, and the rest of his leftover pizza. He pursed his lips, paused, and opened his veggie drawer. Untouched iceberg lettuce stared back at him.

Tallis thought to himself that he ought to start making healthier choices. He stood there, fridge door open, pondering for a moment about how curious it was that the human body can simultaneously be so resilient yet so fragile. Opting for the healthier choice, he grabbed the head of lettuce and closed the fridge, only to open it a second later and snag the bottle of ranch from the door.

He ripped off a hunk of lettuce and drizzled some ranch across it. He was pretty sure this was called something like a wedge salad and that was what fancy people ate at expensive restaurants.

After his wedge salad breakfast, Tallis cleaned himself up, got changed, did some light cleaning, and made a trip to the grocery store after deciding he wasn't in the mood for pizza for lunch again.

The rest of his day was uneventful. He bounced between random tasks around the apartment-- not having any plans, but unable to sit still. Every time he sat for longer than a moment without keeping himself occupied, his mind drifted, and every time it drifted to the same image: that beautiful girl at Illusion.

He didn't know why he couldn't get Big O out of his mind. Sure, she was pretty, and yes, Tallis was single. He hardly knew her. He didn't even know her real name. But the pure, wild excitement in her eyes had him stuck.

Most men would have thought about her curves, her legs, or even her lips, but all Tallis could think about was her eyes and her smile. It didn't look copied and pasted on like every other girl at Illusion. It looked like she was having the time of her life.

Unable to stand merely thinking about her anymore, he did what any desperate man would do: he looked her up online.

"Show me Big O," he said to his watch.

"Pulling up videos of big O," his TV replied, flipping the screen to an explicit video.

"Ohh!" the random woman on the TV moaned.

"Nope, nope, nope!" Tallis felt his heart race as he tapped at his watch to trigger it again. "Show me Big O at Illusion." He enunciated the last word loud and clear, just to be sure.

"Pulling up search results for Big O at Illusion," his TV said, the video of the woman melting into a webpage on Illusion's official website. The page was labeled, "Our Dancers."

Using his watch to scroll, he sifted past the other dancers on the page until he reached the bottom, where he spotted her photo. She was posed on top of a motorcycle, in no sort of position to safely ride it.

"Big O is our newest dancer!" the webpage read. "She loves animals, shopping, and going out for drinks. Her favorite drink? A gin and tonic!"

"Zoom in on image," he said. The screen maximized her motorcycle photo.

Others would've first spotted her ass-- propped up in a thong at an unnatural angle. Instead, his eyes went straight for her face. In the picture, she was laughing, and it didn't look forced.

He knew she had to be a fun person just by the way she held herself.

His mind kept wandering, first imagining himself smooth-talking her at the bar, buying her a drink, and getting a kiss on the cheek. By the time his nearly hour-long daydream started to come to a close, he was picturing himself taking Big O as his date to Xavier's wedding. He felt a flutter of joy, as if his dreams were real.

The rest of the weekend passed without much event. He wrote a couple poems, went on a walk around the block with his camera to take some photos, and idly passed the time in his apartment.

When his alarm screamed at him to wake up Monday morning, he felt a sense of relief. At least, now, he could break the monotony.

He sat on his couch with his morning coffee, watching the holographic fire in his fireplace, the projected flames dancing around the real logs. Tallis let his eyes go out of focus, entranced by the shimmering shades of orange. His watch chimed, dragging him back into reality.

On his way to the subway, he wondered if Big O had ever been to his sector. Or, better yet, Sector 12, with Opulence and all the other glossy buildings. The city never ceased to amaze him, but he imagined it would blow Big O's mind. He got the sense she had a similar passion for beauty as himself.

Ms. Iris greeted him as usual, with outstretched hand and distracted eyes. This time, she was reading something from a tablet in one hand while she stood, waiting for Tallis to surrender her coffee.

"Did you have a good time this weekend with your new toys?" she asked without looking up. The corner of her lip twitched in a suppressed smirk.

Tallis felt the blood flood to his cheeks as he stammered, unable to get a word out.

"I'm kidding. I'm not judging. We've all got our things. I'm just giving you a hard time."

"Oh," Tallis huffed an uneasy "hah."

He turned to walk to his desk, pausing, turning back to Ms. Iris, and blurting out a quick, "It was for a friend."

"I'm not sure what you intended by that," she said, finally looking at him. "But it doesn't sound any better when you word it that way."

He scurried to his desk, dropping his things below the tabletop and logging into his computer.

Thunk.

"I need these by lunchtime," Ms. Iris said, eyeing the stack of documents she dropped on Tallis's desk.

"Yes, ma'am."

Tallis did his best to stay focused all day, knowing Ms. Iris and the CAs were counting on him. At least, that's what he told himself to stay motivated.

Right around the time he closed the folder on the last document, his watch buzzed, and Xavier's name popped up. He hit the "accept" button.

"Hey, man," Xavier's voice came through the watch. "Got any lunch plans?"

"I've got a frozen burrito and a slice of cheesecake I've been thinking about all day. Why?"

"Wanna meet up at Sprouts?"

"Is that the new plant-based place in Sector 11?"

"Yup. I saw another ad for them and I've been dying to try their new grilled cheese."

"That doesn't sound like something that would be in a plant-based restaurant," Tallis said.

"It's made with cashew cheddar or something. I don't know how it works, but apparently, it's not cheese. I just need to know if it's stringy like cheese. Plus, Vanessa wants me to lose a few pounds before the wedding, but I still want to eat food that tastes like... you know... food."

Tallis laughed, and the two agreed to meet for lunch.

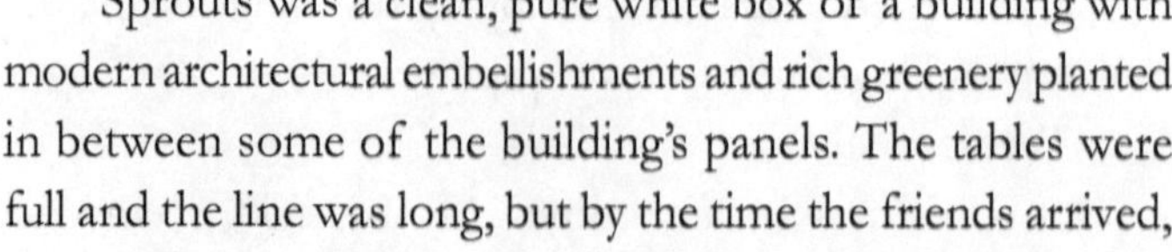

Sprouts was a clean, pure white box of a building with modern architectural embellishments and rich greenery planted in between some of the building's panels. The tables were full and the line was long, but by the time the friends arrived, they didn't care how long they'd have to wait-- they just wanted to eat.

Xavier ordered his non-cheese grilled cheese, and Tallis picked a plant-based burger piled high with vegan bacon. He didn't bother asking how they could call such a creation "bacon."

All the tables were still full after they got their food, so they took it to go and found a nearby bench.

Xavier took a bite of his sandwich, eyes wide and full mouth grinning at the faux-cheese string.

"Live up to the hype?"

"You don't even know!"

"So," Xavier said, swallowing his bite and wiping at some crumbs on his face with the back of his hand. "I've got a question."

"Mmm?" Tallis mumbled, mid-bite.

"You got a date for my wedding yet? I'm not trying to rush you, but you know we need the final guest count soon for the caterer."

"I know, I'm sorry. I didn't think it would take so long. Is that cocky of me to think I'd have found a date sooner?"

Xavier laughed. "Nah, man. That's just confidence."

"Is that what that's called?" Tallis grinned, a piece of chewed lettuce plastered to his front tooth.

"So..."

Tallis took another bite.

"Do you?" Xavier pried.

"Do I what?"

"Bro! Do you have a date or not?"

Tallis froze, his mouth full. He held a finger up while he pretended the bite he took was bigger than it really was. Chewing slowly, he tried to find a way to hide his embarrassment at failing to find a wedding date.

"Tal," Xavier urged, his smile flattening.

"I do," he blurted before he realized what he was saying.

That wasn't exactly what Tallis had in mind, but it was too late now.

"Woah! My man! When were you gonna tell me about her?"

"I was going to," Tallis lied. "You just beat me to it."

"Way to go, man! I'm happy to see you putting yourself out there finally."

Tallis smiled, his eyes and mouth failing to agree on an emotion.

"I mean, you're a good-looking dude—please don't take this a weird way. I just mean you fit that look of what's conventionally attractive or whatever. You're just too damn nervous sometimes. People are attracted to confidence! Just happy to see my best friend working up the nerve to ask a lady out, that's all."

Tallis nodded. "Thanks."

"You should invite her out to dinner with you, me, and Vanessa," Xavier said, giving him an encouraging pat on the shoulder, leaving a small grease stain.

Tallis eyed the grease stain and looked back up at Xavier, his mind racing.

"Sorry about that."

"No worries."

"We'll be out of town this weekend. Vanessa has a work trip, and I was able to take off to go with her. How about next weekend? We could go to Glitz?"

"That's a bit out of my budget," Tallis said-- the first truthful thing so far.

"Don't worry about it! It's on us."

Tallis's face felt flushed. "Sounds good. Thanks." He felt like his words were lodged in his throat, reluctant to come out.

❖

After they finished lunch, Tallis made his way back to the office to finish out the workday. His paperwork stack shrunk slower than ever as he wrestled with his daydreams— all of them consisting of various plots to ask Big O to be his wedding date.

The CAs came waltzing through the door, and Tallis used it as an excuse to look up and stop pretending to get work done.

"Nice work on the REM article, man!" one of the CAs said, slapping another on the back. "That's some freaking wild stuff. Wish I got to cover that story!"

"It's totally different when you see it in person," the writer said. "These people are so sad. It makes for a fun read, but that drug does some crazy stuff to your mind. Some of these people are so far gone, they don't even know what's real anymore."

"Is it true they can customize it?"

"What? Customize REM? Yeah. Tia's supposed to catch a video talking about some of that this week."

"And this shit's legal?" another one of the CAs asked.

"Yup."

The CAs were all seated in the conference room at this point, and before Tallis could catch any more of the story, Ms. Iris joined them, glaring briefly at him as she shut the door behind her.

By the time the workday was just about done, Ms. Iris made a beeline for Tallis's desk. She let out a guttural huff when she saw the incomplete pile of paperwork, knocking Tallis out of his daze.

"I don't pay you to be an office decoration!" she crowed. "I don't care if you *think* you can sit around and look pretty. It doesn't excuse this! You have to actually *work*. Did you get anything done?"

She riffled through the smaller stack on his desk, her eyes scanning over his work.

"You get paid good money to do this paperwork. You did practically nothing today! This stuff needs to be done, and we can't afford to wait on it. And I'm not paying you overtime for something that should have been done during office hours. You're going to stay and get this done. Got it?"

"Yes, ma'am." The embarrassment stung, but he couldn't argue with her disappointment.

Without another word, she waddled out of the office, shutting most of the lights off behind her and leaving Tallis in the dead office with nothing but his desk lamp and the harsh glow of his computer screen.

Tallis buckled down and got the paperwork done. He had to keep pulling himself from his own thoughts, but by ten at night, he closed the folder on the last spreadsheets, placing the completed stack in front of Ms. Iris's closed office door.

He left the office, walking outside into dark skies and neon lights. Following the thinned crowd into the station, he shuffled onto the subway as per usual. Only this time, he disregarded the blinking "Sector 8" above the door. Several people got off, a couple others boarded, and the subway was off.

Sector 7. Blink... Blink... Off again. Sector 6. Sector 5. Sector 4. Sector 3.

Tallis was one of the only people left on the subway at this point, and all remaining passengers stepped off, including Tallis.

This terminal was darker than the ones he was used to, and far grungier. There were bags and piles of trash tucked in every corner, holos and posters advertising "thirsty ladies" and "dancers for hire" all through the area.

Along his path out of the station, he side-eyed an older gentleman crouched over on the tiled floor, digging through the pockets of an unconscious younger man. He pulled a small empty vial, uncorking it and tipping it back, his tongue sticking out to try catching the only remaining drop.

The man slumped backward, seated as he stared off with a blank face, his eyes seemingly trained on Tallis.

While any rational stranger to Sector 3 might have quickened their pace and left the old man, Tallis couldn't help but wonder what was going on. He slowed, gawking at the man as he kept walking toward the exit. The man gasped, sucking back tons of air before letting out a maddening giggle.

"No good, no good, no good," the man muttered, shuffling over to a trash can to dig through it, presumably for another vial.

Tallis was almost at the exit when the old man noticed him and scurried over, grabbing at both of his hands and whipping Tallis around to face him.

"Why aren't ya dancin'?" the man asked, his breath reeking of old milk.

"Excuse me?" Tallis asked, pure curiosity and confusion in his voice.

"This is a party! I know there aren't a lot of people here yet but come on! Dance!"

"I really do have to get going," Tallis excused himself. "I hope you have a fantastic party though!"

"Don't forget a goody bag!" The man shuffled over to one of the garbage bags near the younger man's unconscious body, plucking one up and giving it and a large smile to Tallis.

Politely, Tallis gave a half-smile back, taking the bag before exiting the station and dropping the bag beside a garbage can around the corner.

He paused, taking in his surroundings above ground. When the bachelor party group was here, they didn't take the subway, so Tallis was in a different part of Sector 3. He realized this wasn't the brightest idea, but he had never done anything exciting before. Surely this counted as exciting, right?

He looked up and down the dark street, spotting the occasional flickering neon sign—many of which were red triple X's, others were green plus signs, and there were a few unfamiliar symbols. One symbol in particular that caught Tallis's attention was a purple neon eye, dimly illuminating an alley as he continued down the street. He slowed to a stop, intrigued by the unblinking purple eye. He found himself entranced, taking cautious steps down the empty alleyway.

Now standing right below the sign, he could see the chipping paint below the eye: *Dream Depot*.

"Well? Are you going in or not?" a raspy voice startled him.

He spun around. A mop-haired woman in a skin-tight cheetah bodysuit let her cigarette bounce on her lip as she repeated her question.

"Uh," Tallis said, undue anxiety creeping under his skin and crawling like bugs. "No. Sorry."

He hurried back the way he came, looking over his shoulder, only to find that the woman must have disappeared into the shop.

Continuing down the street, he could eventually see the flashy facade of Illusion. His palms started sweating and he realized he had been digging his nails into them as he walked closer.

A thin woman in a pink bikini and long blonde braids greeted him at the door, holding it open for him. He walked past her, stopped, and took a few steps back.

"Excuse me," he said to her.

"Mmm?" She smiled.

"I'm wondering if Big O is working tonight."

"Should be! Have a great time!" She turned her attention back to the guests walking toward the door.

"I was wondering if I could talk to her," Tallis continued.

"Ask the front desk, sweetie."

Tallis paused for a moment, stopping himself before pushing further, instead turning back to the inside of the club and looking for the front desk.

The front desk turned out to be a small booth tucked away in the front-most corner of the club, practically in the dark. Tallis approached the booth, which was staffed by a brick of a man in a black vest and slacks.

"Can I help you, sir?" the man asked Tallis, who clearly looked lost.

"I need to talk to Big O."

The man chuckled. "It's your lucky day. She's working the private rooms tonight."

"Private rooms?"

"Yeah. They're back behind that curtain." The man pointed across the club to a curtained doorway with a holographic dancer poised in front of it.

"What exactly are the private rooms for?" Tallis asked innocently.

The front desk guy clearly found this question entertaining, but when he saw Tallis was being genuine, he replied, "They're for private dances. That's all. Groping is only allowed above the waist, you get a room for a ten minute time block unless you pay a premium. You got DigitPay?"

Tallis nodded, his hand migrating to his watch.

"Great. Just go to the machine, scan your payment, and go sit inside and wait. When the dancer's time ends, you gotta leave. You linger, you get kicked out. Don't linger."

"Got it," Tallis said. "Thanks."

Tallis turned and walked toward the private rooms, the front desk guy watching him for a moment before looking back down at his phone under the counter.

Once through the curtains, Tallis was in a small room with a door to his left and an ATM-looking machine in front of him. He tapped the screen on the machine, waking it up.

The screen displayed "Available Dancers" centered in the middle of an on-screen button. Tallis tapped the button, and the screen populated with the 3D image of a dark woman with a head full of long braids. The name "Lola" displayed above her image, and there were arrows on either side of her. Tallis tapped the right arrow and another woman's image displayed. He clicked through a few more ladies before Big O smiled back at him on screen. He tapped her image, and a bubble popped up.

Would you like the premium package for additional time?

Tallis hoped he'd be capable of saying everything he wanted to say before his time ran out. He selected "No," and the disclaimer agreement popped up.

Accept.

He let the machine scan his watch. Then the words "ROOM 4" displayed on the screen before disappearing and returning to the main menu.

Tallis let out a little "huh." He turned his attention away from the machine and made his way through the door, opening it to reveal a long, narrow hallway. The ceiling was a screen on which pink and purple patterns danced and illuminated the hall. All along the right wall, there were curtained rooms with holographic numbers floating in front of them. Tallis made his way to the number four and stepped through the heavy curtain.

The private room was simple. There was a plush booth seat in a U-shape across from him with nothing else but a small screen on one of the walls. He took a seat, crossing his leg over his knee and taking a deep breath. When he realized the screen had words on its display, he leaned forward, squinting and reading:

There are 3 clients ahead of you right now. Make yourself comfortable and please be patient.

Even after he had finished reading the screen, Tallis remained hunched forward, his leg bouncing beneath his rested elbow. He started to look around the room for an air vent, wondering why it felt so hot in the room. He spotted one almost directly above him.

He stood, but too quickly, his vision filling with little stars as he steadied himself. When his eyesight cleared, he stepped up on the booth seat and held a hand up to the vent. There was a soft flow of cool air wafting out. Stretching up further, getting on tiptoes, he pawed at the vent. He began fidgeting to see if it could open anymore, and while he was, the screen let out a sharp *ding*.

Tallis jumped at the sound, losing his balance and landing on the hard floor with a thud. The back of his head hit the floor, and he let out a pained groan. Embarrassed with himself but grateful nobody witnessed anything, he brushed himself off and sat back down.

His hand wandered to the back of his skull, inspecting the bump forming as he looked over at the screen again, noticing the number three had changed to a two. As soon as he had processed this, his heart turned to brick. He coughed, his heart making up for lost time by beating rapidly beneath his shirt.

Tallis leaned forward again, this time placing his face into his palms. Looking down at his tennis shoes as he bounced his legs, he started playing through make-believe scenarios in his head.

How would he greet her? Was "hello" too formal, but "hey" too casual? Should he smile? Play it cool?

He imagined them having different conversations. He imagined her enjoying his company so much that she promised not to tell anyone if he lingered past the time limit. He also imagined her seeing his face, recognizing him from the other night and running out of the room, assuming he was a stalker.

He felt his face grow cold and then hot again the longer he sat. His stomach seemed to do a flip with each thump of the club music through the walls. Time dug its nails in—every minute aching.

When the screen dinged again, acid raced up Tallis's throat and he caught it in his mouth. Without even looking at the number one on his screen, he rushed out the door, bolted down the hall and out of Illusion, and then puked in a trash can outside the club.

That was certainly not one of the situations he had been imagining.

Back at his apartment, Tallis washed up and went to bed, but he was unable to fall asleep. Not that it would have mattered much, as he had about two hours until it was time to get up and get ready for work again.

Tallis hardly got to shut his eyes before his alarm crowed. Letting out a pathetic whine, he reached over and shut it off. A dull pain throbbed in the back of his skull. After gingerly rubbing at it, he remembered the lump, then he remembered the puke, then he remembered he was completely and utterly alone.

That day at the office, he struggled to focus, his mind continually wandering to his embarrassment and how, next time, he'd keep his cool.

His email chimed and he sat up, scrolling over and checking it.

FWD: Time for the Job of Your Dreams

Dear valued employee,

Have you dreamed of joining the Creative Anchors in their adventures?
We're looking for our next Creative Anchor! The position is open internally first, and if we don't find a worthy candidate, we'll expand our search outside. If you're looking for a career that allows you to explore every corner of the city, chasing exciting opportunities for stories, photos, and videos, this is the opportunity you've waited for.

To apply, please submit your application to Iris Haberdeen by next Friday.

Tallis's already distracted mind moseyed off to mental images of exploring the different sectors. He kept having to snap himself out of it as the stack of documents at the corner of his desk grew.

The next few hours were a constant battle of Tallis's attention span, until he eventually broke down and decided to take a leap. He was going to try for the open position, even if Ms. Iris told him he'd never have a chance.

"Ma'am?" Tallis peeked around the corner of Ms. Iris's office.

Ms. Iris muttered, her gaze fixated on her computer screen.

Tallis still stood at the door, waiting for a true response.

"Stop staring," she finally said, "and spit it out."

"I was wondering if I could talk to one of the CAs."

This was enough to get her attention. Her eyes flickered up to meet his and her lips pursed. "Why?"

"I'm still interested in that open CA position, and I would like to talk to one of them to get some better insight to really see if it's a good fit. See what the day-to-day is like."

"Tallis," Ms. Iris said with a huff. "I already told you—"

"I know," he interrupted. "I understand, but I really, really think I have what it takes. I'm going to work on my portfolio and the application this week, but I would really like to talk to one of the CAs."

Her mouth opened, and Tallis threw in a last-minute "please."

She closed her mouth, taking a deep breath instead. The silence made Tallis uncomfortable, but he held his confident pose.

"Ok," she said. "I'll check their schedules and see who's available this evening."

"Thank you so much!" Tallis couldn't hold back his smile.

"But it's on your own time. You clock out for this, got it?"

"Yes, ma'am."

She looked back down at her computer, clicking away at some keys for a moment, scanning over the screen. "Tiabelle's available toward the end of your workday. She specializes in video, but she's been with the team for a few years, so she has a good sense of what we're looking for. I'll book an appointment at the office for her this evening."

"Thank you, ma'am," Tallis said again.

"Mmm."

Tallis scurried back to his desk, where he remained hard at work for the rest of the day. He didn't want to let Ms. Iris down, especially after she just did him a favor, however reluctant she may have been.

It was reaching the end of his workday, and Tallis's document stack had shrunk down to just a couple residual folders. Just as he was submitting his last document for the day, he heard a loud voice from the other end of the room.

"What's with the appointment, Iris? What did Marcus say about me this time? Please don't make me do another safety seminar—you know I'm careful already!"

Tallis looked up to see a leggy, tan woman with long, ratty blonde hair and a half-shaved head.

Ms. Iris stepped out of her office to meet Tiabelle with a grin. "Nothing like that, Tia." Her smile quickly sunk. "Though you have me concerned. What did you do this time that Marcus could possibly want to report?"

"Nothing!" Tiabelle cheesed.

Ms. Iris raised an eyebrow and paused. "Anyways… I scheduled a brief appointment for you here because one of my office workers is interested in the open CA position and wanted to ask some questions. He's that one over there," she motioned toward Tallis over at his desk. "Make sure he keeps it quick—you've got more important things to do."

Tiabelle waved a goofy salute with two fingers to her forehead.

"I'm out for the day—have a good one." Ms. Iris locked up her office and waddled toward the elevator.

"Tia," Tiabelle held out her large hand to Tallis before he had a chance to fully stand from his chair. "Don't worry— sit! I'll pull over a chair."

"Uh—I—alright."

She flopped into a nearby office chair and used her feet to roll toward Tallis.

"My name's Tallis, by the way."

"Nice to meet ya! Heard you wanna join the team."

"Ye—"

"What's your specialty?" she jumped right in.

"Writing and photography. I think I like writing more, but I really love both."

"Sweet! So, let's get right to it. What questions ya got?"

"What's your average day like?"

"No such thing."

Taken aback, Tallis tried to think of another question, or at least a clarifying question.

"Every day is a little different," she said. "Some days, I might be capturing interviews with people who use different products, or I might be getting clips of kids at school to help promote a charity event. Or other days—and these are my favorite—I'll be on a commercial shoot. Some ads are simple, get some shots of people using the product or whatever. Other days, we go big, we go dramatic. Some days, I bungee off the sides of skyscrapers with my camera, or I go up in the helicopter to catch a good aerial shot."

"Oh wow," Tallis said breathily.

"I mean, it would be a little different for you as a writer and photographer. You'd do some of the crazy stuff for photoshoots, but our writers are the ones who get to meet some really wild people. You might write about an interview with the billionaire business owners in Sector 15. One of our writers had to do a "week in the life" piece about one of them once. He spent the day going to lavish parties, lounging at luxury pools, and going to fancy restaurants. Then he wrote about it. Other days, you might be going to Sector 2 and writing news pieces about rising crime rates in the outer sectors."

"That's insane." Tallis felt his face turn warm and a smile creep across his face as he imagined the possibilities. He would never be stuck at a desk again.

"What else ya got for me?"

"What's the interview process like? From what you remember from yours, at least."

"It's rough." She chuckled. "I'm not gonna lie to you. They grill you. And it isn't just one interview either. The first one is rough because they wanna weed out the weakest candidates as quickly as possible. They'll go over your portfolio a bit in that first one, too. They wanna make sure you've got a creative flair—something different than the rest of the team. Everyone brings their own unique flavor. That requirement also pertains to your personality, so make sure you let that originality truly shine!"

Tallis nibbled at the inside of his cheek. "Tell me about the best day you've had on the job so far."

About an hour had passed before Tia looked at her watch.

"I really need to get going, but I hope this helped!" She shoved back against the floor with both feet, propelling herself and the rolling chair back to its original location.

"It did, thank you so much!"

"Happy to do it! Hope to see you on the team soon, Tallis."

"Me too."

Back at his apartment, Tallis decided to forgo the idea of a shower and a proper dinner, instead spending his time digging through his photo files and written pieces, organizing his favorite ones into a digital portfolio and relabeling everything for clarity. When he was satisfied with the final product, he pulled up the official application document. About two hours and an accidental nap later, Tallis had finished the application itself, attached his portfolio and resume, and let his finger hover over the "send" button for a solid minute before hitting it.

He looked at his watch. Looks like it was about to be another night of minimal sleep.

Frustrated with himself for taking so long but feeling relieved that the first step was out of the way, Tallis brushed his teeth and crawled into bed. Just as he was about to drift off, his brain reminded him that the next step would be the interview, and his heart started racing.

Instead of minimal sleep, Tallis got none.

A few days went by without any word of the application from Ms. Iris. On his way home from work on Thursday, Xavier gave him a call, and the buzz of his watch made him sputter, as if his heart was trying to crawl through his esophagus. Once he registered the name on the call, his heart sank back into place.

"Hey, Xavier," he answered.

"Hey, man! I know this is a bit late notice, but mine and Vanessa's trip got postponed. Would you and your date want to get dinner this weekend instead?"

There went Tallis's heart in his throat again.

"I know you guys probably aren't anything crazy serious

yet, but I'd just love to meet her. If that's alright. You don't even have to call it a double date! Just say it's 'meeting friends' or something."

Tallis struggled to find words.

"Sunday would work best for us," Xavier clarified.

"That's probably fine. I can ask her," Tallis sputtered, unable to come up with an excuse, aware that Xavier would know he had nowhere else to be over the weekend.

"Great! We'll meet you at Glitz. Seven sound good?"

"Unless she says otherwise, it's a date."

"Sweet. See ya then, bud. Can't wait to meet her!"

"Yeah," Tallis nearly whispered.

Xavier hung up, and Tallis turned around immediately, right before stepping into his apartment complex. He made his way back the way he came—toward the subway.

With long, shaky breaths, he tried to encourage himself not to think too hard about it. "Just go in there, wait your turn in the room, and talk to her when she comes in. No big deal," he whispered as he stepped onto the subway car.

Once again, Tallis was on his way to Sector 3. The man with the trash bags wasn't there this time to stop him, so he kept his hurried pace toward Illusion, trying not to let anything distract him along the way. That is, until he was stopped by a man outside Dream Depot, the purple eye on the sign flickering in the dark alley behind him.

"You're awful pretty to be walking around here by yourself," the man slurred, stumbling toward Tallis.

Tallis tried to disregard him, turning back to the street and continuing on his way until the husky man stepped in front of him, wiggling a small glass vial inches from Tallis's nose.

"Join me," he said with a foul-smelling grin. "I could use some pretty friends here."

Tallis instinctively swatted the vial from his face, accidentally knocking it from the man's hand. It landed on the asphalt and shattered, leaching shimmering purple liquid into the ground.

"Shit," Tallis said, eyeing the liquid and then eyeing the man.

"What'd you have to go and do that for?" the man said with alarming coolness.

"It was an accident, I swear."

"That was supposed to be for you. I was sharing, you prick!"

"I'm so—"

"Get lost!" the man spat.

Tallis scurried out of the man's way, hurrying down the street, not slowing down until he was greeted by the increasingly familiar sight of Illusion.

Without stopping to smile at the woman at the entrance, he blew through the door and power-walked straight to the private rooms. He selected Big O at the machine and paid. It assigned him to room number two.

He pushed his way through the curtain to his room and sat down, refusing to look at the number on the screen. With each beep of the screen, he felt a rush of cold flood his veins, but he continued to ignore the number ticking down on the screen. After seemingly forever, a delicate-looking hand with carefully manicured nails reached through the curtain, parting it just enough for Big O to come walking through in a shimmery teal G-string and matching pasties.

Tallis's entire body went cold, yet he couldn't stop

sweating. Words felt like cotton in his throat, and he stood to his feet without thinking.

"Hey, sexy!" she chirped, flashing her contagious smile.

"H-hey."

"I'm so glad you're here! Tonight was pretty lame until now."

"Really?" Tallis felt his heart flutter.

"Yeah!" She squeezed his arm playfully and then grinned. "Oh my gosh! Check out those biceps!"

"Wait, what?" Tallis said, looking down at his arms.

"Do you work out?"

"No."

"Oh," she said, her smile fading for a split second before returning. "You just must have good genetics! You've got really sexy arms."

"Th-thank you," Tallis said. "I guess."

"You want a dance, honey?"

"Uh. I actually wanted to talk to you about something."

"Here," she ushered him back to the seat, "sit down. Get comfortable!"

Tallis mindlessly sat down, trying to collect his words.

"I think you're really beautiful—"

"Thank you!"

"And I think you have a really genuine smile," Tallis tried continuing, but Big O straddled him, moving her warm chest toward his face. His gaze shot down to the pasties and then back up to her eyes. "I'd really like to get to know you."

"So, get to know me, babe!" She grabbed one of his hands and placed it on her waist as she started gyrating and running her fingers through her hair.

"I mean—"

She spun around, curving her back as she grinded on his lap.

Tallis sighed, frazzled. "My best friend is getting married soon—"

"I remember! You were with that party that was here the other day. I'm so happy for him!"

"You remember us?" Tallis's face grew warm and he tried to suppress a smile.

"Of course I do! Can't forget a handsome face like yours."

He let the grin work its way through as he beamed at her. "You're sweet," he said.

She giggled artificially.

"So, I was meaning to say… I don't have a date to the wedding."

"Oh no! I'm sure a stud like you could get any girl out there to go with you!"

"Well, see, that's the thing," Tallis said. "I was wondering if you'd go with me?"

"That sounds like fun! I bet you'd be a fun date for any girl!"

"So, you'll go with me?" Tallis couldn't hide his awkward smile. "Wow. Umm… I was also wondering… I sort of told the bride and groom I already had a date, and they want to meet you. Just a fun dinner with friends. So, I agreed to this Sunday. We have a table reserved for seven o'clock at Glitz. I get if it you can't go or don't want to. But don't worry— dinner's on them at least."

"That place is so fancy! Have you ever been?"

"Once. It's been a while." He desperately tried to think of ways to keep the conversation going when he recalled reading about her favorite drink on Illusion's website. "But if you go with me, I'll buy drinks. Do you have a favorite?"

"I love a good gin and tonic. Can't go wrong! What about you?" She spun around again, continuing her dance, Tallis's hand stationary on her waist exactly where she placed it.

"Rum and Coke is usually my go-to, but I'm not picky. I'll make sure there's a gin and tonic ready for you when we go to Glitz. I'm so glad you're coming!"

The screen beeped, and Big O eased off of Tallis's lap, squeezing his arm one more time before she turned to leave.

"Wait!" Tallis called right as she stepped one foot out the curtain. She paused, her head pivoting to look toward him with a small smile.

"Yes?"

"I still don't know your real name," Tallis said.

"Just call me O," she said with a tainted sweetness to her voice. She disappeared out of the curtain, and before Tallis could catch her, she was already in another room.

The rest of the week went by painfully slow. The workdays crept by, and the hours at home alone were spent aimlessly writing plotless stories just in an effort to fast forward to Sunday. Friday evening rolled around and Tallis was mindlessly scrolling online when his watch dinged. He looked down to see an email notification. He tapped his watch a few times, transferring the message to his TV.

CREATIVE ANCHOR OPENING

Tallis,

We're reviewing all applications for the Creative Anchor opening. Please be patient while we narrow down our candidates. Thank you for your application.

Tallis felt his stomach flip. It suddenly felt far more real than when he simply submitted his resume and portfolio.

The hiring team officially had his application, and there was no going back. When he thought about calling Xavier to tell him, he decided to wait and share his news when he'd see him at dinner.

Tallis was in his dressy dinner clothes by lunchtime on Sunday. By mid-afternoon, he already had his shoes on, ready to go. His productivity was absolutely shot—every time he tried to sit down and focus on some project or another, his mind would wander, his heartrate would skyrocket, and he'd start watching the clock again. Every so often, his hands would migrate to his hair without a thought, and his fingers would fixate on any hair that felt out of place. He'd stop everything and abandon his computer to instead face the mirror, hair goop in hand in an attempt to secure the disobedient strands.

Glitz was in Sector 15, which Tallis was unfamiliar with, so when seven o'clock grew closer, he decided to leave a bit early.

On his way to the station, his nerves got the best of him, and his feet seemed to stop communicating with each other as he tripped over them on flat ground, stumbling and falling in front of a few people passing by. He apologized to them softly, as if the spectacle had disrupted their walk, though no one bothered to glance his way. He brushed himself off. His clothes, fortunately, were hardly dusty and were otherwise unscathed. His palm, however, had a minor scrape, which he ignored.

The subway was emptier than usual, so he took a seat near the doors, which slid shut just as his butt hit the seat, and the subway zipped off toward the next sector.

A couple stops later, an older woman climbed aboard and sat beside Tallis, who was sitting hunched over, elbows on knees, chin resting on clasped hands.

"Everything okay?" the lady asked, her face scrunched.

Tallis turned to look at her, confused, but followed her gaze to his leg, which was bouncing with rogue nerves.

"Oh," he said, his leg freezing. "I'm okay, but I appreciate you asking." He smiled genuinely. It wasn't often you met strangers who cared about you in the city.

Clearly unsatisfied with his answer, the lady spoke again. "Going anywhere fun?"

"I am, actually," he said. "Going to a nice dinner."

"How lovely! Meeting with family? Friends?"

"It's a double date," he said. "My first time out with this girl."

"That's so exciting!" She beamed at him, placing a hand briefly on his shoulder. "You're going to have such a nice time."

"Thank you. I really hope so."

The subway jolted and began to slow to a stop for the next station, to which the lady stood and wished Tallis the best of luck before disappearing out the doors.

When they finally reached Sector 15, Tallis hurried out the door as if it would snap shut and trap him inside.

Sector 15 was one of pure wealth and glamor. Unless you were of the top 1% economically, or merely a visitor to the lifestyle, you had no business in Sector 15. Even the station for Sector 15 reeked of elegance, with quartz walls and floors, leather seats, and hologram ads for things like fancy wines and luxury home decorating services. Xavier and Vanessa made good money, but even they must have squirreled away extra cash to afford the double date at Glitz, which only flooded Tallis with more anxiety.

He reached the front of Glitz about a half hour early, but somehow, he didn't feel any more at ease. Knowing the reservation likely wouldn't allow him early seating, he opted to instead wait in the restaurant lobby.

The lobby's tall ceilings were ornamented with decorative glass balls and an immense chandelier made of natural-looking crystals. The massive fountain in the center of the lobby seemed like it was practically the size of Tallis's entire apartment, and it seemed to glitter as water spouted from the top, raining down into the pool below.

After sitting in one of the uncomfortably rigid chairs for only a few moments, Tallis grew antsy again, popping onto his feet and instead approaching the fountain. He looked down into the base of the fountain, admiring the decorative crystal work even below the surface of the water. He began to wonder if the staff at Glitz would ever allow someone to bring a camera to simply take pictures in the lobby, but he quickly assumed they wouldn't.

Just a few minutes before seven, Xavier and Vanessa walked like a celebrity power-couple through the doors and into the lobby. Vanessa placed her hand delicately in the crook of Xavier's arm before the two of them glided toward Tallis, who pulled his attention from the fountain to go meet his friends.

"Hey, Tallis! Long time, no see." Vanessa said, her voice rich and warm. There was always something soothing about the way she talked, Tallis thought.

"Vanessa," he greeted, hugging her. "You look stunning."

She thanked him as Xavier welcomed him with a hug as well.

"Your date still on her way?" Xavier asked.

"Yeah, I suppose so. She has a long ride to get here, so she might just be running a little late."

"Does she know we have a reservation?" Xavier asked.

"She does. I'm sorry—"

"Nah, man. No problem. I just meant we could go ahead and get seated so they don't give up our reservation to someone else. I'm sure she'll understand. Just text her and let her know we're inside."

"Oh, yeah," Tallis said, his voice fading. "Of course."

The three of them made their way inside, getting seated at their table. The waitstaff placed cloth napkins in their laps before offering them a sample of the wine of the day.

"Has she texted you back?" Xavier asked after their wine had been poured.

Tallis hesitated, pretending to look at his watch, knowing full-well that he didn't have Big O's number in the first place. Hell, he didn't even have her real name.

"Not yet," he said.

"No worries, bro. I'm sure she's on her way," Xavier said with a soft smile. "So… tell us about her!"

"She's the most beautiful woman I've ever seen," Tallis said.

Xavier and Vanessa laughed.

"I know, that's super corny and cliché. But, like… I don't just mean she's pretty. If joy was a person, that's what it would look like. She's always smiling, and it never seems like it's to put on a front. She lights up the room."

Vanessa let out a little "aww" and looked at him with her hands clasped in front of her chest.

"That's awesome, man!" Xavier said. "I'm really happy you finally found someone, even if it's nothing super serious…yet."

"Tha—wait. What do you mean, 'finally?'"

"I just mean, like… I've known you a long time, dude. And you've only had like one girlfriend. And it didn't last that long."

"Two."

"What?"

"I've had two girlfriends." Tallis grinned and sat back in his seat, taking a sip of his wine.

Time slipped away, and the group eventually decided to order their food. Xavier apologized to Tallis, feeling impatient, but everyone agreed they were starving and it had been long enough.

When the server brought Tallis his alfredo, he continued sitting back in his seat, sipping his second glass of wine. Conversation continued, Tallis growing further detached with every passing minute until he was practically watching his alfredo get cold.

"I don't think she's coming," Xavier said. "I didn't wanna have to say it, but you're breaking my heart sitting there like that. Plus, it'd be a damn shame to let that pasta get cold." He chuckled awkwardly, the tension unwavering.

Tallis sighed. "You're probably right." He leaned forward, his shoulders loose and hunched as he picked at his dinner with a fork.

"Where did you meet this girl, anyways?" Vanessa asked.

Tallis shoved a forkful of alfredo in his mouth, hoping

to delay the answer as if it made a difference. Vanessa and Xavier just stared at him in anticipation as he had to cover his overly full mouth to avoid flashing chewed food.

He decided to get straight to it. No sense in lying.

"I met her at Illusion."

Xavier burst out in a belly laugh and Vanessa looked between the men, confused.

Tallis took another bite of pasta while Xavier collected himself.

"I'm sorry, man. You met this chick at a *strip club*?"

"Mmmhmm. Yup." Another bite.

Vanessa's mouth gaped open as she rested her elbows on the table and leaned forward, as if someone was about to spill deep secrets.

"It's not a big deal," Tallis said. "She's allowed to work wherever she wants. She's making a living, and I respect her for it."

"I mean, sure, *you* respect her. But do all her clients?" Vanessa asked.

"How did you even get a stripper to agree to a date?" Xavier asked.

Tallis shrugged. "I dunno. I went to one of the private dance rooms in the back so I could talk to her one-on-one, and I just sorta asked her."

"Oh, honey," Vanessa cooed, her voice laced with condescension and a little amusement. "Those girls will do or say anything in those private rooms to get a good tip. They get paid more to flirt with you."

Tallis felt his heart sink and his stomach churn. He set down his fork and pushed his plate away.

"I'm so stupid." He rested his head in his folded arms on the edge of the table.

"You are *not* stupid." Vanessa defended. "You didn't know any better, and you just wanted someone special in your life. I think that's sweet."

"She's probably actually really ugly in proper lighting." Xavier jabbed.

Vanessa shot him a warning glare, and he sat back with an "oops" face.

"I think I'm just going to go home," Tallis said, sitting up, his face red with humiliation.

Xavier nodded and Vanessa placed a hand softly on Tallis's shoulder.

"Call us if you need anything," she said.

Tallis returned a half-hearted smile before turning and leaving, dropping his napkin in the chair.

When Tallis got home, he checked his messages and saw one from Ms. Iris.

No work tomorrow. Apparently fifth floor has some emergency repairs needed, and they said it's going to be loud. Just take the day.

Yes, ma'am. He replied before sitting on his couch for a moment with a sigh. After wallowing in self-pity for a few moments, he decided there was no sense in staying up late.

He took a long, hot shower, just standing in the scorching water and staring at the wall. He had so many thoughts buzzing in his mind that they just merged together and sounded like static. His whole body felt heavy. When his fingers turned irritatingly pruny, he finally shut off the water, dried himself, and went to bed.

The next day, Tallis slept through the morning and afternoon, right into the evening. If it weren't for the aggressive knocking at his door, he could've slept even later.

Groggy, he tapped his watch screen to see who was outside his door. The small screen showed Xavier and Vanessa's faces, looking at the door's camera with big smiles, waving.

"We know you're in there!" Tallis could hear Xavier through his watch.

Xavier's comment stung. He knew his friend didn't mean anything by it, but it almost seemed to rub it in Tallis's face that he was alone and pathetic. Of course he was in his apartment. Where else would he be?

Tallis rolled over, letting his feet fall to the floor with a thunk. He stood and shuffled to the door, unlocking and opening it. He greeted his friends' smiling faces with a sleepy grunt.

"I'm gonna cut to the chase," Vanessa said, her voice almost squeaking. "We have a brilliant idea."

Tallis stared back expectantly, rubbing a crusty bit from the corner of his eye.

"We would like to buy you a pet!" She clapped her hands.

The couple watched Tallis, their smiles fading as he took too long to process.

"A pet? Like… an animal?"

"Yup!"

"Why would I want an animal?"

"Companionship! Your apartment feels too lonely. Imagine coming home to a happy little buddy who would be excited to see you every day."

"I don't like dogs," Tallis said. "Xavier knows that."

"It doesn't have to be a dog," Xavier replied. "What about a cat?"

Tallis shrugged.

"They've got those AI pets now too," Xavier suggested. "They're basically fictional animals, but they're robots. No mess, no feeding."

"Yeah," Vanessa said, raising an eyebrow and facing Xavier. "And no real feelings or love. We aren't buying him a robot."

"I don't know, guys."

"C'mon. At least come to the store with us. No harm in looking. If you don't see anything you like, you don't have to get anything."

Tallis looked back and forth between the two before eventually agreeing.

"Get dressed," Vanessa said. "We'll be downstairs whenever you're ready."

Tallis threw on some clothes and brushed his teeth. As he moved about his apartment, he wondered where he would keep a litterbox, food, water, toys. Would he need a scratching post?

When he was done, he joined his friends in the apartment lobby. There was a pet store in Tallis's sector, but Xavier and Vanessa said they had heard about a bigger, better one in Sector 12, so they took the subway.

Despite working in Sector 12 for quite some time, Tallis had never seen a pet store. He wondered if, perhaps, he was just unaware, until Xavier directed them down an unfamiliar street of shops and boutiques. They stopped when they reached a large, flashing neon sign covered in pawprints.

"Ready to make a new friend?" Vanessa asked, trying to contain herself, her smile creeping back onto her face.

"I'm ready for breakfast," he said, half-jokingly. "I'm starving."

"Breakfast? It's dinner time, Tallis," she said. "Come on, let's go!"

"Vanessa, calm down a little. You're gonna freak him out," Xavier laughed. "Sorry, man. I told Vanessa we can get a puppy after the wedding, and she hasn't stopped talking about it since."

"Sorry—I'm just excited. Hang on," she said, rummaging in her purse and pulling out a fat, round lollipop. She handed it to Tallis. "It's not much, but I like to keep candy on hand in case I ever need a little bit of energy. I like this brand— you can suck on these ones for probably a good couple of hours."

"Thanks," he said, ripping off the wrapper and popping the lollipop in his mouth, the stick wiggling as he sucked.

"Now that breakfast is served..." Xavier said, tapping his foot.

"Let's get this over with," Tallis said, still feeling distant. He felt as if he was letting his feet make decisions—the rest of him was just going along with the motions.

They stepped inside the large store, and immediately were enveloped in the smell of wet dog, canned cat food, and hay.

Tallis moseyed down the main aisle aimlessly, with Xavier following beside him. Vanessa, meanwhile, had already hurried off toward a display window looking into a room full of puppies. She gasped and squealed at each puppy, and Xavier looked over at her for a moment, a soft smile on his face.

"Where do you wanna start?" Xavier asked, turning back to Tallis. "Wanna look at cats? Birds? Maybe a guinea pig or something?"

"Wherever," Tallis said, passing by a fish tank full of tropical fish darting back and forth. He stopped, mesmerized by the flash of colors zipping around the tank.

"Bro," Xavier said, pulling Tallis along. "We're not getting you fish. You can't even pet them."

"I mean, you technically can."

"Dude, you know what I mean."

The two walked into the reptile room. It took Tallis all of thirty seconds before he had enough of that.

"No snakes or lizards?"

"Nope," Tallis said with a shiver.

"Hey, at least we're narrowing things down!"

After visiting a room full of bunnies and ferrets, the cat room, and the bird room, Tallis had pretty much determined they weren't going to find him a pet, and he was okay with that.

"We done yet?" he asked.

"Almost," Xavier said. "There's still one more room."

"Not that one, please!" Tallis said, staring down the insect room across from them.

"Absolutely not." Xavier said with a sputtered chuckle. "I don't do spiders—even *I* won't go in there. Only way we'd pay for anything related to bugs is if it's paying to have someone kill them. Big nope."

Tallis breathed a sigh of relief. "Aside from that and the dog rooms, I think we've hit them all."

"Not yet. They've got an upstairs."

Tallis's shoulders slumped.

"Chill. It's one room. The rest of the upstairs just has some random specialty feeds and stuff. It won't take long."

"Fine."

Tallis followed Xavier reluctantly up the stairs. The upstairs was dimly lit, minus the entrance of the new room. Unlike the other rooms, this one was lacking a sign about the animals he could expect.

"What is this room?" Tallis asked.

"You'll see! The pictures of this room online looked awesome."

Tallis followed cautiously behind Xavier. Like all of the other rooms, they stepped into an entrance room, letting the door shut behind them while they used the hand washing station. Since almost every room allowed the animals to roam freely and interact with people, the pet store required people to wash their hands before and after visiting each room.

After drying their hands, they stepped through the second set of doors, into the unnamed room. This new room was full of small trees and patches of grass and dirt. Little bowls of fruits, nuts, and eggs sat positioned at the bases of several trees. When the door closed behind them, a few foxes scurried out, running over to sniff the newcomers.

"Hiiii!" Xavier said with an excited squeak, squatting down to scratch one of the foxes behind the ear.

"It's a fox room?" Tallis said, a small smile creeping on his face. "That's kinda cool. Didn't expect that!"

"Not just foxes," Xavier said. "Just roam around a bit. The article I read said they usually have some other random animals in this one. Foxes, sugar gliders, skunks, spider monkeys, hedgehogs. Oh, and one of the commenters suggested we be careful not to step on them."

Tallis walked around the room, checking the ground before each step, paranoid about squishing a little hedgehog. When he finally spotted one, he pulled the lollipop—which was rather small at this point— out of his mouth, letting his arm down while he knelt and touched the top of the hedgehog with his other hand. The hedgehog hardly seemed to notice him as he gently pet it with a knuckle.

"You're kinda cute," Tallis told the hedgehog. "I like your tiny little ears." He felt a smile creep onto his face.

As he stood back up, thinking to himself how he might like a hedgehog as a pet, he moved his hand back up to his mouth to continue sucking on his candy. When his hand neared his face, he realized the lollipop was gone. His brow furrowed as he looked at his now-empty hand for a second before looking down the ground, thinking maybe it fell from his grip.

Further confused by the missing candy, he did a 360, looking around the room until he spotted a raccoon sitting in a low tree branch just a few feet away from him. The raccoon clutched Tallis's lollipop and stared at him with her tiny black eyes. She moved the lollipop up to her mouth, giving it a couple nibbles without breaking eye contact.

Tallis crept up to the grey thief slowly.

"That's not yours, buddy," Tallis said, getting close to the raccoon and pointing to the lollipop. "I'm not even sure if that's safe for you to be eating."

The raccoon, still staring at Tallis, reached her empty little black paw out to Tallis, setting it on his outstretched finger.

"Okay," Tallis said, his voice a bit giddy. "You're really freaking cute." He chuckled.

The raccoon put the remainder of the lollipop in her mouth and stretched both arms out to Tallis, who stepped closer. She pawed at his shoulder, as if testing it for a second, before climbing and holding onto it.

Tallis could hear Xavier and Vanessa growing closer—or rather, he could hear Vanessa approaching as she babbled gleefully to Xavier about a fluffy brown puppy she got to hold.

"You find anything you like?" Xavier asked as he walked up.

Tallis turned to face him, and Xavier and Vanessa both spotted the raccoon clinging to Tallis's upper arm at the same time.

The smile on Tallis's face answered their question. The couple gathered up some starter supplies in a basket for Tallis and his new friend, while Tallis spoke with the specialist at the checkout counter about caring for raccoons. The specialist tried to pull the raccoon from Tallis's shoulder to put her in a carrier, but she held on tight, refusing to budge.

"Is it okay to bring her home like this?" Tallis asked.

"Yeah, I mean, as long as you don't let her run off. She's a sweet girl, but she's not totally trained or anything. She's litterbox trained, but not much else," the specialist answered.

After Xavier and Vanessa paid and bagged up all the new goodies, the group made their way back to Sector 8.

As they approached Tallis's apartment, Vanessa asked Tallis

if he had any ideas of names for his pet. He did a quick search on his watch to see what raccoons were symbolic of— after all, Tallis was a sucker for symbolism and deeper meanings —but when his search didn't reveal anything interesting, he had to resort to natural creativity.

He looked over at the furball clinging to him, taking the soggy lollipop stick from her mouth.

"I was thinking of calling her Lolli," he said, flicking the stick into a trashcan outside his building.

Vanessa clapped her hands. "Yes! That's so cute. I love it!"

They made their way up to his apartment. Xavier and Vanessa helped him set out some toys, a litterbox, and food and water bowls. When everything was prepped, they decided to head home.

"Thank you, guys," Tallis said, giving Lolli a little scratch on the head. "That was a really nice thing to do. You didn't have to buy me all this."

"Just call it an early birthday present," Xavier said.

"My birthday isn't for months."

"I said 'early,' didn't I?"

They said their goodbyes, and Tallis retreated into his apartment.

"I bet you're hungry," Tallis said to Lolli, who was still hanging onto him. "It's been a big day for you."

Tallis poured a bowl of kibble and set it beside a bowl of water. Lolli turned her gaze from Tallis to the bowl, shimmying down his arm and plopping onto the ground. She scurried over to the bowl and Tallis was finally able to stretch his shoulder.

"The pet store people said you like apples, so if you finish your dinner, you can have an apple. Deal?" Tallis walked over to the kitchen sink to wash off an apple and chop it up in advance. He put the tiny fruit pieces in a baggy and shoved the bag in his pocket.

When he was done cutting up the fruit, he looked back over at Lolli, who was dipping her food in her water bowl before setting the soggy kibble on the floor and chowing down, leaving wet crumbs all over.

"Oh," Tallis said, processing. "Are you gonna do this every meal?"

Lolli looked up to him, holding another handful of food in her water bowl. Tallis couldn't help but to laugh. He admired her adorable ingenuity.

"I'm going to take a shower while you eat. Will you be okay on your own?"

She simply stared back at him and dropped her handful of wet pellets on the hard floor with a spatter.

"Cool. Be good. I'll be fast."

Tallis was never fast in the shower. No matter how short on time he was, he'd always manage to get trapped in a daydream as the hot water pounded rhythmically against his back, leaving him red. This time was no different. By the time he put his 3-in-1 in his hair, he was already in a trance, a ballad stuck in his head as he imagined spinning Big O around the dancefloor at Xavier and Vanessa's wedding. Just as he dipped her and was about to kiss her, there was a loud crash from his living room.

He immediately shut the water off, wrapped a towel around his waist, and stepped out of the shower. He looked around the corner of the bathroom into the living room.

Lolli sat on the floor, surrounded by what used to be a glass vase. She looked up at Tallis, holding out a paw with a little glass shard embedded in the pad of her hand.

Tallis ran over, scooping Lolli up while carefully avoiding the glass on the floor. He hurried her to the bathroom, setting her on the edge of the sink while he rummaged for his rubbing alcohol and some bandage.

"I'm not really sure how to do this," Tallis admitted, carefully pulling out the glass piece and immediately blotting the cut with some alcohol. "I mean, I've patched myself up, but like… I'm not sure if this is ideal. Better than nothing, I suppose."

He wrapped Lolli's paw up with bandage, and she looked at it in disgust, flapping it around for a moment. She tried to set it down to stand on it but picked it back up and looked at it again.

"Sorry," Tallis said. "How about some apple?"

After Lolli managed to rip off her bandages twice, chewed on Tallis's toothbrush when he wasn't watching, and hid some of his socks in the couch cushions, Tallis decided it would be best to keep her in her crate whenever he was going to be away, at least until she was fully trained.

When Tallis had to get up in the morning for work, he set some food in a bowl of water to soak for Lolli while he had his morning coffee. He set her pre-soaked food in front of her, and she simply poked it with her little finger, turning and looking at him with a blank stare that could only be interpreted as confusion and disappointment.

"What? Now you don't like your food wet?" Tallis asked. "It's perfectly fine! It's the same as the food you put in your water, I just figured you'd like it."

Her food made a soft squelch as she poked it again.

Tallis grumbled, checking the time. "You're going to make me late for work. You're gonna have to eat in your crate this morning."

He poured some new dry food and a separate water bowl, setting them and Lolli in her large crate in the living room before locking up and hurrying off to work.

⸻ ‹O› ⸻

"You seem awfully chipper," Ms. Iris said without looking up as Tallis handed her a coffee.

"Ma'am?"

"You normally shuffle in here. I think this is the first time I've heard you pick up your feet while walking." She looked up and handed him a stack of documents.

"I adopted a pet," Tallis said.

"Oh. I figured you just got some use out of that toy you brought to work the other week."

Tallis's face flooded with redness as he floundered for words.

"Joking," she said, looking at him without a tinge of emotion. "Sort of. Anyways, I need the Gillian Street documents finished before lunch, so get cracking."

"Yes, ma'am."

While Tallis worked, he wondered if the hiring team had a chance to look over his application yet. He pictured them carefully observing every piece of it with excited eyes, agreeing to call him right up for an interview. He also pictured them reading his resume, spit flinging from their mouths as they laughed uncontrollably at his stupidity for thinking he had a chance. Both possibilities gave Tallis terrible anxiety.

Tallis managed to get the Gillian files to Ms. Iris right on time, but his focus waned as the afternoon went on. His daydreams transitioned from thoughts of his application to mental images of bringing Big O home to meet Lolli. After all, he figured she was probably an animal lover. Then, he began to feel a hint of guilt about poor Lolli sitting in her crate alone all day. He'd have to remember to leave the TV on for her or something tomorrow.

That evening, Tallis let Lolli out of her crate before he even set his bag down. He pulled some apple pieces from a container in his fridge and handed them to her. She carried them off to his desk on the far side of the living room, sitting beside his keyboard while munching.

Tallis sat at the desk with her and pulled up some emails on his computer. After reading a couple junk promotions, he got up to get a snack for himself. He plopped onto the couch and turned the TV on with his watch, flipping it to some program about the process behind synthetic meat.

Just when the show got to the packaging process, an email notification popped up on the corner of his TV, reading, "Your Application."

Tallis felt his palms begin to sweat as he jumped up to run to his computer. Before he could reach it, Lolli finished her last apple piece and stood, shuffling a couple steps and sitting on his keyboard. She pawed at the mouse, ears twitching with every click.

"No!" Tallis screeched at her, his frantic swatting was met with a little grumble as Lolli hopped down from the desk.

He scrolled through his emails and even through his trash, desperately looking for the email but unable to find it.

"What did you do?" he yelled, looking once again through his emails, refusing to believe it was gone.

Lolli sat on the floor at his feet, staring up at him. She stuck her arms up.

"Not right now," Tallis said. "I don't want to play with you."

Lolli's arms were still outstretched as he walked away, lying down in bed while he wondered what to do next.

He thought maybe it would be best to email Ms. Iris and explain the situation, so that was precisely what he did. With the addition of repeated apologies and promises to never let it happen again, he sent the email off. He nibbled on a hangnail while he stared at his screen, as if she was bound to reply right away.

Tallis thought that perhaps this was a sign. Maybe this was the universe sparing him the pain of rejection. Rejection can't hurt if your raccoon deletes it before you ever see it, right? He felt overwhelmed, his chest heavy and his stomach upside down. He imagined Ms. Iris checking her email and feeling so disgusted with Tallis that she deactivates his access into the building entirely, unwilling to even tell him he's fired. After all, it was careless to leave his computer unlocked like that. As he began to panic, Lolli charged at him, launching herself onto his lap as if her snuggles would make everything okay.

The next day crept by and all Tallis did was lie in bed, legs flopped over the side as he stared at the ceiling, images of his boss's disappointment growing more and more intense in his mind. It wasn't until Lolli crawled into bed with him that he finally realized the time.

"Damn, Lolli," Tallis said, looking at his watch. "I'm sorry. I'm mad, but I'm not going to starve you. You must think I'm a jerk."

He stood, holding his arm out and allowing her to scurry up to his shoulder for a ride to the kitchen.

Tallis skipped his own dinner, opting to take a shower and go straight to bed instead. He felt too sick with nerves to force anything down, even though he knew he would feel worse in the morning with an empty stomach.

Worse is precisely how Tallis felt in the morning. With a pounding headache, every step of his walk to work seemed to echo in an empty skull. Despite the throbbing in his head, he couldn't help but stop on his way to Bru, distracted by little pink ripples in a puddle.

He loved the city, even though so many people around him seemed miserably complacent there. The city itself was beautiful, but Tallis felt that people would truly fall in love with this place over and over again if they just took the time to look at the little works of art around them. Tallis's favorite happened to be the way the light for Buzz's Elecrosuite reflected in the puddle that always formed in the dip in the sidewalk.

He pulled his camera out of his work bag, snapping a few pictures of the puddle. One of the photos perfectly captured the moment a water droplet touched the puddle's surface, and Tallis wished he had taken that photo before submitting his portfolio. Not that it mattered now.

The closer he got to work, the more he felt his deep heartbeat could be heard by everyone around him. He rounded the corner to bring Ms. Iris her coffee, but instead, he was met by her closed office door.

He stood, puzzled for a moment with her coffee in his hand. Her office lights were off. He turned and went to his desk, pulling up his email to make sure he didn't miss some sort of message from her, but he saw nothing. He checked his watch, seeing no missed calls or messages there either.

Two of the CAs walked in shortly after him and went straight toward the conference room. Tallis hopped up from his seat and ran clumsily toward them, startling them in their conversation.

"Excuse me," Tallis said. "Do you guys know where Ms. Iris is today?"

He was met with a shrug and a headshake as the two CAs closed the conference door when he left.

Naturally, Tallis couldn't just assume Ms. Iris was sick. Ms. Iris didn't get sick. Not knowing the consequences of his deleted email ate him alive. Even if she were furious with him, he would've rather her come to the office and blow up at him. Somehow, her absence and the unknown of it all stung worse.

That day, Tallis managed to use his anxiety to his advantage, staying extraordinarily focused on doing enough work to validate his continued employment, rather than letting himself wallow in his disappointment. The self-loathing could wait.

While flipping through his documents for the day, he spotted a spreadsheet with the word "REM" printed in bold at the top, with "Dream Depot" below. Tallis recognized the name, but he couldn't place where he had seen it before. He also remembered hearing about REM, thinking back on the meeting he overheard not long ago. REM was some kind of drug—he knew that much. One of the CAs said something about it being customizable, but how would that even work?

He skimmed over the document, hoping for some information, but it was just a list of B-roll shots from the video Tia captured. All Tallis was meant to do with this document was log the hand-written shot names and video lengths into a continuous spreadsheet of video clip data. He set the paper down, disappointed. With a dramatic huff, he adjusted his posture and got to work.

For the first time in a while, Tallis finished his stack of documents and cleared his email inbox before the day was even over. At that point, it was obvious Ms. Iris wasn't going to assign him things from home, so he could've simply gone home for the day. Instead, he wrote up an overly sentimental and heartfelt apology letter. He tried to word it in a way that took responsibility, rather than try to garner undue pity. He was about to hit the send button on the email before deciding this would best be printed old-school. After printing it and signing it by hand, he slid the letter under her door.

It was only about a half-hour before his usual quitting time, so Tallis decided to log out of his computer and head home a bit early.

On the subway ride home, an overweight man in stained sweatpants sat on one side of him, and a mother sat on the other side with two toddlers in her lap. One of the toddlers kept pulling at Tallis's sweatshirt, while the other was flicking boogers near his feet. The fat man on his other side subtly lifted a leg for a moment before lowering it again. Moments later, the smell of eggs filled the subway. Despite the chaos around him, Tallis felt empty. He didn't feel any particular way about his current situation. He just sat, staring straight ahead.

When the subway stopped at his station, he pried himself from the toddler's grip and wiggled his way out from the man's fat overlapping on his seat. He popped out the door just as it was about to shut again.

Once he was home, he let Lolli out of her crate and she scurried right up his arm, bumping her nose against his cheek as if to say, "Where were you all day?"

Tallis chopped up an apple, eating a few slices himself and sharing the rest with Lolli. While they sat together, Tallis started tracing back in his recent past. He knew Lolli had deleted that email about his application, but he didn't blame Lolli. But… if he hadn't adopted Lolli, it wouldn't have happened. He thought back on why he adopted Lolli but realized he can't blame Xavier or Vanessa either. They just wanted to get him some companionship because he seemed lonely. But why did he seem lonely? He thought some more, growing fixated on how Big O never showed up for the double date. His anger at her only lasted like a quick spark before he began to see who he felt was truly at fault: himself.

If he hadn't been so stupid, he thought, he would've known she wasn't going on a date with him. Heck, he probably wouldn't have gone to Illusion on his own in the first place.

He had spent the past several weeks completely immersed in the idea of being with her, and to simply forget about it felt odd. The longer he thought about it and about her, the more he began to think he needed closure. Tallis wasn't ridiculous. He knew there was never anything between them that needed closure, but he felt like perhaps seeing her one last time and telling himself this was absolutely it—the end—would offer the ending he needed.

"I think I'm going to go out tonight," Tallis said to Lolli. "I hate to leave you alone some more, but you're not quite ready to go out yet."

Lolli stared back at him from his upper arm with her little black eyes.

"Oh, don't look at me like that." Tallis melted.

He handed her another piece of apple, which she grappled with one hand and happily munched.

"I won't be gone long. An hour or two, tops. I'll get you an extra special treat tomorrow, okay? And we'll work on more training this weekend so you can start going out with me."

After he snuggled with Lolli on the couch for a bit, he set her back in her crate, this time with her dinner and some fresh water.

"Oh!" he said, stopping in his tracks before leaving. He turned, pulling out his work bag and digging out his camera. "I almost forgot, I wanted to show you something."

He clicked through the photos on his camera, pulling up the pictures of the pink puddle from earlier that morning, holding the screen out to her.

"I wanted to show you this. Sometimes, you can see a whole lot of the city reflected in a puddle, and it's almost like an alternate little universe. I like to think about what might go on in that little world. Plus, I thought it was pretty, and I know you're probably bored cooped up here all day. Once we work on some training, I'll take you to see all kinds of pretty things outside." He tilted the angle of the screen. "See it?"

Lolli seemed to look at the screen and back at Tallis. He wasn't sure if she understood, but he told himself she did.

"Alright," Tallis said, putting away his camera. I'll be home in a bit."

He gave Lolli a little wave as he made his way out the door, once again hopping on the subway to visit Illusion.

Tallis knew he'd been visiting Illusion too often when the girl greeting at the front door addressed him with a "welcome *back*."

He avoided direct eye contact, shuffling through the door and making his way to the bar. He kept his head low, and in doing so, he noticed the strange pattern of circles with dots in the centers on the floor. Tallis wondered why the floor would have an eyeball design, but the more he thought, the louder his common sense whispered to him that the pattern was most definitely not eyeballs, but rather a repetitive design of boobs.

At this realization, he felt strange for staring at the floor and immediately looked up, just in time to nearly collide with one of the dancers.

"Sorry!" he said, backing away from her as she threw him an eyeroll before leaving.

At the bar, Tallis sat, once again falling victim to the farting chair. He was no less embarrassed this time as the first.

"What can I get ya, love?" the bartender asked him, leaning over the counter and playing with a strand of her black hair.

"I'll take a kamikaze, thanks."

"Shot or cocktail?"

"Shot."

She went to work, pouring things into a shot glass and setting it in front of him, watching him as he tossed it back with a little shudder.

"Another?" she asked.

"No, thanks." He tapped an icon on his watch to tip the bartender and she thanked him with a nod. Just as she was about to turn around and continue reorganizing supplies, Tallis called to her.

"Just a quick question," he said, leaning into the counter. "Is Big O working tonight?"

"I'm not sure," she said. "Try the big stage. Show's starting soon."

"Cool—thanks."

Tallis made his way up the stairs to the upper stage—the same one as the bachelor party. He took his seat at an empty booth toward the back.

After a while of waiting, the MC called everyone's attention to the stage. There was a quick announcement about some new menu items, and then the MC introduced the first dancer, a girl named Honey.

Honey worked her magic on stage, but Tallis was worlds away, trying to say goodbye to all the made-up images in his mind of him having a great time with Big O at Xavier's wedding. His mind wandered, completely disregarding the purpose of his visit this time. Instead of using this as some sort of closure to a fantasy, he zoned out, imagining some of the kinds of outfits she may have worn as his date. He felt like she would look stunning in green, and he would've gladly saved up to buy her an extravagant dress just so she could feel beautiful. He tried to tell himself it was her loss that she didn't take him seriously.

The show continued, and Tallis hardly paid any mind to the girls dancing their way across the stage. By the time the guests voted on their favorite dancer from the show and she did her victory lap, Tallis's mind had finally made its way toward saying goodbye to what never was. He gave up, standing from his seat and abandoning a basket of complimentary chips.

He stepped outside Illusion. During his time indoors, it had rained. At this point, it was misty outside, and the sidewalks and roads seemed to catch every glimmer of light from the signs on the street. Tallis took a deep breath, inhaling the chilly, wet air as he looked around at his water-speckled surroundings, which seemed to sparkle in the night.

His attention turned toward a nearby bar. He realized he was being unrealistic to expect Big O to actually go on a date with him, and he felt bad for revisiting her work several times, but he was proud of himself for taking a step in the right direction from that point on. For that, he deserved a drink.

The inside of the bar had tall ceilings with tons of small bubble-shaped, dim lights. The bar was at one far end of the room, and the other end was full of plush lounge chairs, low to the ground. Many of the lounge chairs sat beside equally short tables with hookahs on them. The air was a bit foggy and smelled sweet.

Tallis took a seat at the corner of the bar, ordering a strong drink and resting his head in his hand. He glanced up occasionally at the bartender, a bald man in a shirt with torn sleeves and a tattoo of an octopus on his bare shoulder. Tallis began to wonder how far bald people go when they wash their faces, since there's no hairline to define the edge.

By the time Tallis was just about done with his drink, the door opened and in walked Big O in a dressy black coat. She sat in the middle seat at the bar, greeting the bartender with a sweet smile and a quick flutter of her long eyelashes.

Before he could address his objecting thoughts, Tallis stood and quick-stepped to a seat closer to Big O. When she realized he had crept closer and sat just two seats away from her, she tensed up, leaning away from him and holding her hand over her Cosmopolitan.

"Can I get you something else?" the bartender asked, his voice noticeably gruffer this time as he crossed his arms at Tallis.

"Umm," he hesitated. "Gin and tonic, please."

The bartender's stare lingered a moment longer before turning and prepping Tallis's drink.

"Hi," Tallis said to Big O, who had just poured a little vial of blue liquid into her drink.

Her eyes narrowed.

"Sorry," he said, realizing he was coming off creepy. "I just—I recognize you. We've met before, and I just wanted to chat. Please don't leave—you don't have to talk to me again after today."

"You're one of my clients, aren't you?" she asked, removing her hand from the top of her drink just long enough to take a sip.

"No—I mean… technically. I guess. I really was just trying to get to know you though."

"Yeah, 'get to know me' like all my clients wanna know me."

"What?" Tallis thought for a second. "Oh! No! Not like that!"

Big O's brow furrowed, and she looked confused.

"I mean…" Tallis sighed. "What I mean to say is that I wanted to get to know you as a person. I've never seen someone have so much fun while they're working."

"My job can be fun, I guess," she said.

"You have a beautiful smile. Your eyes light up, and it's really cute."

Her mouth opened to speak, but Tallis threw in an "I hope that's okay to say."

Big O's posture softened slightly, and she took another sip of her drink just as the bartender passed Tallis his gin and tonic.

"Where are you from?" she asked.

"Sector 8. You?"

"Sector 3," she said with a light giggle. "Here."

"Oh. Duh." Tallis blushed, taking a generous gulp of his drink and almost choking.

There was an awkward silence for a few minutes before Tallis spoke up again.

"You missed dinner with me and my friends."

"Oh."

"I mean, I guess I should've known better. I didn't really realize what was going on in the moment, and that was really stupid of me. I'm sorry for putting you in that position."

"That's alright," she said. "I hope you had a good time at least."

"I mean, they bought me food. Can't be that bad if there's free food, right?"

She laughed. "Right."

"So, what do you do when you aren't working?" he asked.

She hummed and nibbled at the corner of her lip, her maroon lipstick unaffected. "Nothing too interesting. I like reading, shopping, exploring… I guess."

"You like reading?" Tallis reiterated, a smile growing on his face as he shifted his posture toward her. "Me too. I actually really enjoy writing even more."

"That's cool!" She smiled, her shoulders relaxing. "What do you like to write?"

"A little of everything, I suppose. Short stories, blog posts and research articles, poems, whatever I'm in the mood for and whatever I have motivation for."

"That's really cool."

"Thanks."

The two turned their attention back to their drinks, and a small group of newcomers at the far end of the bar stole the bartender's attention. Big O twirled a little black stir stick around the remainder of her drink, her eyes out of focus. Tallis nibbled on his straw, throwing occasional glances at her from the corner of his eye. He caught a glimpse of the dainty golden chain woven through several small holes along the outside of her ear. He wondered if the little dangly bit at the end ever made her ear itchy. That image devolved into him picturing her stopping in the middle of one of her dances at Illusion to scratch an incurable itch on her ear to the point that she looked like a dog with fleas.

When she finally spoke up again, he jumped in his seat, startled out of his daydreaming.

"Did you grow up in Neuvale?" she asked.

"Sort of," Tallis answered. "I was born a few hours outside the city. Tiny little town that had more cows than people. I moved here when I was four, so I don't remember it much."

"Does your family live in the city now?"

"No, they moved back after I graduated high school."

"Oh," she said, her eyebrows lowered and her soft smile faded. "So, you're all by yourself?"

"I mean, I have friends—like the one getting married. And I recently adopted a pet, if that counts."

She perked back up, grinning. "You have a pet? What kind?"

"A raccoon—"

Before he could tell her about Lolli, she let out a shrieking gasp, tapping her fingertips together rapidly with a little bounce in her seat.

"Raccoons are my *favorite!*" she said. "What's its name?"

"Her name is Lolli."

Tallis shared the story of how he came to meet Lolli, and how she had kept his apartment life interesting ever since. The entire time, she watched him and listened, her big eyes crinkled at the corners as she smiled at his stories.

"She sounds adorable!"

"She is." Tallis nodded. "I didn't think I wanted a pet, but she keeps things exciting. I guess I'm not all that exciting myself."

"I'm sure that's not true."

Tallis scoffed.

"Well, your challenge for the week is to do something exciting." she said while pulling a stray hair off her lap. "And then you can tell me about it over drinks this time next week." The corner of her lip twitched upward as she flicked her eyes up to observe him.

Tallis stared back at her. He wondered if she was just flirting because she was used to doing it for work.

"You good?" she asked, her smile fading.

Tallis gulped and nodded rapidly. "Yup, yup, all good!"

She raised her brows, her lips flat as she continued looking back at him.

"Wait… were you serious? You," he motioned to her, "wanna go out for drinks with *me?*"

"I didn't think I was being that discrete. Yes, that's what I was getting at."

"Holy cow."

At this, Big O looked over to the bartender, who was holding back laughter as he watched the train wreck with crossed arms.

"I mean, if you're sure," Tallis said. "Yeah. I'd love to."

"Fun! Same time and place next week then. You better do something exciting to talk about. And I wanna see Lolli, so get some pictures for me." She stood up, tapping a miniature screen on her necklace to tip the bartender.

Just as she was almost out of earshot, she stopped and turned back to Tallis and smiled.

"My name's Odessa."

The next morning, Tallis woke up and stared at himself in the mirror for a solid few minutes, trying to discern if the previous night's events were just another figment of his imagination. He knew it was real, but it felt too good to be true. The realist living in his head told him it would just be a repeat of the dinner date, but the dreamer Tallis had faith.

His excitement woke him up earlier than he was used to, so he took the time to check his emails after feeding Lolli. The most recent email in his inbox was titled "FWD: Your Application" and was from Ms. Iris. His heart nearly stopped as he clicked to open it.

The email was forwarded, but the only text above the forwarded email itself said, "Don't let your raccoon near your computer anymore. Congratulations."

His eyes flew over the words until he found the line he wanted to see: "We'd like to set up a time for an interview."

Tallis read the email over and over, sure that he must have misread. Some sort of unnatural, excited yelp burst out of his mouth, and he stood from his desk, unable to contain himself. He paced across his room, hands woven through his hair and heart racing. He reached a finger to his watch, about to call Xavier before stopping himself. It was too early to bother him, but he'd have to see if his friend could meet him for lunch later.

Considering he woke up ahead of schedule, he took his time that morning. He put Lolli up in her crate, giving her some extra scratches and goodies before making his way to Bru to pick up Ms. Iris's coffee, stopping at his favorite pink puddle along the way. The dip in the concrete and Neuvale's consistent rainy weather made it basically impossible for that puddle to ever truly disappear. He tapped the water's surface with his shoe, sending wide pink ripples across it as he let out a contented chuckle before continuing on his way.

Once Tallis was in the office, he delivered Ms. Iris's coffee, trying to bite back his smile so he would seem cool and professional.

"Congratulations, Tallis," Ms. Iris said, looking up at Tallis for once when she reached for her coffee. "Your portfolio intrigued the entire hiring team. When did you schedule your interview for?"

"Thursday at four, ma'am. And thank you."

"End of the day?"

"Yes, ma'am."

"You're going to look exhausted. Your clothes'll get wrinkled from sitting all day. You didn't think this through, did you?"

"Oh…"

Ms. Iris sighed, taking a sip of her coffee. "Take a long lunch Thursday. Go home at two o'clock and freshen up."

Tallis didn't realize he was clenching his teeth until that moment. His clench loosened and he stared back at her, blinking a couple times to see if this was real.

"Are you just going to stare at me? Get to work. Got some billboard invoices in early—there's a stack of 'em on your desk."

"Yes, sorry," Tallis said, stepping out of her office, only to peer back inside to throw in a quick "thank you."

At his desk, he focused on the skyscraper of documents beside his computer, determined not to disappoint Ms. Iris. He set a goal for himself: complete a quarter of the stack, and then he'd allow himself to call Xavier to tell him the exciting news.

Inevitably, Tallis took longer than he intended. He reached his goal, but only after having to shake himself from several daydreams of his interview—sometimes imagining the hiring managers accepting him on the spot, other times picturing them all falling asleep after his answer to just the first question.

Tallis dialed up his friend and waited for an answer, his leg bouncing in his seat. When Xavier finally answered, Tallis didn't even wait for the "hello" before blurting out, "Let's get lunch today."

"Shoot, dude." Xavier chuckled. "You alright?"

"Yeah, just gotta tell you something."

"Not dying, are ya?"

"No, nothing bad. Promise. It's good. Look, I'll even pay for your food."

"You're lucky I'm off today," Xavier said. "I've been swamped at work. Plus, you know I can't turn down free food."

They scheduled their lunch outing, and Tallis went back to his documents. Shortly before he was about to head out to meet Xavier at the restaurant, the CAs entered the office, more focused and hurried than usual as they all gathered around the table.

"The deadline's today, Tia," one of them said. "What took so long?"

"Sorry," Tia said, flicking the conference screen on and navigating to a video. "This shit's way more intense than I thought and it took a long time to really do it justice."

She played the video, and Tallis allowed his gaze to wander over the top of his screen to watch the video.

"*What if reality could be whatever you wanted?*" Tia's recorded voice narrated as the video showed some clips of scenic areas around the city. "*That's exactly what the creators of Reality Enhancement Modification, or REM, wanted to achieve.*"

Next were some shots of storefronts. "*Stores have popped up all around the lower sectors, touting REM as the solution. 'Why escape reality,' they say, 'when you could simply change it?'*"

One of the CAs moved, obstructing Tallis's view of the screen. "*REM is fully customizable for the individual. Change how you see yourself, how you see your family, how you see strangers. You can pick what you want your surroundings to look like, the kinds of smells you want to sense around you. And even after completely altering your own reality, you are still capable of interacting with everyone else's reality as if nothing is different.*"

Tallis's watch buzzed with the reminder he set to make sure he left on time to meet Xavier. He pulled his attention from the video, grabbing his things before heading off to lunch.

The two friends agreed to meet at BBQuisine, a barbeque restaurant that arguably had the best ribs in Neuvale. When Tallis got there, he walked past the holographic pig getting chased by a butcher—he felt it was a bit crude, but he loved the food there.

"What's up, my man!" Xavier beamed at Tallis, wrapping him in a quick hug with an arm slap across the back. "Let's get some food, I'm starving."

Tallis nodded, wanting to get seated with food before spilling his exciting news. He wanted Xavier's full attention to be on the conversation, and when his friend was hungry, there was nothing else he'd think about but food.

They walked through the front doors and stood in line at the counter to order. The restaurant was fairly dark, with little Edison bulb lights strung up on wires from the tin roof ceiling. The queue line was bordered with rusty troughs, which held some discarded paper menus.

They ordered their meals and grabbed a table.

"How's wedding stuff going?" Tallis asked, trying to stall while they waited on their food.

Xavier let out a dramatic sigh, his cheeks puffed out and his eyes big. "It's going." He let out a single laugh. "It's just coming up quick, ya know? Vanessa's got me coordinating with the caterers and the baker while she handles putting together some of the little decorations with her sisters. There's so much stuff—I just thought we'd have like… food… and a cake… and alcohol. And like, her dress and my suit. I didn't realize there was more stuff than that."

One of the workers, a pimply teenage boy with the uniform of pig ears and black apron, set their tray of food in front of them before scurrying off to deliver food to more tables.

"Oh… my… GOD!" Xavier moaned. "Do you smell that? Per-fect-ion."

Xavier ripped into his rack of ribs like a savage, BBQ sauce smearing across his lips. After he tore his way through half of his tray of food, he started to slow down and eventually leaned back in his chair with a sigh.

"So, when are you gonna tell me your news?" he asked.

"Didn't wanna interrupt you." Tallis said. "It looked like you were having a moment." He eyed the pile of bones in front of Xavier.

Xavier shrugged and grinned. "Alright. So… spill!"

"I applied for the empty CA position and they want to interview me."

"That's phenomenal, Tal! I mean, I'm not surprised. But that's so exciting!"

"Thank you." Tallis couldn't help but to smile. "I've wanted this for a long time. I've always thought being a CA would be the most exciting job on the planet. They get to go everywhere, do everything. And they do stuff that's actually fun. I'd be able to make money off the kinds of things I do in my free time!"

"That is the dream, isn't it?"

Tallis nodded.

They continued picking at the remainder of their food for a little while before Xavier spoke up again.

"So, aside from the super awesome news," he said. "Anything else new with you?"

Tallis's mind immediately flashed to the other night at the bar with Odessa.

"N-no. Nope. That's about it."

◆——◆◇◆——◆

Thursday eventually crept up, and by then, Tallis had already rehearsed about a hundred practice interview questions he found online. He added some of his new work to his portfolio to take with him, and he set out his interview outfit that morning.

Tallis was on edge the entire workday in the office. He felt like he was being watched by a thousand sets of eyes, when in reality, the office was incredibly slow that day. Since he was to take a long lunch break to get ready for the interview, he nibbled on a sandwich at his desk while he worked during his usual lunch time. He hardly ate half the sandwich—it felt like every bite was getting lodged in his throat. His forehead started to collect little beads of sweat, and he realized he was death-gripping his computer mouse. At 2pm, he packed up his stuff, threw Ms. Iris a little "thank you" and "see you later" before rushing out the door.

When he got home, he turned the TV on for background noise and let Lolli out to roam around freely while he showered. He had worked on her training more than usual that week as a way to distract him from his nerves, and she was taking to it better than he expected.

When he got out of the shower, Lolli was sitting on the couch, munching on an apple slice while she stared at whatever random show was playing on the TV.

Tallis smiled to himself when he saw her. She looked content and comfy, leaned up against a soft blanket he left bunched up on the cushions. He put on his suit, ran some mousse through his hair, and spritzed himself with a single spray of cologne.

He ran through his checklist in his head. Portfolio. Copies of his resume. Phone and watch on silent. When he checked the time, he realized he hardly had any time to spare if he was to arrive ten minutes early like he wanted. He looked over at Lolli, preparing to put her up in her crate again.

"Do you like this show?" he asked. Upon closer observation, it appeared to be some sort of true crime show.

Lolli turned to look at him for only a second before turning her attention back to the screen.

"Alright. I'm going to trust you today, okay? Please don't make me regret it. Be good." He scruffed the fur on her head and left, locking the door behind him.

Tallis ignored every urge to stop and admire the way the sun was glinting a brilliant orange light off the glass of Opulence. He was cutting it close on time, but he was going to get there right when he wanted to if he stayed focused.

The email instructed him on precisely which floor, hall, and room to wait in. When he arrived, he entered a little glass box of a waiting room, with a few chairs lined against two of the walls, and a water cooler in the corner opposite them.

The rest of the floor seemed dark compared to the waiting room, with its flickering florescent light. The longer Tallis sat there, the longer he thought perhaps he got the date and time wrong. Several times, he pulled up the confirmation email again, checking over and over to see that the date and time lined up with present time. When 4:05pm hit, he was fully convinced this was all part of some cruel joke designed to make fun of him for thinking he had a chance. But still, he waited. Just in case.

At 4:08pm, the lights in the office flickered on and a tall, broad-shouldered man walked down the hall, stopping in the waiting room door. He smiled at Tallis, who stood so abruptly he stumbled, reaching out to shake the man's hand.

"You must be Tallis!" the man said. "My name's Bill. You ready?"

"Yes, sir," Tallis said, flashing the man a nervous, toothy smile.

Bill led Tallis through the empty office space and into a larger glass room. Instead of a claustrophobic waiting area, this one had a tall ceiling and softer lights. There was a long conference table and about a dozen people seated all along one side of it. The only familiar face was Ms. Iris's, at one of the far ends of the table.

Bill motioned to a singular seat across from the dozen. Tallis swallowed the lump in his throat before sitting back into the chair, not expecting it to have wheels. It rolled back about a foot, catching him off guard. He used his feet to scoot back up to the table, his face hot.

Tallis set his portfolio in front of himself. Bill took his seat across from Tallis.

"Is that your portfolio?" he asked, pointing.

"Yes, sir."

"May I take another look at it?"

"Of course!" Tallis reached over the table, handing Bill the portfolio. "I've been working on some new stuff in my downtime, so you'll see some new pieces in there as well."

Bill and the interviewers to either side of him picked through the printed photos and written samples for a while with Tallis watching them, chewing on the inside of his cheek. Whenever one of them would look up at him, he'd throw on a quick smile and nod back.

"Tallis," Bill said, closing the portfolio and handing it back. "You have a fantastic way of capturing the simple beauties of Neuvale. Your vision is stunning, and as the viewer, I can really feel your sense of awe with some of these. Great work!"

Tallis smiled uncontrollably. "Thank you, sir. I really appreciate that."

Bill nodded, directing his attention momentarily to a folder in front of him. He flipped through some pages and clicked his pen before looking up at Tallis again. Then, he asked the dreaded first question: "Tell me a little about yourself."

Fortunately, Tallis had rehearsed this. He told them a brief intro about where he grew up, where he went to school, and how he likes taking pictures and writing in his free time. The entire time he spoke, several of the interviewers scribbled frantically in their notebooks, while others stared mercilessly at him.

When he finished answering the question, he sat, fingers interlaced on the desk. His posture was unnaturally straight with a smile to match. While waiting on the ones who were still writing, he allowed his eyes to wander to Ms. Iris—one of the ones staring at him. When his eyes met hers, however, she put her hands to her sides in a sort of meditative pose, closing her eyes for a second and taking a deep breath before staring intently back at Tallis. He looked back at her, unsure of why she needed the spontaneous meditation session. Her expression flattened and she pointed subtly at Tallis, then mimed a deep breath, complete with hand motions. Tallis let out an almost audible "oh!" when he realized her message. He took a deep, slow breath in, and exhaled, just in time for the next question.

"Tell us about your experiences working for Opulence," Bill instructed.

The interview continued without much surprise. Tallis had correctly assumed most of the questions they asked, and he felt confident that he gave them enough information on the ones he hadn't anticipated. His confidence grew slowly over the course of the interview, up until the final question.

"What makes you the best choice for the open CA position?"

Tallis expected this question, and he began his rehearsed answer without hesitation.

"I'm a creative thinker and a hard-worker. I get all of my work completed by or before deadlines. I spend a lot of my free time taking pictures and writing, so I have a lot of experience and show initiative to learn."

There was the usual silence after this question, but after a moment of watching and waiting for more, Bill spoke again.

"I don't mean for this to sound rude, Tallis, but let me rephrase: Why should we call you back for the second interview? The reasons you gave us are, I hate to say, fairly generic. If we called back every interviewee that gave an answer like that, we would never narrow down the candidates. We're looking for someone exciting. A storyteller who can captivate an audience. An answer like that isn't gonna do it."

Tallis's heart fluttered and he coughed, as if to set it back in rhythm. His eyes scanned each interviewer, landing on Ms. Iris's, as if he were drowning and he expected her to have a lifesaver on hand.

His mouth opened and closed a few times, but it couldn't grasp at words.

"Thank you for your time," Bill said, his tone deeper than before as he broke his gaze, checking a couple boxes on a paper in front of him.

"Wait!" Tallis said before he realized what he was doing.

All the interviewers looked up to face him and he froze.

"Yes?"

"I have a date with a stripper."

A couple of the interviewers suppressed laughter, one in particular biting her lip as she grinned, turning her face away from the table and trying to calm herself. Tallis wasn't sure if they were laughing at what he said or at the general train wreck in front of them.

"Excuse me?" Bill asked.

"I have a date with a stripper tonight," Tallis said, "and if you call me back for the second interview, I'll tell you how it went."

The silence was suffocating. Tallis began to grab his things, ready to bolt if they told him to leave immediately for his inappropriateness. The interviewers stared at him for only a moment, but to Tallis, it felt like an entire day. Just then, a smile stretched across Bill's face, as well as many of the other interviewers—even the corner of Ms. Iris's lip twitched upward.

"Now, that's what we're talking about!" Bill said.

Bill and the other interviewers thanked Tallis for his time, letting him know they'd be in touch with him one way or another about the second round of interviews. While Bill escorted Tallis back through the office privately, he patted Tallis on the back and wished him luck on his date.

When he got home, he was surprised to find Lolli sleeping in the exact spot he left her on the couch. A little corner of one of the couch pillows had clearly been gnawed on, but aside from some small, frayed holes, there was no other damage to the apartment.

"I'm so proud of you!" Tallis said, scooping his sleepy pet up. "You did such a good job."

Lolli's mouth stretched wide in a yawn as she wiggled onto his shoulder.

Tallis checked his watch. It was about dinnertime, and he still had a couple hours until his date with Odessa. He prepped a grilled cheese for himself, setting out Lolli's kibble and water before he sat on the couch to eat his sandwich.

As soon as he took a bite, hot cheese stringing onto his chin, his watch started buzzing and Xavier's profile picture popped up on his TV. He tapped his watch, leaving a greasy fingerprint.

"What's up?" Tallis answered, Xavier's video feed loading onto the TV screen.

Xavier was sitting beside a pool, some sort of orange cocktail in one hand. Vanessa's face popped into view behind him and she squealed.

"How'd it go?" she asked before Xavier could speak.

"I think it went alright," Tallis answered.

"Just alright?" Xavier asked. Vanessa's smile faded.

"I mean, they seemed to like me well enough, I suppose. They said they'd be in touch."

"Oh, Tal," Vanessa cooed. "I'm so sorry."

"Vanessa! What the hell?" Xavier glared at his fiancée. "That doesn't mean he won't get the job!"

"It's alright," Tallis said.

"You should come hang out with us this evening. De-stress after your big interview!" Vanessa suggested.

"Erhm…" Tallis hesitated. "I appreciate that. I think I might just get to bed a bit early. I didn't sleep well last night. Thanks, though."

"Suit yourself," she said. "We'll talk to you later!"

They hung up, and Tallis redirected his attention to Lolli, who was nuzzling up against his arm.

"Wanna go on an adventure?" he asked her. She replied with a little blink and a mindless nibble on his shirt sleeve.

Before it was time to leave for his date, Tallis made sure his hair was gelled, his button-up ironed, and his teeth brushed. He even found time to run a brush through Lolli's fur.

Once he was ready, he grabbed his keys and a pocketful of treats for Lolli.

"Ready to go?" He held out his arm to her and she scurried up to his shoulder. "Hang on tight."

Tallis made his way to the subway station, Lolli bouncing on his shoulder with each step. He stood on the platform and gave Lolli a little head scratch while waiting for the subway to pull in.

"I think you'll really like her too. She's really fun and pretty and sweet. She said she loves raccoons, so she might like you more than she likes me. Which I'm not sure if that's saying much yet."

Tallis smiled and handed Lolli a treat from his pocket. She chewed with her mouth open, little chunks of mush falling to the tiled floor.

The subway arrived, and Tallis was able to grab a seat right away. Since it was rather late on a weeknight, crowds were sparse. While sitting, Tallis began running through greetings in his mind. What was the most nonchalant way to say hi to Odessa? What could he say—and how—to let her know he's interested, but not too eager?

In his daze, Lolli wiggled her way off his shoulder and scampered across the top of the seatbacks of his row. She nearly made it to the other side when Tallis was ripped from his daydreams by a scream.

His head spun, looking for Lolli. She was digging through some lady's furry purse and pulling out a packaged snack when he spotted her.

"What were you thinking?" he called out to Lolli, storming over and snatching her up.

"If you can't control your *rodent*," the lady spat, "it should be exterminated!"

Tallis's face grew hot as he turned back to face her.

He held his tongue, eyeing her furry purse and imagining her skinning a furry sewer rat to make it.

Just then, the subway reached Tallis's stop. He walked toward the doors, waiting for them to roll open. Once they did, he stepped out with Lolli bouncing on his shoulder, completely unaware of the woman's harsh glares.

Tallis and Lolli reached the entrance of the small bar from the last week and stepped inside. Odessa wasn't there, but Tallis expected this—after all, he was thirty minutes early.

He sat in the same spot at the bar as before and ordered a gin and tonic.

The bartender stared back at him for a moment, his eyes wandering to the raccoon on Tallis's shoulder. "Anything for your date?"

"Umm," Tallis thought. "I don't remember what she ordered last time. I'll just wait 'til she gets here. Thanks, though."

"I meant—" he pointed to Lolli.

"Oh." Tallis blushed. "She's okay, thanks. Unless you have some apples or something?"

"We have carrots and celery."

"She likes carrots."

The bartender nodded, turning his back to Tallis while he made a gin and tonic with a side of carrots. He handed Tallis the drink and held the plate.

"Is she friendly?" he asked.

"Lolli?" Tallis turned to face his pet, who was now sitting on the barstool beside him. "She's super friendly."

The bartender picked up a carrot from the plate and slowly held it out to Lolli. She wrapped both her front paws around it and looked back at him.

"She won't eat it until you let go."

"Oh." He released his grip on the carrot, and Lolli began nibbling on her snack.

After a while, the doors opened. Odessa stepped inside, wearing a short cocktail dress. Her hair was parted to the side, exposing her woven chain piercing. She stopped, picking up one of her feet and adjusting her tall heels.

"Over here!" Tallis called, waving. He immediately cringed, feeling like all of his ideas of how to look cool had been flushed down the toilet with his one awkward gesture.

Odessa gave a dainty wave and a smile, adjusting her other shoe before coming over and sitting next to Tallis.

"Sorry," she said, fidgeting with her shoes again when she sat. "New shoes. They're horrible."

"Take them off," Tallis suggested.

Odessa's eyes narrowed.

"Uh. I don't mean that in like… a foot fetishy way. Sorry. I just mean…" Tallis gulped air. "I feel like it would be better if you were comfortable."

She smiled, observing his rambling for a moment before she reached down and undid the straps on her shoes, letting the heels fall to the floor with a heavy thunk.

"Much better," she said.

Tallis turned back to face the bartender, calling him over. When he turned, Odessa was finally able to see Lolli, who was contentedly munching on her snack while still sitting on the barstool beside Tallis.

She squealed, and Tallis nearly fell out of his chair.

"Are you okay?" he asked, eyes wide.

"I didn't even realize you brought her!" She pointed to Lolli, her finger wiggling as she bounced on the barstool. "She's beautiful!"

Tallis released some tension with a light chuckle.

"You said her name is Lolli, right?" she asked.

Tallis nodded.

"Hi, Lolli!" she said in a softened voice. "It's so good to meet you! Your daddy told me all about you."

Lolli stared back at Odessa.

"Can I pet her?"

Tallis nodded, reaching for Lolli, who sunk her tiny claws into her barstool.

"Come on," Tallis said, trying to pry her off the stool. "She just wants to say hi."

Lolli let out a mix of a growl and a whine, to which Tallis released her.

"Sorry," Tallis said, turning to Odessa. "She's not normally like this."

"It's okay. I get it. She's probably just overwhelmed. Do you bring her out often?"

"Nope. This is her first field trip."

"Aww," she cooed. "No wonder! She's just scared, I bet."

Tallis and Odessa talked for a while about work, family and friends, and hobbies. He learned that Odessa had a knack for baking, and her sister lived across the country and they hadn't spoken in two years.

"Wanna move over there?" Odessa pointed to the plush chairs around the hookahs.

"I mean, we can. Why?"

"I wanna smoke."

"Oh. Sure."

The two moved over to the hookah table, Lolli still sitting on her barstool, picking up little crumbs of carrots that had dropped from her mouth earlier.

"So, you said you have an interview for a new job?" she asked.

"Had," Tallis corrected. "Today, actually."

"That's exciting! Did you get the job?"

Tallis laughed. "I don't know yet. They don't usually tell you that sort of thing so fast. I mean, I hope so, but I'm not so sure I'm what they're looking for."

"What do you mean? I'm sure you'd be great at it!" She paused to take a long drag off the hookah, held it, and puffed out a cloud of smoke from her mouth and nose. "What is it for?"

"It's called a Creative Anchor. They're basically the crew that gets to go out and do all the exciting stuff. They go wherever the action is and write stories and articles about it, take amazing pictures and videos… stuff like that."

"Why wouldn't you be what they're looking for?"

Tallis scoffed, a soft smile in the corner of his mouth. "I'm not exactly exciting or adventurous."

"Well… we can work on that!"

"How so?"

Just then, there was the jarring sound of glass shattering. Tallis and Odessa both looked up to see the bartender swatting at Lolli, who was clinging to a high cabinet of cocktail glasses. As she tried to scurry higher, she knocked another glass down at the bartender, shattering it on the floor.

Tallis shot out of his seat and almost tripped on his race to the bar.

"I'm so sorry!" Tallis said as he flew around the corner of the bar counter.

He reached up for Lolli, holding his hand open.

"Come here!" Tallis said sternly. "*Now.*"

Lolli looked down at him, her tail flicking around.

"What is your problem?" Tallis said with a growl.

He turned to the bartender and asked for a carrot. The man obliged, handing one over to Tallis. Carrot stick in hand, he held it up to Lolli.

"Look! A treat! Not that you deserve it right now."

Lolli blinked at the carrot, still for a moment before shimmying down the cabinets and onto his arm. She held her carrot stick and munched contently.

"This is her first time out of the house. We've been working on training." Tallis apologized to the bartender, whose mouth was practically in a snarl.

He stepped out from behind the bar, Lolli now clinging to his shoulder as usual.

"I have to go," Tallis called over to Odessa. "I'm so sorry. I won't bring her next time."

He realized his words and his face grew hot. "I mean. If there's a next time. I'm sorry. I shouldn't assume. That was—"

"Next week?" She smiled back at him.

"Next—yes! Perfect. Yes. Absolutely!"

She waved goodbye and Tallis left the bar with his ill-behaved raccoon.

That weekend, Tallis didn't spend much time with Lolli. He couldn't decide if he was angry with her, embarrassed about the date, or disappointed in himself for not realizing she wasn't ready to go out that long. When Xavier called him up to hang out Saturday night, he jumped on the opportunity, leaving Lolli with one of her favorite TV shows and a fresh bowl of food.

Xavier and Vanessa invited Tallis to check out their new backyard pool. They had it built just a few months prior, and as the weather was warming up, the couple was spending more and more time in it. Tallis knew a little part of Xavier wanted to show off, but that never bothered Tallis—he was more than happy to celebrate his friend's accomplishments.

Xavier and Vanessa had an elegant house in Sector 13. Both of them worked, and both made good money. They dated for years before finally getting engaged, so they had time to build up their wealth together.

"Good to see you, man." Xavier greeted Tallis at the towering, solid oak front doors. "Come on in!"

Tallis stepped inside. It was pleasantly warm outside that evening, but when the cool indoor air touched his skin, it sent an immediate shiver across his whole body.

"I see you got some new artwork," Tallis said, motioning to a car-sized painting of a tropical beach along the foyer wall. "Looks nice."

"Thank you! Vanessa picked that one out. Friend of a friend of a friend did that one. Cool, huh?"

Tallis nodded, following Xavier further into the house. The two stepped into the living room, with its tall ceilings, glowing from three suspended ring lights. The living room was full of floor-to-ceiling windows looking out at the city. Vanessa was in the open kitchen, prepping three bright blue cocktails. When she spotted him, she beamed. "Hey, Tallis!"

"Hey, Vanessa," Tallis said with a little wave.

"I'm going to go get changed upstairs," Xavier pointed. "You know where the towels are. I'll be back in a moment."

Xavier trotted upstairs and Tallis made his way to one of the downstairs bathrooms to change into his swim trunks. When he came back out, pool towel in hand, he joined Vanessa out in the back. The sun was setting, but the couple had market lights installed around and across their pool, keeping it illuminated in a soft glow at all times. The pool was a simple oval, but it had a short waterfall feature along one side of it, and several palm trees surrounding the area.

Vanessa handed Tallis one of the cocktails.

"Blue Hawaiian," she said before he could ask. "I made them a bit strong, sorry."

Tallis chuckled. "Not something to apologize for."

She smiled, walking to Xavier as he stepped out, handing him a drink.

"We've been dying to hear more about your interview." Vanessa said, taking a seat at the edge of the pool and dipping her long legs in the water.

"Let the man relax a little!" Xavier said, setting his drink on the ground. "I'm sure he doesn't want to talk about work all the time."

"No," Tallis said. "It's okay."

Xavier ran and jumped into the deep end of the pool, a surge of water soaking the concrete at the edges. He popped back up to the surface, running his hands over his face and hair. "Damn! Feels good tonight!"

Tallis stepped into the shallow end, still clutching his drink as he walked through the water over to his friends.

Vanessa and Xavier looked at Tallis expectantly, but Tallis had been distracted by the reflection of all the small white market lights in the crystalline water. He traced his hand along the surface of the water, turning the reflections into little white ripples.

"Tal?" Xavier urged.

Tallis looked up, still grazing his hand along the water surface. "What?"

"The interview."

"Oh! Sorry. It went well."

"You pretty much already told us that," Vanessa said.

"Not much to tell. There were more people there than I thought. It was a bit awkward. And I had to wait a good while 'til they called me into the room. They seemed to like my portfolio, but I think I bored them."

"Why would you say that?" Vanessa asked, her voice poorly feigning surprise.

"Well, they called me generic at one point."

"Are you serious?" Xavier's surprise was genuine. He looked offended.

"They asked why they should pick me, and I told them I'm creative... a hard-worker... stuff like that. I don't know. I thought I sounded professional, but I guess it was lacking personality and interest. It's fine." Tallis shrugged and looked back down at the water.

"That's it? I'm sure it went better than that!" Xavier said.

"I mean, I think I saved myself. They seemed happy with my last answer, so maybe I've still got a chance."

"What was the last question?" Vanessa asked.

"The one about why they should pick me."

"I thought you said they didn't like your response?"

Tallis wondered if he should change the subject.

"Aren't they looking for the exact opposite of generic?" Vanessa pried.

"Yeah. But I panicked and threw out the best thing I could to seem interesting."

"Which is?"

"I told them I had a date planned with a stripper, and if they called me in for the second interview, I'd tell them about it."

Vanessa and Xavier stared back at Tallis, their mouths gaping. They exchanged a look before focusing back on Tallis.

"So now what? If they call you back, you'll tell them about how she stood you up and made your friends wait forever for dinner?" Xavier said. "Or are you just gonna tell them about how you misinterpreted her fake flirting and just *assumed* you had a date?"

Tallis's brow sunk as he looked back at his friend.

"Sorry, bro, but what were you thinking?"

"I *did* have a date with her."

Xavier's brows furrowed and he lowered his chin, staring back up at Tallis. "Yeah. Okay. I'm sure you did."

"I did!"

"They don't wanna hear about your pervy dreams, Tallis!"

"I'm not talking about a dream. I really did go on a date with her. The night after my interview. We got drinks. I brought Lolli with."

Vanessa's eyes were bulging as her gaze flickered back and forth between the two men while she sipped on her drink.

"Sure you did."

Tallis crossed his arms.

"Swear," Xavier demanded.

"I swear."

"What the hell were you thinking?"

"What's that supposed to mean?"

"She's just trying to gouge you for more money. She's not just a stripper, is she? She's probably a damn hooker. How could you be so stupid?" Xavier shot.

"She's not," Tallis said. "We just got drinks. She's really fun to talk to. Nothing else happened."

"Yet."

"Nothing's *going* to happen! I just enjoy her company—"

"She knows that! How do you think she makes her money?"

"I didn't pay her to go out with me—"

"You better not have sex with her. Hookers have all kinds of diseases. You'd be better off swimming in the sewers."

"What the hell is your problem, Xavier?" Tallis finally raised his voice.

"I don't have a problem! I'm just trying to look out for my best friend! You deserve the best and paying a hooker to pretend to love you isn't that."

"She's not a hooker!"

"You don't know that. How much do you even know about this girl?"

"Why can't you just be happy for me? Sorry I don't have the kind of money you have. Sorry I'm not about to get married and live happily ever after. Sorry I'm not interesting or fun or successful or anything people want me to be. But God, Xavier. I thought of all people, at least you would be happy for me."

"I'd be happy for you if you found a *real* woman. Or a man, heck! Just not a prostitute!" Spit flung from his lips as he spoke.

"I'm going home," Tallis said, setting his drink outside the pool and lifting himself out of the water.

"Tallis," Xavier called out without moving. "Wait—"

By that point, Tallis was already drying off. He threw the towel against the back wall of the house on his way inside. He could hear Vanessa hollering something to Xavier about, "Why did you have to be such a dick to him? He was being vulnerable with you and you chewed him out!" It didn't matter—Tallis wasn't going back, and no one came after him.

Once Tallis was back home, he slammed the door shut behind him and walked straight to the shower. Hot water pelted his back, and he rubbed his palms against his eyes several times, as if he could wipe away the past few hours. He replayed the evening over and over in his head, each time imagining what would have happened if he said something different. What if he hadn't said anything at all about the interview? What if he had said he had lied to the interviewers, and he really didn't have a date with a stripper? What if he just made up something more generic about the interview, but still told them about Odessa? He could have pretended she was a different girl, not the same stripper that already hurt their friend.

Tallis spent so long in the shower daydreaming that the water began to run frigid before he noticed. He dried off and stepped out, wrapping his waist in a towel before walking out to the living room.

Right outside the bathroom door, he spotted Lolli, sitting on the floor and looking up at him. Before he could say anything, Lolli scampered over to her empty food bowl. She sat beside it, glancing down at the bowl for a moment before looking back up at Tallis, who had followed her.

"Right," he said. "Sorry."

He filled her food bowl and changed out her water, giving her a quick scratch on the head. Unfortunately, Tallis was self-aware enough to know he wasn't going to sleep that night, so he threw on some lounge pants and fell back on the couch. Lolli's program must have ended ages ago, and now some cheesy sitcom was on.

"Are you watching this?" he called over to Lolli. He peered over the back of the couch at her, catching her dipping her full paws of kibble in her water. "Ah, I see you're busy."

Tallis changed the channel, putting on some sort of documentary about the history of candy. He found it fascinating that a pharmacist developed the first candy machine. He imagined putting jellybeans in a pill bottle and thought it would be a brilliant business plan. He supposed there wouldn't be much of a market for it, except for medical personnel with a love of jellybeans.

Just then, his watch chimed. He glanced down, seeing a long text from Xavier that started with an "I'm sorry." Tallis skimmed over some of it, focusing on one specific part: *I know it's hard being the single friend in a group.*

He rolled his eyes. Xavier didn't know what it was like to be single, and they both knew that.

Tallis swiped the notification away with the tip of his finger and went back to his candy documentary.

After she was done eating, Lolli crawled up the back of the couch and moseyed her way into Tallis's lap for snuggles and head scratches.

"I forgive you for the other day," Tallis said to her. "You weren't ready for such a big adventure, and I shouldn't have put that kind of pressure on you."

He ruffled her fur around her neck, and she flattened her ears.

"Sorry." He stopped. "I do hope you like Odessa though. I know you were scared the other day and you were already overwhelmed. I'm sure after some time, you'll understand why I like her so much. After all, she thinks you're beautiful. That's gotta count for something, huh?"

Lolli disregarded everything he was saying, instead opting to lick at the wet crumbs of food stuck between her fingers. When she had finished cleaning herself, she leaned against his hip and dozed off.

After a couple hours of agonizing over each little thing he thought he could've said or done differently, he eventually fell asleep too.

The rest of the weekend went by without much excitement. At least, nothing the average person would find exciting. Tallis, on the other hand, found it oddly pleasing how he had the exact right amount of wheat puffs left in the box for the exact amount of oat milk he had in his fridge. After his riveting Sunday breakfast experience, he felt extra motivated to get some things done around his apartment. When he went to start a load of laundry, he was surprised to find his last load of laundry still in the wash.

"Oops." He peeled a stiff hand towel from the inner wall of his washer, bringing it to his nose and giving it a whiff. A grin crept across his face when he realized the towels didn't smell like mildew. Chucking the stiff but clean towels into the dryer, he turned his attention back to his newest load of laundry.

As he loaded the washer, he thought to himself what fantastic yet simple inventions washers and dryers were. He imagined himself going down to a muddy stream and trying to wash his button-ups by hand, shuddering at the thought. They'd probably smell like real rainwater, instead of his similarly titled detergent.

Monday was a rainy day—just enough of a trickle to quiet the sounds of traffic and passersby. Tallis didn't mind the rain. In a city full of concrete and glass, rain was one of the few natural things that ever seemed to make an appearance in his life.

On his way to Bru to pick up Ms. Iris's coffee, Tallis stopped periodically to take pictures of plump raindrops resting along sleek metal stair railings, neon shop signs, and car windshields. He even managed to sneak a picture of the way raindrops beaded on a ginger woman's hair as she stood, waiting on her ride at the street corner. While in line for the coffee, he flicked through his new photos, admiring the way each raindrop captured different colors and reflections of the city around his subjects. To Tallis, each raindrop looked like its own little world.

After retrieving Ms. Iris's coffee, Tallis turned to leave, spotting a young man in the corner of the coffee shop, uncorking a tiny vial of green liquid. Tallis stopped, pretending to adjust the lid of his coffee while he peered over at the man, who tipped the vial's contents into his drink, giving it a stir. He thought it was odd, but as the man proceeded to drink his coffee like anyone else, Tallis stopped staring and continued on his way to work.

Once in the office, Tallis handed Ms. Iris her coffee. He tried to put on an extra-friendly smile, as if it could help his odds of a second interview. Ms. Iris, as usual, didn't look up.

"Don't you have something to do?" she asked as he

continued to stand in her doorway. "If not, I can *give* you something to do."

"Sorry," he said, still standing there for a moment before retreating to his desk.

⬥⸻⟨◉⟩⸻⬥

The rest of the week went by in a similar fashion. Rainy weather, few words from Ms. Iris, and predictably mundane work every day.

At the end of the workday Thursday—the day of Tallis's second date with Odessa—he finally worked up the nerve to ask Ms. Iris about the status of his interview.

"You'll be contacted one way or another," she said while typing.

Tallis sighed lightly, adjusting his bag on his shoulder. He turned to leave, but stopped as Ms. Iris spoke again, this time a little louder.

"If it's any consolation, they're still on the first stage of interviews."

"Excuse me?"

"We have several applicants who still haven't had their first round of interviews. Second interviews won't be scheduled until all the first ones are done." Tallis looked at her as she spoke. Was she trying to comfort him? "We're accepting a limited number for the second round, so we need to have the full set of first rounds done."

"Thank you," he said, trying to contain his smile.

"Okay." She refocused on her computer.

"You're staying late today?" he asked.

"More updates on that REM story from the other week. It was a popular one, so we're doing more digging. I'm trying to line up some interviews with people who actually have experience with this drug."

"Sounds exciting," Tallis said. "Let me know if there's anything I can do to help."

"Mmm."

Tallis stepped away and made his way out of the building after wishing Ms. Iris a good evening.

He pulled up Xavier's contact page on his watch to call him and tell him there's still hope for the job, but felt a weight in his stomach as his mind flickered back to images of his best friend insulting him at the pool. At that, he swiped off the contact page, going about his walk to the subway.

Before heading out to meet Odessa that night, Tallis made sure Lolli was set up with plenty of food and water, an apple treat, and her favorite program—some sort of detective show that had been playing reruns all week.

Tallis kissed Lolli on the top of the head, handing her a little apple slice.

"I'll be home later tonight. Behave."

She stared back at him, nibbling on her fruit.

Tallis checked his hair one last time in the mirror, smoothing down a rogue strand of hair that had stuck up. He grabbed his camera bag, throwing the strap over his shoulder and walking out the door, locking it behind him and hurrying down the stairs.

He left early for his date, wanting to stop at a little store near his apartment on the way to the subway. His local corner shop was a simple white box of a building, with irritatingly bright LED light strips lining the entire ceiling.

Tallis paced the aisles, expecting the perfect gift to jump out and bite him.

He wondered if Odessa was more of a flowers girl or a chocolates girl. Or maybe she'd rather have a bottle of wine? He picked up just about every box of candy in the sweets aisle, looking it over and trying to imagine Odessa enjoying the candy inside. For some reason, he struggled to imagine her enjoying a cheap box of candy.

Just when he was about to give up, he spotted a display of plushies near the register. Odessa certainly didn't seem like the sort to like stuffed animals, Tallis assumed. It wasn't until he noticed the furry little raccoon plushie that he changed his mind.

He picked up the stuffed raccoon, with its cartoonishly large yellow eyes with flecks of golden glitter. After paying, he was about to leave the store when he realized he didn't have a pretty way to display the present for Odessa. He turned back around, dipping down into the giftwrap aisle and returning to the register with a teal giftbag and matching tissue paper. Just then, he had a last-minute idea.

"Hang on," he said, leaving his stuff on the register counter as he ran down the craft aisle, stopping at a display of ribbons.

Lifting his watch into view, he tapped out a search: "Color symbolism."

The search pulled up some information about the meanings behind different colors, and one in particular stood out to him: yellow. Apparently, it was symbolic of happiness and optimism. Whether or not Odessa would casually know the symbolism didn't matter to him. He just liked knowing there was a deeper meaning behind his choice.

With the yellow ribbon in hand, he went back to the register once again to pay.

"Do you have any paper?" Tallis asked the girl behind the counter, who looked back at him with blank eyes, smacking the gum in her mouth. "Just a piece of plain paper."

"Yeah."

"Can I have one?"

"Yeah, whatever." She reached under the counter, grabbing a sheet of paper and handing it to him.

"Can I borrow a pen, too?"

Her eyes narrowed.

"I'll be quick, I swear."

"You'll hold up the line."

Tallis looked behind him at the empty store. She continued to smack her gum and stare at him.

"Please," he insisted.

She rolled her eyes, reaching under the counter again and tossing the pen onto the countertop.

"Thank you."

Tallis quickly wrote out the word "Lolli" onto a small section of the paper and handed the girl her pen.

"Thanks again," he said, grabbing his things and leaving.

Once outside the store, he tore off the section of paper with Lolli's name, poking a hole in either end of it and weaving a piece of ribbon through it. He took the stuffed raccoon out of his shopping back and affixed the makeshift collar around its neck, setting it inside the gift bag and covering it up with tissue paper.

He checked his watch. He would be cutting it close, but he was confident he could make it to the bar on time. With a bit more speed to his step, Tallis made his way to the subway.

As he descended into the underground station, Tallis

was met by a crowd of girls in black dresses with pink sashes. He stopped in his tracks, surprised to see so many people out on a Thursday night. As he crept closer, trying to work his way over to the edge of the subway tracks, he noticed the sashes all said "Clara's 21st birthday bash" in white script.

There was hardly enough room to wiggle between any of the girls, let alone reach the subway platform. Tallis settled for where he was at, standing and waiting for the subway to arrive.

Once it pulled up and the doors slid open, few people exited, but the band of birthday bashers swarmed forward, crowding into the subway. Just as they finally stopped shoving their way past Tallis, he stepped forward to try to wedge his way on board and the doors slid shut in front of him. The subway zipped off to its next stop, leaving him alone in the station.

"No!" Tallis hollered after the subway before grumbling to himself and resigning to a nearby bench to wait for the next ride.

Every few seconds, he'd peer at his watch again. He wished he had Odessa's number so he could at least apologize in advance. Minutes crept by slowly, with no subway in sight. It wasn't often that Tallis had to wait on a second subway. He wasn't even sure how far apart they arrived.

Ten minutes had passed, and Tallis was beginning to panic. His leg was shaking, and he couldn't stop nibbling on a hangnail. When the subway finally pulled in, he shot out of his seat and nearly had his nose to the door before it could welcome him inside.

He hurried in, opting to stand instead of sit. He was too antsy to sit.

The subway continued its path. Was it moving slower than usual? Tallis swore it was.

When the subway finally stopped at Sector 3, Tallis was once again nose to the door, ready to run. The doors slid open and he zipped out, nearly barreling into an elderly man waiting to board.

"Sorry!" he shouted back at the man, refusing to stop as he sprinted out of the station and down the street, giftbag in hand and camera bag bouncing at his hip.

He reached the entrance of the bar, threw the doors open, and tried to wipe the look of exhaustion from his face. Tallis was mentally prepared to see Odessa storming out of the bar, offended that he would waste her time, but instead, he was met by a moderately empty barroom with no Odessa in sight.

He quick glanced at his watch. Fifteen minutes late. She may have left a long time ago.

Defeated, Tallis slunk over to the bar, easing himself onto the stool and letting his head fall into his hands.

"Should I give you a minute?" the bartender asked.

Tallis groaned, slowly lifting his gaze. "Give me a shot, please."

"Of?"

"I don't care."

The bartender turned to the bottles, selecting a few and mixing them into a shot glass. He topped the shot with a dollop of whipped cream before sliding it toward Tallis, who now had his face in his arms on the bar counter.

"I wouldn't do that if I were you," the bartender said. "I've been using the same rag to wipe these counters all week."

Tallis lifted his head, his lip snarled in disgust as he pulled his arms from something sticky on the bar top. "Isn't that some kind of health code violation?"

The bartender shrugged.

Tallis's eyes traveled down to the pretty little shot in front of him. He picked it up, sucked the whipped cream off the top, and tossed the rest back into his mouth.

"Oh my God," Tallis said, inspecting the inside of the empty glass, "that was like a little dessert. What was that?"

"A blowjob."

Tallis stared back at the bartender. "Ha-ha," he said flatly.

"I didn't come up with it," he said, his hands splayed in innocence. "That's just what it's called."

"Who would call it that?"

"Someone with a sense of humor."

"I suppose."

Tallis thought for a moment how impressive that, while some shots taste like pure acetone, others could taste like a miniature treat and enough of them could still get someone drunk.

"Can I have another?" Tallis asked, wiggling his shot glass.

Three shots in, Tallis's eyes began to wander. He looked over at a lone guy sitting at one of the hookahs, puffing little rings into the air. He wondered how that man learned such a trick. Did he discover it on his own, or has that knowledge been passed from friend to friend? He then looked over at two women, sharing a large cocktail and giggling together as they took turns showing each other their phones. It was then that Tallis's gaze drifted, focusing outside the glass door and spotting a beautiful blonde in a trenchcoat. She was quick-stepping in her stilettos, the door nearly catching her as she pushed forward unsteadily to open it. When she entered, she met Tallis's eyes and beamed back at him.

"I was worried you'd have left by now," she chimed at him as she approached.

Cognitive capacity stunted by alcohol, Tallis simply looked back at her, confused for a moment.

She didn't seem to notice. "I didn't mean to be so late. I was working in the private rooms today. A client paid for a bunch of extra time at the last minute. So sorry about that!"

"It—"

"Wow! Started without me?" She interrupted, eyeing the empty shot glasses.

"Turns out your date really likes blowjobs," the bartender said.

Tallis's eyes widened, but Odessa simply chuckled at this statement, sitting down and ordering one herself.

"Man," she said as the bartender passed her a shot, "I haven't had one of these since college!"

"You went to college?" Tallis asked.

Odessa turned, her smirk unmistakable. "Why do you look so surprised?"

"No!" Tallis's face beamed red. "I'm not surprised. I just—"

"You didn't think a stripper could be educated," she said. "I get it."

"No! I don't think that! I—"

"We're all high school drop-outs with daddy issues, hmm?"

"Absolutely not!"

"I bet you think these are fake, too," she grabbed her boobs, staring directly into Tallis's soul.

He hunched over, looking like he'd simply disintegrate if she said another word.

"I went to college, my dad and I still get lunch at least once a month, and these are totally real, albeit enhanced by a big push-up bra."

"You don't have to defend yourself to me," Tallis said, forcing himself to look up at her again. "I didn't make any of those assumptions about you. Honestly."

"I'm giving you a hard time, Tallis," she said, her voice soothing him like hot tea and honey.

"I'm sorry."

She forced a soft smile, opting for silent observation as he squirmed in his seat, debating what to say next.

"Oh!" He perked up, reaching for his giftbag on the bar floor. He pulled it up, a thin piece of the paper from the bottom of the bag sticking to the floor and tearing. "This is for you." He handed her the bag.

She let out a light gasp, her hands shooting out for the bag. Tallis watched, noticing how her hands ripped the tissue paper out without any dignity before plunging her dainty fingers in, pawing for the gift. When she felt the soft fur of the plushie, she yanked it out and let the bag drop to the floor, forgotten.

Tallis thought to himself how peculiar it was that people get so excited at the sight of a giftbag, but as soon as they get their hands on it, the bag itself is immediately deemed trash. After all, they don't even know what's inside the bag. They get excited, and for all they know, it's an empty bag.

Odessa cooed, squeezing the stuffed toy against her very-real boobs in a tight hug.

"I love it!" She took a closer look, noticing the paper tag and ribbon collar. "Aww! You even made it a collar! It says Lolli! That's precious."

Tallis tried to act nonchalant, biting his lip to hold back his proud grin.

"I'll bring her back on another date eventually," Tallis said. "She needs a bit more training first. So, for now, you've got this Lolli instead."

"'Another date'?" Odessa raised an eyebrow, smirking.

"I mean—"

"We'll see how you do on this one, first," she played.

"I'll do my best."

"I have an idea," she said. "Do you trust me?"

"I mean, I just met you, sort of."

Clearly not the answer she was hoping for or expecting, her expression flattened.

"You said you wanted to do more exciting things, didn't you? So… do you trust me?"

"Oh," Tallis said. "I trust you."

She smiled and perked back up.

"Good. Come with me."

She paid the bartender and ushered Tallis out the door with her, stepping into the dark street. It was misting outside, and the neon lights lingered in every tiny drop in the air. Odessa grabbed Tallis's hand, the feeling of her fingers wiggling between his sending a ripple down his chest.

She tugged his hand, her pace quick as she guided him back toward the direction of the subway.

Tallis's attention kept flickering between things. One moment, he was entranced by the vivid colors reflecting on the slick asphalt. The next, he was watching the way Odessa's blonde hair bounced—weightless—with every hurried step.

"Where are we going?" he finally asked, adjusting his camera bag on his shoulder as they walked.

She hushed him, not looking back at him as she continued to lead. When they reached the alley with the glowing purple eye, she took a sharp turn.

Tallis looked up at the sign, remembering it labeled as Dream Depot, and he began to wonder what kind of business would have such an obscure name. He thought it sounded like a mattress store, but it was a rather odd place for that. As Odessa pulled open the door, she tugged him inside, letting the door slam them into darkness. This definitely wasn't a mattress store.

Dream Depot was a store, but Tallis was unsure what they sold. The ceilings were low, and the small shop was full of shelves that looked like they belonged in a bookstore. As Odessa guided him toward the aisles, he noticed the shelves didn't host books, but rather, long glass tubes, with bright lights illuminating each one in different colors from above.

Odessa walked over to a barrel at the end of one of the aisles, reaching down and pulling out two empty glass vials. She handed one to Tallis with a soft smile.

"What's this for?" he asked.

"Welcome to my favorite place in the world!"

"A store?"

"It's not just *any* store. This store can make your dreams come true."

Tallis loved idealizing things, but even he didn't follow what Odessa was saying.

"Come here," she said, beckoning him as she tucked down one of the aisles.

Each aisle appeared to have a different color scheme. She chose the aisle full of bright yellows, walking about halfway down before stopping at one of the big glass tubes.

"You can technically start with any color. Yellow is the most fun, if you ask me. It's called 'costuming'."

"Should I be taking notes?"

"Smart ass."

Tallis chuckled.

"Anyways," she continued. "Costuming is what you want others to look like. You'll still be interacting with real people in real time. This only changes their aesthetic. So, you find whichever one sounds best to you, an—"

"I'm lost," Tallis interrupted. "I don't mean to cut you off, but I truly don't know what you're talking about."

"This," she motioned with her arms, "is called REM. It can change the way you see the world. *Literally.*"

"I've heard of this stuff," Tallis said, soft enough that Odessa didn't hear him.

"And don't worry," she said, "it's totally legal. A lot of places and people frown upon it, but it's legal, and it's safe. It's just something to spice up life. Life is boring, ya know? It's full of shit. Other drugs are bad for you—it's no better than coating shit in sparkles. It's glittery, but it's still shit. This though? This is the real deal."

"It's safe?" Tallis asked.

"Yup. I just said that."

Tallis nodded in confirmation. "Just checking."

"I mean, sometimes you can basically have the REM-equivalent of a 'bad trip' or whatever, but they almost never happen. It's really only if the vials aren't properly cleaned. Which, I mean, they aren't always spotless, but even still… even a vial that's not totally cleaned isn't going to necessarily cause a bad dream. Sometimes it's totally fine—just won't have the effect you picked out. Other times, it might be enough to mess with the mixture you put in there. You really shouldn't have two things from the same row. Like costuming. If there's enough left in the bottle, it could technically cause some weird effects. Only ever put one of each thing in your vial. Don't put two in there or they can interact and it's a bit more unpredictable. I had one once where people looked like clowns. I definitely didn't want that. Bottle was dirty or something."

"So, when you say, 'bad dream,' does it only work when you're sleeping?"

"No. The opposite. It's just called a 'dream' or a 'bad dream.' Slang, REM's marketing, who knows where it came from."

Tallis was infatuated with the idea. The thought of the drug made him uneasy, but he couldn't deny the itching curiosity he felt as he looked at the labels on the yellow glass tubes.

"I'm going to make one of my usuals," she said, continuing her presentation. "You can pick whatever you want, and I can help. But I want everyone to wear ballgowns and fancy suits. Think Victorian. So that's this one, here."

She put her vial to a tiny nozzle at the bottom of one of the tubes, holding in a little button as yellow liquid trickled into her vial.

"Oh!" she said, pulling her vial away. "I almost forgot. See these lines?" She held the vial up close to his eyes, pointing to tiny black lines all up the vial like a measuring cup. "Don't overfill. Each color gets one section of the vial. Again, doesn't matter what order."

She noticed Tallis's furrowed brow as he inspected the lines on his vial.

"Nothing bad will happen if you mismeasure," she reassured. "It's just that if you get too much costuming, you might not have enough room for setting, or scent, or something else, so it won't work as well. That's all."

Tallis sighed, his posture relaxing.

"How did you learn all this?" he asked.

"Some of it through experience, a lot of it through the shop owner. They'll teach anyone the ropes, but I figured I'd give you my own lesson. Special access!" She winked. "Go on! Pick your costuming."

Tallis rubbed at the glass vial in his fingers as he meandered, checking out every single yellow tube's label. He stood, dazed by the glow of the drug in its tubes—each one looked identical to its neighbors, but the labels revealing that they were, in fact, entirely unique. He tried to wrap his mind around it all, but instead ended up imagining the mad scientist that must have invented REM. Tallis figured the scientist must live in his head just like him. How else could anyone come up with such a bizarre drug?

"Are you going to look at every label in every aisle?" Odessa asked, crossing her arms and swirling the yellow liquid in her vial.

"Sorry."

"We can always come back another time and you can try something different. Don't worry about checking out every single one of them today."

Tallis nodded, standing in place for a moment in thought before returning to a tube near the beginning of the aisle.

"This one sounds fun." he called over to Odessa from the other side. She finally perked up, trotting over to meet him.

"*Vegas*," she read. "That *is* a fun one!"

Tallis put his vial to the nozzle and held the button. The liquid dripped slowly, and he squatted down to watch for when it precisely hit the first line. Once it did, his finger flew off the button as if it caught fire.

"Good," Odessa confirmed when he looked back at her. "Time for setting."

Setting turned out to be an aisle of blue tubes.

"Setting can be a bit tricky to get used to, so let me know before you pour so I can make sure you're doing a good one for beginners."

Tallis nodded and began scanning some of the blue tags until he found one that piqued his interest. He flagged Odessa down and she burst out laughing.

"Absolutely not!" She laughed some more, shaking her head.

"What's so funny about 'beach'?"

"If you're not used to REM, it'll make you walk funny. You can always tell people who picked 'beach' because they walk like they think they're in sand. They pick their feet up all dramatic. It's hilarious!"

Tallis chuckled at the thought, then scooted away from the beach tube and continued looking.

A few minutes later, he flagged Odessa down again.

"How about this one?" He pointed to one labeled *fiesta*.

"Yes!" She started clapping. "That one is so much fun! It'll pair really well with the Vegas costuming, too."

Tallis filled his vial to the next line with the blue liquid.

Odessa continued to guide him through the aisles, helping him select things like scents, sounds, and flavor. When they finished, they went to the counter to pay.

"Are these together?" the man at the register asked, eyeing Tallis's and Odessa's vials.

"Yup." Odessa answered right away. "I'll cover your first one," she said to Tallis.

"Oh," he said. "Thank you. You didn't have to do that."

"My treat!"

"What colors?" the man asked.

"Pink for me!" She turned to Tallis. "What's your favorite color?"

"Green."

The cashier held his hands out expectantly, and Odessa snatched Tallis's vial, handing both over the counter. The man turned to the wall behind him, dropping in a couple drops of different liquids into either vial, turning the murky black-brown of all the mixed colors into uniform pink and green before handing them back.

The cashier processed Odessa's payment and spouted off a few routine disclaimers about their purchase, but Tallis was too distracted to hear, focusing instead on the wet smacking sound the man kept making as he chewed his gum between every syllable.

"Thanks!" Odessa's hair flipped as she turned on her

heels and strutted toward the door, guiding Tallis out behind her by a hand.

"What now?" he asked.

"Now, we go back to the bar."

Once back at the bar, Odessa sat at one of the tables with a hookah. Before Tallis could sit, she pointed to a hookah at the next table over.

"Oh," he said, taking a seat at the table next to her instead.

"No!" She giggled. "I meant grab that hookah. Sorry! We need two separate ones for this."

Tallis's face grew red with embarrassment, but Odessa didn't think twice about the exchange. She simply scooted her hookah over to make room on the table.

"Trust me," she said, "you want to keep vials separate. I've just found it's best to use separate hookahs entirely." She shrugged, pouring her vial into part of the hookah.

"Do they clean these things after each person?" Tallis asked, wondering if his hookah's previous user smoked REM.

"Yup! The owner of the place is a friend of a friend. It may look a little run down, but believe it or not, they take good care of their equipment here."

Satisfied with her answer, Tallis watched her, mimicking her actions with his own. He observed and waited for her to make the next move.

"Now," she said, "you don't always have to smoke it. This is just one of my favorite ways. Personal preference. Some people like it in their morning coffee. If you decide to do it again after this, you can do whatever you want. But for now, I'm in charge." She smirked and winked.

Tallis felt warm, and he was sure his eyes just about popped out of his skull.

Odessa laughed before reaching for the hose and putting her lips around the mouthpiece. When she pulled it back away, she blew out a cloud of vapor that smelled faintly like cinnamon.

"Go on!" she chirped, waving her hand frantically toward Tallis's hookah.

His hand's shaking was undetectable to Odessa as he reached for his own, putting it to his lips and inhaling. Almost immediately, he spat out the mouthpiece, choking and sputtering. While gasping for air, he managed to spout a raspy, "it really tastes like coconut."

Odessa's smile failed to travel to her eyes as she leaned over to take the hose from Tallis while he caught his breath. When he stopped choking, she instructed him on the proper way to use the hookah, her words laced with condescension. Tallis picked up on this and immediately felt guilty for embarrassing her in public. He was certain she must think he was an idiot.

"It's okay," she said, smiling softly. "Try again."

Tallis nodded. Maybe he read her reaction wrong. She watched him patiently as he hesitated for a moment before giving it another go. Much better.

"That coconut taste is really nice when it's not choking me," Tallis said with a dopey smile.

"There ya go!" She took another hit.

"How long does this stuff take to kick in?"

"Depends on the person and how long you've been

doing it. It takes about half an hour for me. It'll probably take fifteen minutes or so for you."

"Will it be obvious when it does?"

Odessa chuckled. "Yeah. It'll be real obvious."

She wasn't exaggerating. After exactly twelve minutes, Tallis noticed a strange, feathered headdress on the bartender. He did a double-take, taking a closer look. He could've sworn the bartender was wearing all black when they arrived, but now he was wearing a sequined orange suit.

"Woah," Tallis muttered breathily.

He looked around, spotting the few other bargoers in similarly glitzy attire. He sat upright in his chair, turning to face Odessa.

"Already?" she asked, making assumptions by his face. "That was quicker than I thought."

"Damn!" Tallis said as he saw her, her original outfit replaced with a shimmery pink dress.

She sat back, slouched down in her seat as she watched Tallis, who had turned again to look at the rest of the bar.

"Shit!" he exclaimed, sitting up even straighter. The dark, dull barroom had been transformed in the short time he was looking at Odessa. The tables were all still there, but instead of sticky and dingy bar décor, he was looking at bright table spreads with colorful banners and flags draped across them. Colorful lights strung across the ceiling in a complicated web began to twinkle, casting oranges, reds, blues, and greens all around the room.

"So?" Odessa pried. "Whatchu think?"

"This is incredible!"

"See?" She finally sat up, her face beaming. "I told you!"

"I want to see what the rest of the street looks like!"

"Hold your horses, Tallis," she said, taking one more puff before standing. "I'll pay. Stay put."

Tallis was too busy gawking at the wall behind him at this point. Originally plain brick, it now appeared adorned with vibrant posters. "God!" he yelled, the few people in the bar turning to look at him. "It smells *awesome* in here!"

Odessa giggled to herself as she approached the bartender to pay. When she finished, she returned to Tallis, who was touching everything around him to feel if it was real. To him, it was.

"Come on," she said. "Let's go explore."

"Okay!" he followed her, his head spinning like an owl's as he took in every possible sight.

They stepped out onto the street, and Tallis's jaw dropped.

"Are you seeing this?" He gaped, looking up at the sky. To Tallis, the sky was alight with small fireworks and colorful flag banners strung across the street from the tops of buildings as if the entire city was celebrating together. To Odessa, the world looked entirely different. And to everyone else, it was the same as it was every day—dark, dirty, and damp.

Tallis chased after every new sight, wanting to get a closer look. His smile was wide with each new discovery. When he stopped beside a dumpster in an alley, Odessa hurried after him.

"What are you looking at now?" she asked, stepping closer to him as he squatted on the ground, giggling.

"Look at these. Are these some kind of ground firework? A festival toy or something?" Tallis's finger followed one of several golden balls, rolling across the concrete.

Odessa gasped, her smile dissipating as she yanked Tallis up. "No, no, no! Those are rats. Learned that the hard way. For me, they look like abandoned kittens right now, but I know they aren't. Let's get back to the street," she urged.

"You were looking at the wrong thing! I was talking about the—"

"I know what you were talking about," she interrupted. "Trust me. Rats. Remember, when you see stuff on REM, it's still something real, the REM just makes it look different."

Tallis shuttered and wiped his hands on his pants, grateful she stopped him. He followed her back to the main street, craning his neck to look in all directions.

They both stood in the middle of the street. She pulled him in close, but Tallis was completely unaware of her advances. Instead, he was gawking at the view down the street, which appeared completely illuminated by the fireworks overhead. He pulled away from her, grappling for his camera bag, unzipping it and pulling out his camera.

He squatted, angling his camera upwards to capture the tops of the buildings and the sky, snapping a picture. "I want to remember this."

The next morning, Tallis sat up in bed, flipping through the pictures on his camera, only to see the lifeless streets of Sector 3. No fireworks. No banners. No people in sequined costumes.

He laid back down with a sigh, nearly squishing Lolli, who had wiggled her way behind him to mooch some of his warmth.

"Sorry," he said, scooping her up and setting her to his side. Her fur ruffled, she flattened her ears and glared at him.

Fortunately, before Tallis went home for the night, he managed to get Odessa's number. He tapped his watch, pulling up her contact page to text her, but wrestled with himself to resist the urge. He didn't want to appear desperate.

He cycled back through the photographs, feeling a sense of loss. Just then, his watch buzzed.

The CAs have some team building activities planned in the office today and they're going to be all over the room making a mess. Feel free to take the day off.

He replied to Ms. Iris's text with a simple *Thank you.*

Just as he was lowering his wrist, the watch buzzed again.

Doing ok? a text from Odessa read.

Tallis's smile stretched across his face as he sat upright, throwing his feet over the side of the bed and rereading her message before replying.

Doing ok. That was crazy last night.

He looked over his reply before sending it, cringed, and deleted it.

Yeah. Can't believe that stuff is legal.

Deleted before sending, again.

Yeah. You?

That was better. Good enough, at least. He hit send before he could doubt himself again and sat there in bed, staring at his watch. The longer he sat there, the more he thought about Odessa and how he hasn't felt so excited in his whole life. He wondered if she felt the same way.

Before she replied, Tallis typed up a second text: *I hope this isn't too forward, but I've been having a really good time with you. I just wanted to know if it would be silly to get my hopes up that maybe this could go somewhere.* He read over it, realizing how crazy he would probably sound. When he went to tap the delete button, his finger twitched at tapped "send" instead.

His eyes bulged out of his head as he frantically tapped at his watch screen as if he could physically drag his message back. He groaned, rubbing at his eyes before staring at his watch, terrified of what she might say.

When a few minutes had passed and she hadn't replied, he sent a third message: *That was stupid. I'm so sorry about that.* Defeated, he realized she probably wasn't going to respond to him at this point, so he allowed himself to get up and start his day.

While he prepped Lolli's breakfast, he checked his watch twice. While he made his coffee, he checked it once. While he showered, he continuously stared down at it, grateful Xavier splurged and bought him the waterproof model. It was when he was logging onto his computer to work on some writing that his watch finally buzzed again. His hand flew up in front of his face and he tapped on the notification.

You're eligible for discounts on your health insurance! Click to learn more.

He grunted, letting his hand and his hopes down.

When an hour had passed and Tallis had written virtually nothing, he stood up to get another cup of coffee, telling himself his lack of focus was from a lack of sleep.

Finally, his watch buzzed again. He felt the shot of adrenaline, but he resisted, keeping his eyes off the watch's screen. Not wanting to get his hopes up for nothing again, he waited to see if the jittery anticipation faded, but when it didn't, he snuck a look at the screen.

Not stupid at all!

He cocked his head to the side, tapping out of the message and back into it, expecting more to load. Disappointed with the brevity but relieved she at least didn't seem to think he was too crazy, he closed out of the message, trying to refocus on his writing.

When creative thoughts failed to grow, he changed tactics, pulling up news articles online from the current CAs. He worked on reading their articles and writing his own versions of them. It was a good exercise and didn't take as much creativity. Perfect for moments like this.

Buzz. Another message.

I had a good time. But I've got to ask… is this your way of asking me to be your girlfriend or something?

Suddenly, Tallis's lungs felt half their size. He couldn't breathe properly, and he struggled to concoct a response.

Fortunately, Odessa seemed to understand his silence. *Because if so, I'd be cool with that :)*

Tallis's chest flooded with warmth. He bit his lip as he focused, tapping out a reply.

You free this evening?

Without giving it as much thought, he hit the send button.

Already? I mean, you just became my boyfriend like 30 seconds ago. You're ballsy.

Tallis was mortified as he speed-typed a response.

No one said anything about another date. Just asking about what you're up to later. ;)

Nice save, she texted back.

You caught me.

He waited a while, watching the screen. When a few minutes had passed and he couldn't bear to wait anymore, he sent a second message.

Would you want to get dinner in Sector 8 tonight?

Almost immediately, she replied. *Can't. :(I have plans.*

No worries. Maybe another time.

After considerable effort to refocus on his writing, Tallis eventually gave up the notion altogether, instead opting to take a walk with his camera.

It was comfortable and sunny out. As soon as he stepped foot outside, he realized it would be the perfect day to take Lolli around for some fresh air, training, and a photoshoot.

Tallis trotted back upstairs to his apartment, popping inside only long enough to bribe her with an apple slice. She scurried up to Tallis's shoulder opposite the camera strap.

"Ready to be my little model?" Tallis asked, giving her a little scratch behind the ear before heading back outside.

There was a small park a couple of blocks away from Tallis's apartment. With a duck pond and some trees lining the sidewalks, it was the closest thing to nature in Sector 8.

Tallis stopped at a bench near the pond. A family of fuzzy little ducklings bobbed on the surface after their mom, and a group of runners jogged past, filling the sidewalk.

Tallis set Lolli on the bench while he fidgeted with his camera settings. A blue dragonfly zipped around her head, and she leaned back to get a better look, nearly losing her footing as she tried to follow the bug with her eyes.

"That's called a dragonfly," Tallis said, looking over the top of his camera and peering down at Lolli. "It won't hurt you."

Lolli continued to track the bug with her stare, and Tallis took the opportunity to snap a few photos of her, arms and paws outstretched to swat at the kamikaze bug.

"I don't want to make your ego too big," Tallis said, squatting beside Lolli and showing her the pictures, "but you might just be the cutest and hairiest model the world has ever seen."

Tallis continued taking pictures of Lolli for a while before lifting her up to his shoulder to keep roaming around the park. He stopped along the edge of the pond, his gaze stuck on a crystalline reflection of towering skyscrapers mirrored across the entire pond. It looked like an oil painting.

He knelt, angling his camera just right to capture the city itself and its reflection, flipping the camera upside down to make the pond appear on top in the image. He snapped a few pictures at every possible angle and inspected each one, underwhelmed by the dullness of the photos. It didn't do justice to the scene before him.

Lolli began nibbling on Tallis's shirt collar.

"You hungry?" he asked. "Me too. I guess that's good enough for today."

He gave one more long look at the pond, as if trying to capture a photograph in his head that could overshadow any of the digital copies.

Tallis and Lolli returned to the apartment, where Tallis fixed them both something to eat. After they inhaled their meals, Tallis took to his computer, where he uploaded his photos to the cloud and to his digital portfolio—after some minor photo retouching to enhance the colors, of course.

He joined Lolli on the couch, flipping to her favorite show and giving her a little pat on the head, to which she flattened her ears in mild annoyance before scratching at the spot he had touched. It was a few minutes into the show and Tallis was already daydreaming about Odessa and where he'd like to take her on their next date. If he could afford it, he'd love to bring her to Glitz, the fancy restaurant Xavier had invited them to. Unfortunately, Tallis's budget was better suited for a classy date at BBQuisine. He tried to imagine Odessa with BBQ sauce slopped on her hands and face, a bit of corn on the cob stuck in her teeth, and hair tied back to avoid dunking in her coleslaw. Though he felt the visual was endearing, he didn't think Odessa was the type to like that sort of thing, especially not so early in the relationship.

After sufficient daydreaming, he began poking through his photos from the day on his watch, stopping on the one with the pond at the top of the frame and the real city at the bottom. Without thinking about it too much, he popped it into a text to Odessa and hit the send button.

He stared at their text conversation, awaiting her reply. When his screen went to sleep in wait, he began to feel like every nerve in his body was on fire. Would she like the picture? Should he have sent some context? Maybe he shouldn't have sent anything at all. She might think he's being needy or clingy.

Just then, his watch buzzed, and he tapped it awake, displaying her response.

Your picture sent upside down. Lol. Cool pic though.

He felt his stomach sink deeper.

It's not upside down. I was just playing with angles. Sorry, lol, it was stupid. It didn't turn out that great.

Before she could reply, he threw another photo into the conversation. This time, one of the pictures of Lolli reaching for the dragonfly. He added the message *Lolli says hi :)* before sending.

Awww! Hi Lolli!

Afraid of coming across weird, he committed himself to not sending another text until she messaged first. Unfortunately, that was the last text he got from her for the day.

⬥——◆——⬥

The next morning, Tallis stopped to get Ms. Iris's coffee like usual. While in line at Bru, he noticed a man seated nearby, tipping a little black vial into his coffee and giving it a quick stir.

Tallis's eyes kept flickering toward the man as he tried to also watch the line in front of him. There were still several people, and no one behind him yet.

"Excuse me," the man called over to Tallis after a few minutes.

Tallis tried to act surprised, as if he hadn't just been creeping.

"Can I help you with something?" the man asked, taking a sip of his coffee.

"No, I'm sorry. It was just… the vial. Nothing. I didn't mean to stare."

"This?" The man held up the vial.

Tallis nodded and the man beckoned him over. He hesitated, but eventually stepped out of line and approached him.

"It's completely legal. I don't know if you're a cop or just a dude who won't mind his own business, but it's legal. So you can just get your coffee and leave me alone," the man warned.

"Oh, no, sir. I'm so sorry for staring. It's just that my girlfriend had me try that stuff for the first time the other day. I'm just curious to learn more. I didn't mean to pry."

"What?" the man's brow furrowed, and he set his drink down, crossing his arms.

"Sorry again, sir," Tallis said, backing away.

The man paused for a moment before speaking up. "Nah, come back here."

"What?"

The man motioned him closer again. "What do you wanna know?"

"Oh! Well," Tallis thought. "Do you mind me asking what combination you did?" He pointed to the vial, attempting to be quick and subtle, but rather, looking as if he lost muscle control in his arm as his wrist and finger flopped awkwardly toward the vial.

"Like I said, it's legal. No need to be awkward about it. I did the gothic costuming in an ancient Greek setting. Wanted something that felt dark but cultured." He smiled softly.

"Ooh," Tallis hummed. "That sounds like a cool combo. What flavor? Can you taste it in your coffee?"

"Yeah, a bit. It's not super strong in coffee, which is why I prefer it this way. I went for lavender."

Tallis thanked the man for his time and his help, apologized yet again for being nosy, and hopped back into line right before a small group of people entered. He ordered Ms. Iris's drink, and once it was out, he continued his trek to the office.

Inside Opulence, he stopped by Ms. Iris's office, handing her the coffee. As usual, she didn't really say anything except a brief reminder about the files stacked up on his desk.

"Congratulations," she said as he started to leave for his desk, "by the way."

"'Congratulations?' For what?"

Ms. Iris looked up, a little smile teasing at the corner of her mouth before she resumed her work.

Tallis's heart rattled in his chest as he hurried to his desk. He looked down at his keyboard, inspecting a small envelope with a blue wax seal stamping it shut. His fingers traced over the smooth paper and the glossy wax as he turned it over, looking for a name, only to find his own in an embellished calligraphy.

He tucked a finger under the flap, carefully tearing it open and removing the letter.

After reviewing your portfolio and further considering your responses to our interview questions, the board has determined you're an ideal candidate for the second round of interviews. To schedule your interview, please reach out to Bill.

Tallis realized his mouth was hanging open and he immediately closed it, looking around to make sure no one was watching him. He noticed a line scrawled in messier print at the bottom of the letter and squinted, holding the letter closer to his eyes.

I look forward to hearing about your date. —Bill

Tallis blushed, reading over the letter a few times, examining each word to make sure he was interpreting it right. Nearly shaking, he tucked the letter back in the envelope and sat down, pulling up his email to reply to Bill about the interview.

While trying to focus on his work that day, he periodically kept getting up, pacing up and down the aisle, sitting back down, pulling up Xavier's contact information, deciding against it, trying to focus on work, repeat. After a while, Tallis pulled up Odessa's conversation on his watch, tapping out a quick message and sending it.

Good news.

The obscure message was enough to get an immediate reply.

???

He waited for a minute, smirking at the thought that he was leaving her in anticipation. After a grand total of two minutes, he replied.

Guess who got a second interview.

Ah! It'll be cool to say you got this far! :)

It'd be cooler to say I got the job. Fingers crossed.

He felt better after releasing some excitement on someone else. With a stretch and a neckroll, he refocused on his growing stack of work. The next document he pulled from the pile was an article about REM. All he was meant to do was document some of the information—article author, date, word count, and the like—but instead, he allowed himself a moment to skim over it. About halfway through the article, the CA who wrote it mentioned something about a setting option labeled "underwater." Tallis made a mental note to ask Odessa about that one the next time they visit Dream Depot.

Later in the day, Tallis got an email back from Bill, confirming his second interview for Friday evening. Now that it was set in stone, it felt real.

The news of the interview had him feeling a sense of inflated confidence. Without much thought, he pulled up Odessa's number on his watch and texted her.

Wanna be my date to my friend's wedding?

He knew he technically asked her when he was originally trying to ask her out in a private room at Illusion, but he half-hoped, half-assumed she had forgotten since it was an illegitimate exchange in the first place.

I'd love to!

A full-blown toothy smile erupted on Tallis's face as

he shot up from his seat. He immediately sat back down, realizing he looked ridiculous.

I'll forward you the digital invite!

She sent back a thumbs-up.

He decided to ride the good feelings and tell Odessa his news.

Scheduled my interview for Friday, he messaged.

It'll be nice to get it over with before the weekend, she replied.

Are you free at all this week? Would you want to get dinner?

Nothing. He watched the screen on his wrist, waiting. When she didn't reply, he tried to shove aside the heavy feeling in his gut that perhaps he was pushing his luck, and turned his attention back to the spreadsheet on his computer. After he got about halfway through entering timecodes for footage for a new soda commercial, his watch buzzed.

Important question: What kind of food? Your answer determines mine.

Tallis grinned, getting comfortable and leaning back in his seat as he replied.

Lady's choice.

Thai?

Sure. After that, we can go on a wok!

Haha ok.

Odessa wasn't scheduled for work on Wednesday, so Tallis researched Thai restaurants and found a cozy looking one in Sector 5. Tallis offered to ride to Sector 3 to meet her and ride back toward Sector 5 together. While working, he found himself distracted at one point, doing more research on the Thai restaurant, eventually setting an image of the restaurant as his computer wallpaper.

Wednesday slunk by, creeping minute by minute. During his lunch break that day, he opted to go shopping for another gift for Odessa. He wanted to get her jewelry or something pretty to wear for Xavier and Vanessa's wedding. Tallis left Opulence, making his way to the shopping center nearby.

It was toasty outside. The sun beamed up from the pavement, absorbing into Tallis's black pants. He became acutely aware of how sweaty his butt was and he wondered if everyone else was experiencing the same thing. As he walked, he spotted a muscular tattooed man strutting down the street in short, tight gym shorts. Tallis was willing to bet his butt was sweaty, too.

On the first level of shops, people rushed across the open walkway, pushing their way toward storefronts of boutiques and specialty stores. Tallis's eyes scanned the shop signs searching for a jewelry store. When he locked onto his target, he made his way through the crowd, getting knocked back by shoulders of fixed-minded shoppers on their way to their destinations.

Once he reached the front of the jewelry store, he reached for the door handle—knotted gold embellished with cubic zirconium. Tallis wondered if this place would be too fancy for his budget. After all, he had never truly had a reason to buy anyone jewelry before. He simply wanted to get Odessa something nice. He felt like she deserved something special and valuable. Tallis felt bad that such an incredible person was stuck earning singles from horny men in a strip club. In Sector 3, no less.

He opened the door, a blast of cool air rushing toward him. When he stepped inside, a slender salesman scurried toward him.

"Hello, sir!" the man's voice squeaked on the word *sir*.

Tallis nodded, his eyes darting away from the man, fixating on a display of bangle bracelets.

"Looking for anything in particular?" The man tapped his fingertips together in front of him as he waited for a response.

"Umm," Tallis hummed. "I'm just looking for a gift."

"Wonderful! Any particular occasion?"

"Not exactly. I just want to get her something nice to wear to a friend's wedding."

"Absolutely! What sort of piece are you thinking?"

"I'm open to anything, I suppose. Nothing too expensive, please."

"Of course!"

"And no rings," Tallis added.

The man nodded. "Understood. Let me show you one of our newest collections."

Tallis followed the man, who walked as if he had a stick up his butt and his life depended on not letting it fall out.

"Viola!" Stick-Butt flourished his arms at the display of glittery jewelry in a glass case. "They're in a modest price range, but this collection is the newest in the Eliza Lacquer collection."

Tallis hunched over to get a better look at the jewelry while Stick-Butt babbled on about the design and creation process. One particular necklace stood out to him. It boasted a teardrop-shaped red stone in the center of dozens of tiny little diamonds. The piece was elegant, and Tallis could imagine Odessa in a stunning red dress at Xavier and Vanessa's wedding, accessorized by the ruby necklace.

"Excuse me—" Tallis interrupted the man's story about

the designer's educational background.

"You've found something you like?" he asked.

"How much is this red one?" Tallis pointed, his finger jabbing the glass and leaving a smudge.

"That's a stunning one! One of my favorites. Perfectly modest price for such an elegant necklace, if I might say. Only $890, but we offer the earrings that pair with it for an absolute steal when you buy them all together—only $1,350."

Tallis unintentionally let out a huffy laugh but stopped himself when he saw the flat expression of the salesman staring back at him.

"I'm—I'm sorry," Tallis said. "That's *way* outside my price range."

"I see."

"Do you have something for under $100?"

Now, it was the salesman's time to laugh. At that, Tallis thanked him for his time and promptly exited the store.

Back out in the shopping center, Tallis continued to mosey about, checking out the front displays of the various stores. While he was peering through a display window, his watch vibrated.

A text from Vanessa read: *I miss you, Tallis! I hope you're doing well.*

I'm ok. Thanks for checking in on me.

I'm so sorry about Xavier. The wedding has him all stressed out, so I don't think he's taken time to sit back and realize what a dick he was to you. No excuses though, and I know I can't really apologize for him. I guess what I'm trying to say is please be patient with him. He'll come around.

I know he will. He sent his message, throwing in a second message that said *Thank you.*

He kept wandering around the shopping center until, just a few doors over, he came across a little boutique with cutesy arrangements of summery outfits and oversized beach bags in the windows. The thing that caught his attention more than anything, however, was a set of simple silver earrings hung at eye-level in the display. They were exceptionally shiny, acting as thin mirrors, reflecting back all of the colors and shapes of the buzz of the shopping center behind Tallis.

He stepped inside the store. Unlike the jewelry shop, no one rushed over to speak to him. Instead, a young woman with a floral headscarf stood at the register, doodling on a discarded receipt and completely ignoring his entrance. Tallis felt himself relax, his shoulders loosening as he walked over to the tall stand of earrings nearest the window. His eyes looked over the different earrings until he saw the hoops, plucking them from their place on the stand.

He wiggled the earrings around in his hand, dazzled by the glimmers of colors and lights reflecting back at him. The earrings would be perfect for any outfit, he thought. After all, they reflect the colors around you—they were like little chameleons. The earrings were pierced through a card with the store's name and a price tag clearly marked for $80. At the bottom of the card, "sterling silver" was embossed in silver font.

Tallis felt giddy at the idea of presenting Odessa with the earrings. They were perfect. Real silver, so they were still high quality, they had a classic and beautiful look to them, and they were oh-so reflective. He essentially skipped to the register, delicately setting the earrings on the counter in front of the clerk.

She looked up at him, setting her pen down and picking the earrings up to scan them.

"That it for you today?" she said in a robotically cheery voice.

"Yes, ma'am."

"Perrrrfect!"

She wrapped the earrings up in paper and placed them in a small blue paper bag.

Tallis paid, took the earrings, and thanked the woman before leaving and making his way back to the office.

The rest of the workday was uneventful. He didn't focus as well as he should have, so his stack of documents shrunk slower than usual, resulting in a late end to his workday. After Tallis finished his files, dropped some folders off at Ms. Iris's door, and collected his things, he made his way home.

Lolli was there to greet him at the door. She sat in the entryway, hugging a toy mouse from the cat section of the pet store to her chest. As soon as Tallis stepped foot through the doorway, Lolli dropped her toy and held her arms up to him. He scooped her up, kissed the top of her head, and set her on his shoulder while he fixed a snack for them both.

Because of his late workday, Tallis had less time than he would've liked to get ready for his date with Odessa. He stripped off his work clothes and exchanged them for black slacks, black dress shoes, and a simple white button up paired with a skinny black tie. In the bathroom, Tallis wet his hair and slicked it back with some mousse. He leaned down and grappled at some pretzel sticks on a plate with his mouth while simultaneously trying to rinse his hands of the hair product.

He grabbed the bag with the earrings from the counter and rushed out the door, only to pop back inside a moment later, stumbling over his own feet on his way to fill Lolli's bowl.

"Sorry!" he called to her as she watched him from the back of the couch. "I'll be back later."

Tallis hurried down the street, toward the subway. A bit of regret crept into his mind. If he hadn't agreed to meet her in Sector 3 first, he would've had more time to get ready.

Fortunately, the subway wasn't too crowded that evening. When it came to a stop, he stepped in and took a seat at the far end.

On the subway now. See you soon, he messaged.

No response, but he figured she was probably walking to the subway at that very moment and would text when she arrived.

Tallis watched the people scrambling on and off the subway at each sector's station until they reached Sector 3. Before the subway could come to a complete stop, Tallis hopped up out of his seat and stood just an inch from the door. As the subway came to a quick stop at the station, it lurched and he lost his balance, falling backward and grappling at one of the standing poles to stop his fall. A couple at the other end of his subway car looked at him and snickered, whispering to each other, but Tallis didn't care—as long as Odessa didn't see. As far as he could tell, she didn't.

He stepped off the subway, smoothing his clothes out and checking to make sure the earrings in the bag were undamaged. When everything seemed to be in place, he took a look around, scanning for Odessa's face. When he didn't see her waiting on his arrival, he began to feel a pit in his stomach, but reminded himself over and over that she was likely just running a minute late and would be there any second.

A second passed, and then another, and yet another. Over 1800 seconds, or 30 minutes, had passed, and Odessa finally came waltzing into the station in skin-tight black jeans and a lacy, corset style shirt. Tallis stood to greet her but found it difficult to muster up a smile.

"I was getting worried you weren't going to show," he said.

"That's a bit dramatic!" She giggled.

"I mean, I thought we were meeting half an hour ago." He looked at his watch and let out a loose and uncomfortable chuckle.

"Don't be so sensitive! It's a few minutes. No big deal. I'm here now! Ready to get some food?"

Tallis nodded, and the two got on the subway, sitting next to each other.

The ride felt longer than Tallis would've expected. The entire time, Odessa was babbling about one of her clients at work once who got so drunk before a lap dance that he threw up on her chest. Apparently, there's an entire protocol for such events at Illusion. Tallis felt like he was floating away from his body. Everything felt distant.

"Are you okay?" Odessa asked when she eventually stopped her story. She looked at him with squinty eyes.

Tallis didn't reply immediately. Instead, he continued to stare off into space.

"Tal?"

"Mmm?"

"What's got you all weird?"

"'Weird?'"

"It's like you're not even paying attention to me. You're just in la-la land."

"Sorry," he said.

They sat in silence a while again before Tallis spoke.

"Why were you late?" he asked.

She let out a single huffy laugh. "Bad REM," she admitted.

He raised an eyebrow and waited for her to clarify.

"Tainted bottle of REM. It happens. I already told you, it's not common—don't worry! The vials are recycled, so sometimes a little residue gets left on there and messes up the dream. You're not supposed to have two settings, or two costumings, or two anything. Just one of each or it can get really wonky. Sometimes a little scary, I'm not going to lie."

"God," Tallis said with a sigh, "are you okay?"

"Yup. All good. I was still coming down from it and it was finally starting to wear off, so I wanted to wait it out before coming to meet you. It basically made it look like everyone was in black cloaks. I couldn't see faces. There was a dark black fog everywhere. Just really ominous." She shuddered. "Gives me chills even thinking about it. Fortunately, I didn't take much, so it didn't last all that long."

The subway display dinged and lit up with the number 5. The two stood from the seat and exited the subway and the conversation.

"So," Odessa said, changing the subject as they climbed the stairs out of the station, "where is this Thai place?"

"I'm not 100% sure. I found it online and I've got

a general idea where it is."

"Lead the way!"

Sector 5 looked like Sector 3 must've looked in its prime. The streets were dingy and full of mysterious shops and trash, but there were far more lights and hologram displays decorating the street. In Sector 5, people actually roamed between buildings, unlike the nearly lifeless Sector 3.

"I think it's this way." Tallis reached for Odessa's hand.

Tallis led Odessa along the street, making a few turns down some smaller intersecting streets, trying to remember the street names he read online. He knew he could look it up on his watch, but he wanted to impress Odessa with his navigational skills, as if those were a high priority characteristic in a mate.

When he reached a dead end, his face flushed. He took a few steps back to look at the nearest street sign again. They were on Trusette Street, and the nearest intersection was Peacelily Way. He remembered seeing something about Trusette, he thought, but nothing about Peacelily.

"Lost?" Odessa asked, arms crossed and a smirk twitching at the corner of her mouth.

"No," Tallis lied. "Just trying to get my bearings."

"Just admit you're lost."

"I just think I missed a turn or something."

"You just gotta keep your head on straight," Odessa said. "You keep daydreaming and not paying attention. That's why you got lost."

"Let's just go back a bit." Tallis started back the way they came, and Odessa followed a few paces behind, trotting to catch up.

A block later, they came across Waterberry Way.

"Found it," Tallis said, turning on his heel and continuing along the new street. "It should be down this street."

"Thank God!" Odessa skipped beside Tallis. "I'm so ready for food. Do you know what you're ordering?"

"I haven't been here before," Tallis reminded her.

"Wait… how'd you know about it then?"

"I already told you I just found it when I was researching places." Tallis looked up at the sign to the Thai restaurant, opening the door and ushering Odessa in before him.

"Oh. I think you just imagined telling me. Well, this'll be new for both of us."

Tallis stepped into the restaurant behind Odessa. Spiced smells danced through the warm air, and he immediately salivated.

"This is so cute!" Odessa squealed. "Look at the fish tank!"

Tallis joined her at her side, watching the tropical fish dart after each other through the fake coral of the tall, algae-covered tank.

"Has anyone helped you yet?" a short hostess asked from behind Tallis, popping his personal space bubble.

He turned around and stepped back a little. "Not yet."

"Come on," she beckoned, her motions frantic.

Odessa and Tallis exchanged shrugs and grins as they followed the woman to a booth against a window. The hostess dropped two menus on the table and disappeared as quickly as she had appeared.

"I already know I'm getting the pad thai," Odessa said, closing and pushing the menu away almost as soon as she had opened it.

"Not into trying new things?" Tallis asked. "That kind of surprises me."

"I *am* into trying new things." She smirked. "But I love pad thai, and some places do it better. I'm on a mission to find the best pad thai in town."

"Where's been the best so far?"

"Sector 2. Really nasty looking little restaurant. You'd think they let actual rats run the place. The sanitation is honestly questionable at best. But damn. That pad thai is otherworldly."

"Well, see, now you're making me want to order pad thai."

"Do it!"

"Done." Tallis slid his menu away too and leaned forward, elbows on the table.

He locked eyes with her, and she stared back at him, her blue eyes intense.

"I got you something."

"*Another* present?" she couldn't hold back her smile.

He leaned back in his seat, reaching into his pocket for the earring box.

"So, I know you've never formally met my friends Xavier and Vanessa—the ones getting married. They're a bit... on the..." he paused, searching for the right word.

Odessa nodded expectantly.

"Wealthy... side. They make good money, live in a crazy nice house, stuff like that. The wedding will probably match. While I was at work the other day, I thought about it, and I wanted to go out and get you something nice to wear to the wedding. I know you're great at your job, but I can't imagine Illusions pays well, especially considering it's in Sector 3."

He revealed the closed earring box, holding it out to her. Her posture had gone from open to totally shut down. Arms crossed, eyebrow raised, leaning back in her booth. After a pause, she reached for the box and opened it.

"They're real sterling silver," Tallis said.

Not looking away from the earrings in one hand, she used the other hand to pull her hair behind her ear, revealing an almost identical earring already on her ear.

"Oh." Tallis sunk in his seat. "I didn't realize you already had them."

"I didn't," Odessa said, pawing at the earring in her ear. "These are white gold."

Tallis stared back, face flushed.

"Were you trying to imply that I'm too poor to afford nice things? Because I *must* just be some broke ass stripper who lives in Sector 3?"

"No!" Tallis wiggled to sit up, leaning forward and reaching for her hand. "Nothing like that!"

"I get it." She closed the earring box and put it in her clutch, turning her gaze back to him.

"I promise, I didn't mean anything like that."

"It's fine," she said. "Let's move on."

Just then, a waiter walked over, setting two cups of water on the table. He looked at Odessa.

"Pad thai," she said.

He looked at Tallis, not saying a word.

"Same as her."

The waiter nodded and darted off.

"Chatty one, isn't he?" Tallis tried to joke.

Odessa was busy picking at one of her loose fake nails, setting it on the table when it broke off.

"After dinner, you should come back to my apartment and say hi to Lolli."

Her eyes flickered up to meet his, and a soft smile grew on her face.

"How's she been doing?" she asked. "Has her training been getting any better?"

"A little bit." Tallis chuckled. "She's stubborn. And an attention hog. I've been trying to work on that so we don't have another fiasco like at the bar. But if I go more than ten minutes without acknowledging her, she starts to act up again."

"She's so cute! And she knows it. That's why she wants attention."

"Sounds like someone else I know." Tallis smirked, reaching for his glass and sipping on his water.

"Tallis!" Odessa smiled and bit her lip. "You're getting ballsy with your flirting."

"Am I?"

She laughed and nodded.

"Is it working?"

"It might be."

He leaned back in his seat, one arm across the back of the booth.

A short while later, the waiter returned with two plates of pad thai, setting them down and dashing off again.

Odessa's face lit up when she saw the food. Without waiting for it to cool, she shoved the first bite in her mouth. Her eyes studied the ceiling as she chewed.

"So?" Tallis asked. "Better than Sector 2?"

She put a finger in the air as she took a second bite, chewing and studying again. Tallis watched, patiently.

She swallowed her mouthful, set down her fork, and looked at Tallis for a moment before answering. "It's a close contender."

"Wow! I'd imagine that's high praise."

"Absolutely. Basically the equivalent of an award plaque."

"Shoot. Guess I better try this award-winning pad thai, huh?"

"I was about to say if you didn't start soon, I'd go ahead and eat yours too."

Tallis pulled his bowl toward him, shielding it.

Odessa laughed, and the two continued eating together.

"So, tell me about these friends of yours," Odessa said. "The ones getting married."

"Their names are Xavier and Vanessa," Tallis said. "I've been friends with Xavier since our first year of college together. We were placed with random roommates freshman year. I was partnered up with some douchebag architecture major who didn't believe in doing laundry, and he was put with some creepy kid who collected hair in jars."

Odessa's nose crinkled. "Hair? Why?"

Tallis shrugged. "Crafts? Hell if I know."

She shuddered. "Icky."

"After the first few months, we both had enough of our sucky roommates. We hadn't met yet, but we both were waiting in the housing office at the same time to talk to the people there about finding a new roommate. While waiting, we started talking, hit it off, and ended up going in together to ask to be roommates."

"Aww," Odessa cooed.

"He met Vanessa our sophomore year. She was in one

of his classes. He didn't notice her until she had to present some kind of project to the class, and he said she was the most beautiful and intelligent girl he had ever seen. They've been together ever since. They both landed awesome jobs right before graduation, got a really nice house together, and finally got engaged about a year ago."

"Why'd they wait so long?"

Tallis shrugged. "Just how it played out, I s'pose."

"Where's their wedding gonna be?"

"Some venue in Sector 15."

"Holy shit. 15?"

Tallis nodded.

"They've got *that* kind of money?"

"Well, yes and no. They're from 13, but I guess one of the perks of holding off on the whole wedding thing was they were able to save up and go big."

"I already like going to weddings, but… gotta say… I'm extra excited for this one."

Tallis felt a smile creep across his face. Before now, he could only imagine taking Odessa as his date. Now, she was sitting in front of him, talking about how excited she was.

They finished their pad thai, split the check, and left to wander the street. They stopped in a couple little boutiques, per Odessa's request. At one point, she saw a flowery little blouse she couldn't stop touching. When Tallis asked if she wanted it, she said she was "thinking about it." He offered to get it for her, and she declined, taking the shirt to the counter—along with several other things—and paid for it herself.

The couple left the store, continuing on their walk

down the street. When they turned a corner, they spotted an ostentatious neon sign greeting them from a distance. As soon as Odessa could make out the word ARCADE, she squeaked and hopped up and down, pointing at it as if somehow Tallis didn't see it.

"Let's go!" she chirped, grabbing for his hand.

Tallis smiled, his focused face fading as he allowed her to pull him down the street and toward the arcade. As they got closer, he noticed a holograph of an old school arcade machine to the left of the door.

She pulled open the arcade doors and the silence of the evening was replaced by ringing bells, buzzing lights, and a mélange of video game sound effects. The games were organized in sections—one row full of classic pinball machines, another with old, pixelated games. There was even a room for full-body virtual reality.

Odessa let her hand slip from Tallis's as she disappeared down one of the aisles. Tallis stood there, just taking in the sights and sounds. A moment later, Odessa reappeared.

"What're you doing? It's an arcade! Don't just stand there. Let's play something!" she said, reaching for him again. "I used to love arcades! I haven't been to one in years."

She guided him toward a tall machine with two joysticks. A pixelated woman in a comically oversized blue sunhat danced on the screen, swinging her purse around like a weapon.

"Play with me?" Odessa asked, already putting her hands on one of the joysticks and some buttons.

"Why not," Tallis said, stepping up to player two's spot. "How do you pay for the game?"

She squatted down and looked at the text on a little

metal plate covering the coin hole. "Looks like they've set them up with DigitPay."

Tallis tapped on his watch, pulling up DigitPay and selecting the game to pay. Just then, the game's music blasted through its small speakers. The original woman in her floppy hat appeared on a street full of boutiques and cafes. Beside her, a nearly identical woman in a pink sunhat popped up.

"How do we play this?" Tallis asked after the game started. Odessa was already smashing away at the buttons as digital salespeople approached the floppy hat women.

"The directions are right there! Don't let the salespeople throw things at you. Hit them away with your purse. The A button is to hit, B is to jump." Odessa's eyes stayed glued to the screen as she whacked away a perfume salesman.

Tallis picked up on the controls quickly, but Odessa was clearly the superior player. When Tallis's avatar got swarmed by a horde of salespeople, she charged over with her purse, swinging at each of them just in time to spare Tallis from losing his last life.

"Get that one with the shoes!" she shrieked at him.

"Oh God! Is she throwing high heels at me? What happened to just spritzing us with perfume or lassoing us with pretty scarves? Shoe lady is violent as hell." Tallis's character narrowly missed an airborne heel as he darted to the corner of the screen.

Just then, another salesperson popped onscreen and knocked Tallis out with a sandal.

"Stop dying!" he yelled at his character. Odessa started giggling, and her giggles quickly transformed to uncontrollable laughter as she lost focus, allowing her character to succumb to the shoe-throwers.

"Video games aren't your forte, are they?" she asked, still smiling.

He shook his head, grinning. "They're fun though."

"That's all that matters!"

"That game is a bit sexist, don't you think? Why are all the old video game heroes men who fight off badass monsters and villains, but then you've got this one… women in cheesy hats fighting with their purses to avoid shopping. Who came up with this one?"

Odessa shrugged. "I just thought it looked funny. I'd say it was!"

Tallis chuckled in agreement.

The two played rounds on a few more machines, including a few one-on-one games. Odessa dominated in each one. When they both seemed to have their fill, they returned to the quiet street.

Moseying beside Tallis, Odessa reached into her clutch and pulled out a small pen, putting it to her lips, puffing out a little cloud.

"Wanna hit?" She offered him the pen.

"At risk of sounding stupid… what is it?"

"Just some REM."

"Oh," Tallis felt his shoulders relax. "What kind?"

"My personal favorite." She smiled, stopping in place and wiggling the pen in his face.

Tallis hesitated for a moment before taking it. He tried sniffing it first, just out of curiosity, but Odessa urged him onward with a "just try it already!"

He took a hit, handing it back to Odessa.

"Let's keep walking while we wait for it," she said softly, reaching for his hand.

The two walked in silence together for a while, looking around at the lights and holographic displays around them.

"So," Tallis said, breaking the peace of their walk. "How often do you do this stuff?"

"You mean REM?"

He nodded.

"Often enough."

"Do you ever get tired of it?"

She chuckled and paused. "No."

"Do you ever start to get reality confused with REM dreams?"

"I mean, once in a while it's bound to happen. One time, I made a new combination and everyone looked like hipsters. Normally, not a big deal, but this one poor guy at Illusion looked way too much like my ex. I gave him an absolute earful. When I came down, he was a clean-shaven man in a button-up, not some scruffy beanie-wearer. Totally not my ex. Needless to say, I didn't really get any tips that night after that outburst."

"Oof. That's rough."

She shrugged. "Made things interesting."

"I'd imagine your job is usually interesting."

"Not as much as you'd think. It's a lot of the same. When you've been in the business a while, you get used to it."

"Well," Tallis searched for words, "I guess that's not a bad thing."

"I guess." Her voice lowered, nearly talking to herself. "Not the kind of job and environment you wanna just get used to."

"Lot of creeps?"

"Understatement."

"That bad?"

She nodded, eyes forward and crossing her arms as they walked.

"Do you wanna talk about it?"

"Not really, thanks."

"That's alright. You never have to."

Tallis put his hands in his pockets and the two kept walking, both in their own minds. He began to reluctantly envision Odessa straddling a greaseball of a man who was literally drooling as he ogled her dancing. He shuddered and she looked over at him with one raised brow.

"Do you mind me asking how you got into dancing?"

"'Dancing?'" She scoffed, recrossing her arms the other way. "You sound like the other girls at work trying to make the job sound elegant or some shit like that. Just call it what it is."

Tallis lowered his gaze. He felt her stare but chose to ignore it as they pressed onward.

"I was going to get my master's."

"Wow. What did you study? What happened?"

"Computer science. Same as my bachelor's. Difference is, in undergrad, I wasn't the only woman in class. There were at least a few of us. When I went on to work toward my master's, I was the *only* woman."

Odessa paused, but Tallis opted not to speak.

"Normally, that sort of thing wouldn't have bothered me. Hell, I had a fantastic scholarship—I felt like I was unstoppable. But I was constantly berated and sexualized. Every time I did well on a test, the guys in class would start spreading rumors that I must have been sleeping with the head of the department. Stuff like that. Even that wasn't the worst of it. The worst of it was when the professors started to believe the rumors and figured I'd be willing to take shortcuts for the grades. It was too much, so I dropped out. I figured I could try a different program after taking some time to look at other options, but when I withdrew, they didn't skip a beat on sending me the bill and kicking me out of campus housing. Because I went straight into the master's program after graduating undergrad, I was able to defer my undergrad debt. But when I dropped out, that deferment stopped and they slapped me with a bill for tens of thousands of dollars on top of my existing undergrad bill. Turns out, dropping out forfeits the scholarship."

"That's not fair—"

"—so there I was," she continued, "23 years old, no job, no home, and massive debt. I'm close with my parents, but I wasn't about to go home and tell them I gave up. Obviously, eventually they found out. But I felt like moving home would be the ultimate stamp on my streak of shame, ya know? In retrospect, I shouldn't have felt that way."

She uncrossed her arms and put her thumbs in her tiny jean pockets instead. Tallis's eyes moved up from her pockets to look her in the eyes, noticing a crown of purple begonias atop her head.

"Since when were y—"

"—and that's when I started looking for jobs. I was able to room with one of my old college friends for a while, but I felt like I was intruding on her life. Her and her girlfriend had their own place in Sector 6 with a dog and a yard and all. Picture perfect. But then there I was. Living on their couch. Mooching their food because I couldn't afford anything without a job. But nowhere was getting back to me. One night, I tried applying at a high-end shop in Sector 13. Just helping in the back room. Nothing that paid much, but it would've helped me move out at least. When I was leaving after the interview, I saw a gorgeous woman in the tallest heels I've ever seen buying some expensive coat like it was just her morning coffee. I talked with her for a little while and eventually I swallowed my pride and asked her what she does for a living. She told me she worked for Illusion. I've been there ever since."

Tallis kept trying to pay attention, but his focus began drifting. All around him, trees erupted from the ground, towering over the city buildings. Night turned to day, and sunlight dappled through the foliage. Concrete gave way to lush grass, and glass windows ruptured, making room for thick vines. For a moment, he could swear the noise of the city was replaced with bird songs and rustling leaves.

When he stopped walking, Odessa grinned and giggled. "You see it?"

"I don't think I've ever seen anything this beautiful."

"It's my favorite." She tiptoed over and reached for his hand to lead him slowly down the grassy path.

Tallis kicked his toes up as he walked, trying to feel the long grass give under the weight of his feet, but the ground beneath still felt like concrete.

"Remember the woman who introduced me to Illusion? She also taught me about REM. I refused to even try it for the longest time. But a job like that gets to you. Every wolf whistle, every grope, every crude jab eats away at you like vultures on a carcass until there's nothing left of you but a shell. I became cynical and numb. I cracked. I tried it and instantly fell in love. I could see the beauty in the world and in life again."

"Is this how you always see the world?"

Odessa laughed, wrapping one of her little arms around his waist. "No. It's my favorite blend. It's a strong one—as you can tell. But I do all kinds of dreams to keep things interesting."

A group of people walked by on the opposite side of the street. As far as Tallis and Odessa saw, they all sported flowing dresses and delicate flower crowns.

"Am I wearing flowers?" Tallis looked down, spotting the hem of a dress flowing around his ankles.

"Of course!" she chirped. "Everyone is."

"At least tell me they're pretty ones."

"I haven't met a flower I didn't like."

"Noted."

Time seemed limitless as they moseyed through the quiet scenery. Except for the occasional passerby, Tallis felt like they were floating on their own planet. Everything and everyone-- Xavier and Vanessa, Ms. Iris, Opulence, Illusion, even Lolli – all felt like part of some sort of ghost story.

"Don't you have to go to work in the morning?" Odessa asked, her voice sharp in the silence.

"Unfortunately." Tallis's shoulders slumped, and he rubbed his face with both hands.

"Sorry. It's just getting late and figured you should know."

"No, it's alright. You're right. I had a lot of fun tonight though."

"Good!" She clapped lightly to herself. "Me too."

"How do you navigate when everything looks like this? Nothing looks the same."

"I'll get you back to the subway. It should start winding down soon anyways."

Odessa was right. By the time he boarded the subway, the greenery began receding from man-made structures and grass died off, revealing the asphalt below. The costuming seemed to be the only lingering effect once Tallis reached his apartment.

He unlocked his door, stopping inside and immediately kicking off his shoes. Lolli sat right at the door to greet him, a crown of little daises sitting crooked on her furry head. Tallis chuckled to himself.

"I wish you could see how cute you look right now," he said to her, scooping her up and bringing her to the kitchen to feed her a late-night snack.

The next day, Tallis woke up early. Not by choice, but rather his inability to get the image out of his head of mother earth taking over the city like it was nothing. He threw on his work clothes, made sure Lolli had breakfast and her TV shows, and made his way out.

On his way to Bru, he came across the puddle outside Buzz's Electrosuite. It hadn't rained in a while, and the puddle appeared to be shrinking. Tallis squatted, taking a closer look at it. He imagined what it would be like to an insect. Did the puddle look like a big pink ocean? His mind conjured daydreams of cozy seaside apartments, aligned against the shore of a neon sea. Nights would be beautiful, and he was sure he would never go inside if he lived in that little world in his head.

Splash.

A man in a tan trench coat hurried along the walkway, stepping right through the puddle, rattling Tallis from his thoughts. He looked at his watch, realizing the time and popping to his feet to rush for Ms. Iris's coffee.

In the office, he scurried to Ms. Iris's desk, nearly sloshing coffee on himself as he stopped abruptly in her doorway. He handed over the drink, and she paused for a minute, looking him over.

"I texted you to get me a scone while you were there," she said, her disappointment nearly burning a hole through her disposable coffee cup.

"Oh." Tallis looked at his watch, seeing the unread notification. "I didn't see it. I can go back and get one. What flav—"

"Don't worry about it. I need you to get to your stack ASAP. There are some documents on top that need to be processed before lunch."

"Yes, ma'am."

Her focus back on her work, Tallis stepped out of her office and went to his desk, pulling the first page from his work stack: a magazine article that needed formatting. He fell back in his chair, holding out the article to read while his computer ran a morning update.

"Reality-Altering Drug Rattles Minds" the title read.

Tallis sat up in his chair, holding the paper closer to get a better look, careful not to miss any words.

Reality Enhancement Modification, commonly referred to as REM, has been taking the lower-level sectors by storm. While its uses are innocent in purpose, it's toxic in practice. Users find themselves unable to distinguish between reality and "dreams"—the term used for the hallucinogenic state resulting from use of REM. Dreamers can pose a threat to themselves and loved ones after partaking in this alarming legal substance.

He stopped reading, his lip snarling up as he wondered who told them such lies about REM. After all, Odessa had been using for years, and she had no problem telling what was real and what wasn't—aside from the one time she thought someone was her ex—and she clearly wasn't a danger to anyone, even herself.

Tallis stood from his chair and stormed off to Ms. Iris's office, his bravado dying off before he was even in her line of sight.

"Yes?"

"I have a suggestion."

At this, Ms. Iris allowed her curious eyes to flick up from her computer screen to meet his.

"This article," he said, shaking the paper, "it's got it all wrong."

"Excuse me?"

"This article about REM. That's not how it works."

At that, she raised an eyebrow and her features relaxed. Her lips twitched into a smile.

"And you know this… how?" she asked.

"I've tried it," he said, straightening his posture. "Twice."

Ms. Iris was silent as she stood from her desk and approached Tallis. When she was far too close for his comfort, she paused before speaking. "You're telling me *you* tried REM?"

He resisted the urge to ask her what she meant by that, knowing full well what she intended, not wanting to hear it for himself.

"Yup—erh—yes… Ma'am." His words trembled.

She let out a huffy chuckle. "Color me impressed!" She took a couple steps back as she laughed.

Tallis stared back at her, clinging to his demeanor. "I think the CAs only have a vague idea of how REM even works. To be fair, I didn't understand before either. And I feel like I learn more every day."

She reached for the article in his hands, and he relinquished it.

"Not that I use REM daily. Only twice, and never before or during work, of course."

Ms. Iris nodded, as if she expected as much. Tallis was relieved she at least trusted him, even if she felt he was bland.

She scanned over the article for a moment, humming the words to herself as she read.

"What's wrong with it?"

"The part—" he walked over, skimmed the page for the part, and pointed, "there. About being unable to distinguish reality and REM dreams, and about being a danger."

She laughed and looked at Tallis like he just said two plus two equals ten.

"It's a hallucinogenic drug. It makes you see things that aren't real, and if you take it too much, you'll get things confused and could be a danger to yourself and others. It's simple science."

"Have you ever even met someone who takes it regularly?"

"I—well, no, but that—"

"Then you don't know. That's simple science." He crossed his arms and quickly uncrossed them. "Ma'am."

She squinted, locking eyes with him without saying a word. Tallis nibbled at the inside of his cheek, stopping as soon as he realized what he was doing.

"I'll talk to whichever one of them wrote the piece and make sure they do some more digging. Perhaps get an interview with regular users."

Tallis nodded, turning to leave and return to his desk.

"I appreciate your dedication to accuracy, Tallis," she said.

"Just doing my job."

"You're damn good at it."

His chest and stomach burned. Pride riddled with doubt crept its way in. On one hand, she complimented him and acknowledged his skill. On the other, perhaps that would make him too valuable in his current position to risk moving him into a CA role. He felt acid singe his throat and he swallowed it back, dropping himself into his seat.

At the end of the day, Tallis wished Ms. Iris a good evening, and stepped into the elevator pod. As he neared the glass doors to exit Opulence, he realized it was pouring rain. Other staff members leaving for the day approached the door as well, meeting the weather with overdramatic groans, as if the earth chose the downpour specifically for their inconvenience. Meanwhile, Tallis simply returned to his desk upstairs to grab his spare hoodie from his desk drawer before venturing into the storm.

Fat drops spattered and soaked into the fabric of his hoodie. While others around him scrambled for shelter and skirted around developing puddles, he maintained his stride. If anything, the simple splish of his shoes against a puddle made him smile to himself.

During his walk home, Odessa texted him, complaining about how the weather made her heels too slick for work and she had to use the bathroom hand dryer before her shift. Tallis texted back about how the rain made him feel like the world was so much bigger and so much smaller all at the same time. He wondered if rain was symbolic of anything, especially when it never seemed to stop.

It's because you're a Cancer. Cancers are water signs!

Tallis wasn't really sure why Odessa thought he was some sort of cancer, or what that had to do with water, but he replied back with a smiley face nonetheless.

He passed the pink puddle outside Bru. It grew notably since his morning walk to work— how long had it been raining? Tallis imagined the same puddle-side village in his mind as before, but now, the puddle villagers were running from the flood.

"What are you looking at?" a little girl asked. She stood on the opposite side of the puddle, her blonde braids saturated, and raindrops bouncing off her purple raincoat.

Tallis blushed. "Nothing. I was just looking at the puddle."

"It's pretty," the child said.

"It is."

"I like to watch the shapes in it."

"The shapes?" Tallis asked. "Oh! Like the reflections?" She nodded.

"I like those too. I like how the light reflects in it and makes colorful ripples. Watch, I'll make an even bigger ripple." He searched the ground for a rock or even just a pebble to drop into the water, instead only finding a cigarette butt. He plucked it from the asphalt and dropped it from waist height down toward the puddle. It landed gracefully, floating atop the water.

"I don't get it," she said after a pause. "It looks like a little boat though."

"I was hoping it would sink and splash. It didn't work."

"It's still pretty."

"Loretta!" a woman called from the door of Buzz's Electrosuite. "What are you doing? Get back in here!"

The girl waved at Tallis and darted inside the shop with her mother.

Back at his apartment, Tallis changed into dry clothes and fixed himself and Lolli a snack before sitting on the couch and shutting the TV off.

"Wanna help me prepare for my interview?" he asked Lolli.

She stared back at him, exchanging a couple blinks before looking back at the blank TV.

"Sorry. I need to focus for a little bit. I'll put it back on later though. Promise."

She seemed to understand as she turned her attention back to him.

"I know they're going to ask why I deserve the job, or why I want the job. I feel like that's some sort of interview requirement. Let's start there."

Lolli started to nibble on her paw.

Tallis cleared his throat. "I think I'm the best candidate for the new Creative Anchor position because I've worked for Opulence for—wait… I've worked *with* Opulence… that sounds better… right?"

Lolli curled into a ball and began to doze off.

"You're right. It's a boring answer. They need something more exciting. I have to prove I'm not boring. I'm original. I'm different. I'm trying to be."

The fuzzy raccoon hiccupped in her sleep.

"I think you should just do the interview *for* me. Honestly, they'll probably like you better. You're more interesting."

Tallis rehearsed some possible interview questions out loud while Lolli snoozed beside him, and when he had finally grown frustrated and anxious enough, he disappeared to the kitchen to heat up some frozen chicken strips and fries for himself. He poured a bowl of kibble and a bowl of water for Lolli, clicking his tongue to get her attention. There was a thunk sound from the living room as Lolli dropped from the couch—followed by a pitter patter as she propelled her tubby body into the kitchen at full speed.

She scooped up a paw full of food and dunked it in her water, holding it there for a minute while she looked up at Tallis.

"Sorry. I'll let you eat. Bon appetite."

When his timer dinged, he pulled his food from the oven and dumped it on a plate with some barbeque sauce. He tapped his watch. "I want to see my friends," he commanded his TV.

The TV pulled up a social media feed of his friends' most recent posts. Some girl he went to high school with had another baby. His aunt was on a cruise. Some guy he met at the store once and hit it off with posted a shaky concert video. Xavier posted a selfie of him and Vanessa posing with a display of cloth napkins. *Picking out custom napkins for the wedding. Who knew that was a thing? #CountingDownTheDays!* the post read.

Tallis stared at the photo of them for a moment. He's always been happy for the two of them, but he always envied that kind of connection. They were clearly soulmates, at least to anyone who believed in that sort of thing. After years by himself, Tallis had often asked himself if maybe something happened to his before they could meet. Odessa was the closest thing he'd ever had before.

He stared down at his watch for a moment before tapping out Xavier's name. *Did you pick the scented napkins or the ones hand-embroidered with pure gold thread?* He read over his teasing text a few times, highlighted it, and deleted it with a sigh.

Just then, Odessa's name popped up on his watch. *Ready for tomorrow?* the text asked.

What's tomorrow? Tallis asked, brief panic flooding his head as he tried to remember where he may have planned a date for them tomorrow before realizing she must've meant his interview. *Shit. The Interview. Sorry. Nerves have got me in a bit of a funk.*

LOL :)

In summary, no, I'm not ready. But as ready as I'll ever be, I guess. I just don't know what they'll ask because I feel like they asked everything they'd need last time.

"What animal are you most like?" Probably. I'm calling it. They're going to bring out all the crazy questions this time. She texted. "I invited the stripper to be my date to my best friend's wedding."

Maybe. LOL. Doubt it.

Definitely a crow.

Why a crow? Tallis asked.

They're creative. They use sticks and things like tools. You're applying for a creative job. You can say you're innovative like a crow.

Huh. Tallis thought for a second before adding more. *Would you say that's the animal I'm most like?*

I guess! I'm not sure. It's a weird question LOL.
True.

Tallis went to bed early that night but spent most of the night staring at the ceiling, wondering if he was like a crow, or how he could become more crow-like. He thought to himself how ridiculous it felt to aspire to be like a bird, especially not in the "want to fly like a bird" sort of way. He had to convince himself for a moment that he's at least as innovative as a bird.

The sun began to rise without permission, and Tallis moaned in complaint. There was no way the night already ended when he never got any real sleep.

How was he supposed to make it through the whole workday on no sleep, let alone string together coherent thoughts in his interview afterward?

Lolli hopped up on the bed and sat on his chest, willing him to stay in bed a few extra minutes.

"Trust me," he told her, "I don't wanna get up either."
She blinked back at him.

"Offer still stands. Wanna do the interview for me?"
Another blink.

"Alright, fine. Someone's gotta make the money around here. I guess it'll be me."

Tallis picked up Ms. Iris's coffee on the way in, ordering himself an extra-large cold brew, knowing it would likely only give him life for half the day. As usual, Ms. Iris reached out for her coffee without looking up from her work. Tallis always thought it would be funny to hand her something ridiculous instead of her coffee, just to see if she would take it and try to sip. Naturally, he would never truly dare.

She took a sip of her coffee and shivered. "It tastes funky. What'd you do to it?" she accused, glaring at him.

"They were out of half and half. I think they used oat milk."

She smacked her mouth a few times as if it would reset her taste buds. "Gross. Oats don't belong in coffee. Who thought that was a good idea?"

"Lactose intolerant people, I guess."

"They should learn to be more tolerant."

"I don't think it works like that," Tallis half-mumbled.

She stared back at him, unamused. "Sarcasm, dear."

"Oh."

She proceeded to tell him about some of the urgent documents he needed to process for the day and let him know he could take a half day, as long as he finished the most important tasks. Tallis thanked her and hurried to his desk to get started.

The first file on his stack was the same article as the one he spoke with Ms. Iris about the day before. He plucked it from the pile and scanned over it. The problematic section was completely omitted. He smiled to himself, sitting upright in his chair.

He only felt better for a short while. When he reached another article in the stack, the headline sent a cold rush through his veins.

The headline read: *Man Plummets Off Building Under the Influence of REM.*

Tallis's eyes skimmed through the article a few times, trying to process. Ultimately, the article talked about a man who had taken an impure dose of REM, had horrifying hallucinations, reached out to some loved ones who brushed it off, and launched himself off the roof of his apartment complex.

He lifted his watch to text Odessa. *Hey, I know you said it's not common to take bad REM, but I'm processing an article for work about a guy who just died on REM.*

Damn, that sucks! Still stand by what I said though. Super uncommon. And even when it happens, it's not like people usually die from it. He probably had underlying issues anyways.

Something about her text didn't sit right with him. He read it over again, trying to give her the benefit of the doubt and see it from her perspective, but it still seemed harsh.

You're just going to brush it off? O, a man DIED.

I mean, I'm not going to dwell on it. I've been taking REM for a long time. It isn't like that.

Tallis sighed, a bit shaken by the thought of the confused and terrified man. He wondered if the guy even knew what he was doing in the moment.

Eventually, he was able to get his mind off the chilling article and onto the other documents in the looming stack of work before him. Not to mention, anxiety about his interview still hadn't subsided.

Sleep deprivation, 20 ounces of coffee, and unfiltered anxiety merged to give Tallis unavoidable jitters all day. By the time he finished the last of the urgent documents, he was nearly vibrating.

"I'd like to go home now," Tallis said, his voice wavering.

"It's not even close to lunchtime," Ms. Iris said, double-checking the time. "You're already done?"

Tallis nodded weakly, setting a folder on the corner of her desk.

Ms. Iris's eyes widened as she reached for the folder. "I was honestly going to be impressed if you'd finished them by lunch."

He wondered if a 'thank you' would be an appropriate response.

"I don't know what I'd do without you sometimes. I don't think I've told you that enough."

Tallis thought back for a moment. He was pretty sure she had *never* told him that.

"Can I go home?"

Ms. Iris looked surprised, but after a brief pause, she dismissed him.

"I'll see you later this evening."

"Yes, ma'am."

Tallis restrained himself from bolting for the elevator. His legs were wobbling, and his body kept tensing up to resist the exhausted and anxious chills continually rippling across his whole body. He stepped onto the elevator, and with each descending floor, his chest felt like it was constricting more and more around his heart and lungs until it was as if there was a box in his torso preventing his lungs from fully expanding.

He began to desperately suck in air, his hand blindly grappling for the wall as he eased himself out of the building. Two steps out of the building and he realized his fingers were beginning to tingle. He leaned back against the wall outside Opulence, sinking down onto the concrete below and burying his face in his arms, which were set across his bent knees.

"Hey," a man called over, "you alright?"

Tallis mustered a subtle nod, face still covered.

The stranger stood beside Tallis, stretching out a hand and almost placing it on his shoulder, changing his mind at the last minute. "Do you want some company?"

"You don't have to," Tallis muttered, "thank you, though."

"I don't mind."

Another nod.

The stranger sat beside Tallis, silent for a while.

"I know an anxiety attack when I see one," the man said. "I could see you go down on your way out the door. Can I try something that helps me?"

Nod.

"Tell me five things you see."

Tallis lifted his head, looking at his new friend and raising an eyebrow.

"Just try it."

"Uhh," he thought, "I see you. I see the hologram for Delta Cola. The crosswalk. A woman with a grey purse. And a hamburger wrapper in the street."

"Good. Now tell me four things around you that you can touch."

"Concrete, brick, glass, and… I guess… my work bag?"

"Three things you hear?"

Tallis paused for a moment. "People talking, footsteps, cars."

"Two things you can smell."

"Cigarettes and car exhaust."

"One thing you can taste."

Tallis tapped his tongue against the roof of his mouth

a few times. "Stale coffee breath."

The man chuckled. "I suppose that works."

Tallis took a slow, deep breath with a soft sigh.

"Better?"

Another sigh. "Definitely. Thank you. Where'd you learn that?"

"My therapist." The man smiled, standing and shaking Tallis's hand. "Maybe I'll see you around sometime."

Tallis accepted the handshake, thanking him again before rising and making his way to the subway.

The entire ride home, he tried to consciously observe everything he was sensing, just enough to stay grounded until he got home. By the time he walked into his apartment, he all but collapsed on the couch.

"Set an alarm for four o'clock," Tallis called to his TV.

"*Alarm set for 4pm.*"

He rolled onto his side on his sofa, covering his face with a pillow, crumbs from one of Lolli's snacks raining into his hair. With a groan, he rustled his hair, shaking the bits out.

As he tried to sleep, Lolli crawled over, poking her little nose under the pillow to check on Tallis.

"I'm trying to sleep," he grumbled to her, covering his face tighter with the pillow to block her out.

He could still hear her little nose snuffling its way under the pillow.

"Leave me alone for a little bit," he begged. "Please."

Sniff, sniff.

Tallis growled, sitting immediately upright, chucking the pillow back onto the couch as he stormed into his bedroom and slammed the door behind him. Just when he finally started to get cozy and sleepy in his bed, he could hear scratching at his door.

"You've gotta be kidding me."

He tried to ignore Lolli as she begged to come in, but unable to tune her out, he opened the door reluctantly before turning back to bed.

Lolli hopped on the bed beside him, sniffing at his hair and retrieving a hitchhiking crumb. She nibbled on the goody and then curled up on the pillow right above his head.

Tallis dozed off at about noon and hardly moved for four hours. When four o'clock hit, his TV started to blare random popular music, progressively getting louder until Tallis willed himself out of bed to shut it off.

He felt at ease for the first time all day as he poured himself a glass of water and relaxed on the couch, watching TV. Everything felt like it was going to be okay, at least for a moment. Unfortunately, the relief dissipated the second he realized he was supposed to be getting ready for his interview.

Once again, he hurled the pillow at the couch, throwing himself to his feet to race to his closet. He tapped the tablet on the wall beside it, selecting some of his best slacks, a bright red dress shirt, and a custom fit suit jacket. Of course, Tallis had been thinking about what he could wear to the interview ever since he got the letter. He wanted to look classy and competent, but he wanted something that was also loud. Something that said "Listen to me! I'm the one you want!" Red felt like the right fit.

He hopped in the shower, keeping the water cool to help wake him up. After drying off, he got dressed and ran some mousse through his hair and grabbed his portfolio and gave Lolli a finger boop on the nose for luck and dashed out the door.

He reached Opulence only two minutes later than he wanted to, but naturally, he was still early. With a deep breath at the door, he stepped inside and made his way to the same waiting room as his first interview.

While waiting, his watch buzzed, reminding him to set it on Do Not Disturb mode. He ignored the message, not even checking to see who sent it, but the longer he sat in silent wait, the more curiosity pricked.

Tallis stood up, peeking outside the waiting room door in either direction before taking a seat and pulling up the message.

Good luck! Let me know when it's done and we can get drinks—to celebrate or to forget the whole thing! Odessa wrote.

Let's hope the former.

She sent back a fingers-crossed emoji.

He turned off his watch, not wanting to risk it going off in front of everyone. Just as he relaxed his arm beside him, Bill filled the door frame.

"Good to see ya!" he boomed, holding out a hand.

Tallis scrambled clumsily from his seat, dropping his portfolio as he reached out to shake Bill's hand.

"Sorry," Tallis said, ducking down to paw for his papers. Bill squatted and picked up a few, handing them over.

"Happens to the best of us."

Tallis nodded, swallowing and nearly choking.

"Ready to go?" Bill asked, standing.

"Yes, sir."

Bill led Tallis down the hall and past the first interview

room, straight into one about twice the size—and filled accordingly.

Clearly noticing Tallis's surprise at the panel size, Bill answered, "The second round of interviews not only includes upper management, but the next level of authority below them. After all, CAs are the lifeblood of our company! It's important that we pick the best ones possible."

He nodded, following Bill into the room and taking a seat in the center. Everyone's eyes fixated on him like magnets, and he felt self-conscious of everything. Was his breathing too obvious? Could they see the sweat on his forehead? He forgot to brush his teeth an extra time before leaving—could they see anything in his teeth?

"So," Bill said from across the table, "how was the date?"

Taken aback, Tallis stuttered for a moment. "The date?"

"The date with the stripper. We filled everyone else in! I'm curious to know how it went. Plus, consider this an ice breaker." He chuckled heartily.

"Oh! It went well. I took her to a bar near the club she works at in Sector 3. I asked her to be my date to my best friend's wedding. Also, I found out she loves raccoons, and I have a pet raccoon at home. Her name is Lolli—the raccoon, not the stripper. I took Lolli with me on the date."

"You took your pet raccoon to a bar to meet a stripper?" asked an older woman beside Bill. Her face was void of any emotion, but as Tallis nodded, a huge smile flooded her face. "That's fantastic!" She laughed. "I love that!"

"Oh," Tallis blushed. "Thank you." He wasn't sure how else to respond to that.

Everyone stared back at him silently, leaning forward in their seats.

"Umm… We were hitting it off really well. Just talking and drinking for a while, but I had to leave early. Lolli was still in her early stages of training. To be honest, she still is. She's a bit of an attention hog, and I wasn't paying attention to her for a little bit, so she climbed up the bar shelves and started knocking stuff down on the bartender. It was such a mess. The bartender was ticked off—I can't say I blamed him. So, I ran over to try to coax her down, and when I finally got her down, I had to bring her home. There was no way she was going to just sit still after that."

"How precious!" One of the new faces cooed.

"Do you want to see a picture of her?"

Unanimous nods from the interviewers.

"May I connect to the screen?" he asked, motioning to the projecting TV at the far end of the room.

"Of course," Bill said, turning the TV on.

Tallis tapped around on his watch, a picture of Lolli filling the TV screen a moment later.

The room filled with "aww"s and excited chatter amongst the interviewers.

"She's a lot of fun," he said before removing the image from the screen.

"Fantastic!" Bill said. "Glad to finally get some answers about that date! I feel like the rest of the interview won't be quite as thrilling—after all, how can you get any better than that? Unfortunately, though, we've gotta get on schedule with the questions."

"Understandable," Tallis said, settling himself.

"First *real* question," Bill said, "if you had to describe yourself as any kind of animal, what animal would you be?"

When the panel finished asking all their questions and Tallis was confident he had answered them to the best of his ability, Bill began to wrap things up, thanking Tallis once again for his time.

"You definitely know how to make a statement." Bill chuckled. "We admire your boldness in talking about your date. You're candid and willing to go for what you think will make you memorable, and that's something we look for in a CA."

"I'm not sure if there's a third round of interviews," Tallis said, "or if this is it before you make your decision, but I'd love to tell you about the wedding the next time I see you all. Preferably as your newest CA."

Bill smiled ear-to-ear, shaking Tallis's hand yet again. "There likely won't be a third stage of interviews, and you were our first of the second round, so you've got some waiting to do before any kind of decision is made. I hope to hear about the wedding sometime, though."

Tallis nodded, thanking them all for their time and

trying to keep himself calm enough to walk out the door at a nonchalant pace, even though he felt like enough adrenaline was buzzing through his veins for him to hit record-breaking speeds.

As soon as he was outside Opulence, an ungodly squeak erupted from his throat, and he couldn't help but smile.

Just got out of my interview, he texted. He wanted her to ask how it went. He wanted to make her curious.

Ah! How was it?

He tried to suppress a smirk as he ignored her message and started the trek to the subway.

While sitting in the subway car, he imagined Odessa staring at their messages unblinkingly, so anxious for his reply.

He managed to hold back the urge to text her back until he stepped foot in his apartment. The second he did, he replied, *I think it went well. Better than I expected at least. I'm scared to get my hopes up, but I felt like I had some more interesting answers for their questions this time around, and they didn't look bored this time.*

No response. He told himself she probably stepped away from her messages for a while. No big deal.

When a few more minutes had passed with no reply, he resigned to changing out of his interview clothes and sitting down for a late dinner with Lolli. Just as he had filled her bowl and sat down with his leftover frozen chicken strips, his watch buzzed.

WYD?

What? He read over her text a few times, wondering if it was a typo.

Sorry, grandpa, meant to text my boyfriend. She added an eyeroll emoji. *WYD means "what are you doing?"*

Oh. My bad. I'm just eating dinner.

Meet me in Sector 4?

What's in Sector 4?

Me.

Tallis left his half-eaten chicken strips on his plate in the living room, changing back into his interview clothes and grabbing his wallet to leave for Sector 4.

It was late and he was still feeling sleep deprived, but it was a Friday, and he survived his second interview. That was enough reason to go out and celebrate.

He walked down the street, his pace and the wind brisk. Although he tried to keep his focus on his destination, he couldn't help but slow to take a better look at the way the city looked that night. The moon was almost cartoonishly large as it framed one of the taller skyscrapers in Neuvale. Moonlight outlined thick clouds, and the purplish white glow made the glassy structures of the city look elegant and ominous, like some sort of comic book villain's lair.

Without his camera, he attempted to be content with just the mental memory of the moment. The urge to capture the view forever was almost strong enough for him to make the short trip back to his apartment, but he didn't want to keep Odessa waiting. After all, he had no idea if their mysterious plans were time sensitive.

The subway station was lifeless, save for a homeless woman and a curly-haired little dog seated atop a pile of ratty blankets in her lap.

Tallis walked past her and a hologram ad for a new superhero movie, stepping into the subway car and opting to stand and hold the hand grip from the ceiling rather than sit.

The subway lurched and zipped down the track, picking up and dropping off a few random people at each stop. By the time it reached Sector 4, the only other person in his car with him was a rail of a woman with greasy pigtails and an oozing sore on her face. Tallis averted his eyes as soon as he saw her, knowing he'd end up staring and daydreaming her entire backstory.

When the subway stop displayed Sector 4, the doors opened and he stepped off, surprised to see Odessa was already there, sitting on a bench beside the stairs. She was wearing a low-cut, tight black dress.

"Oh, hey!" she called, getting up and walking over to meet him.

"Everything okay?" he asked.

She kissed his cheek when she reached him. "Yup!"

"What are we doing in Sector 4?"

"You'll see."

Odessa took his hand and led him out of the station. As her back turned to him, he noticed the open back of her dress, including her huge and intricate tattoo of ivy and flowers. He had seen it before when he first watched her dance, but now that he was able to look at it up close, he noticed the flowers were delicate apple blossoms. Tallis was mesmerized by the way the tattoo moved subtly with each step she took up the stairs.

Once out of the station, she made a sharp turn and corralled him down a street.

"It's not far," she said.

"Should I be nervous?"

"Depends," she teased, biting back a smile.

"On what?" Tallis grumbled as he continued after her until they reached sleek, black double doors against the side of a brick building.

"Depends on *what?*" he repeated.

"Depends on if you're a good dancer or not." She pulled on the silver handle of one of the doors, a rush of cool air and boozy scents swirling together.

"Wait, what?" Tallis's eyes bulged and his heels dug into the ground as she tugged his wrist.

"C'mon!" she urged. "It'll be fun."

"I'm not really a good dancer."

"You don't have to be. I was joking. And don't worry—let's just get some drinks in you first! First drink is on me—after all, I said I'd take you for a drink after the interview."

Tallis semi-reluctantly agreed, the two of them disappearing into the darkness through the doors. When they closed behind the couple, the two were trapped in a dark hallway lined with small white lights trailing along the floor.

"You sure this is the right place?" Tallis asked, looking around as she picked up her pace ahead of him.

"Positive. I've got a friend who works here and gets me in for free sometimes, but only if I take the back entrance. No big deal."

Tallis grunted and let her drag him along. The further down the hall they travelled, the more the walls and floor seemed to rumble, and a rhythmic thumping began growing in intensity. At the end of the hallway, they reached another black door, which Odessa opened immediately. The rumbling and thumping metamorphosized into electronic music, and the air was full of smoke and chemically scented fog from small machines at either end of the club.

When the smoke cleared enough for him to see clearly, Tallis could make out a huge dance floor made up of small screens set together to make one large display. The floor changed patterns—one minute looking like a real aquarium of tropical fish, the next, it looked like everyone was dancing on piles of money, with virtual coins and dollar bills scattering across the screens with each footstep taken on the floor.

"What is this place?"

"It's just a club!" she said when they reached the bar, gently pushing back on his chest to urge him to take a seat.

"I figured as much, but I've never seen this place."

"Go clubbing enough to have seen all the clubs in Neuvale?"

"Erhm… no."

"There ya go!" She turned her attention to the bartender. "I'm feeling a whiskey sour. Get one for him, too!"

"Oh, I don't really like whiskey much," Tallis tried.

"Yes, you do."

Tallis stared back at Odessa, confused.

"It's good. Just drink it. Everyone likes these. They make 'em good here."

When the bartender slid over the two drinks, Odessa immediately took a generous swig, looking at Tallis expectantly.

"Try it!" she crowed while he sat there, stirring hesitantly with the tiny black straw.

He scratched his head, eyeing the drink.

"Here," she said, reaching into her cleavage and fishing out a small vial of pink. She popped it open and dumped the contents into his glass.

"REM?" He held his drink up, watching as the drug's color dissipated into the whiskey.

"Uh-huh." She looked at him, waiting for his move.

"What mix?" he asked

"Not telling."

"Then why would I drink it?"

"Curiosity." She smirked.

"Dammit, you're good." He brought the drink closer to his lips, still hesitating.

"Plus, you wanna be more adventurous. That's what they're looking for in those interviews, right? Adventurous, exciting, interesting people take risks and try new things."

At her words, he took a big gulp of whiskey and REM.

"So? Amazing, right?"

"Absolutely not." He cringed, setting the drink down.

"Chug it! We just need to loosen you up a bit. I don't care what you drink to get there."

"What do I need to be loosened up for?"

She squinted at him, her face grave for a moment before bursting out in laughter when she seemed to realize he was being serious.

"To *dance*, stupid!"

"Oh God," he said through nervous laughter.

"You don't wanna dance with me?" She scoffed, still smiling, teasing.

"I haven't been to a dance since high school, and even then, I didn't go often. Mostly just for the little meatballs they'd serve at the snack bar."

"But you've danced before, right?"

"I mean…" More nervous laughter. "Sure, but my ex-girlfriends can tell you it isn't my strength."

"Don't worry about it! Just loosen up, move with the music, and have some fun!"

"Uh-uh." Tallis crossed his arms and raised his brow.

Odessa crossed her arms right back and furrowed her brows at him, staring him down until his pose softened.

"Fine."

"Yay!" She clapped and then snatched his hand, dragging him onto the dance floor.

They stopped underneath a display of two large, interlocking ring lights. Tallis looked up, admiring the color-changing LEDs for a moment.

"It's pretty in here," he observed, wondering when the REM would kick in.

"It's alright, I guess," she said.

Tallis turned his attention to the changing screen floor, which now looked like flowing lava beneath their feet. The music seemed to shake the room with each bass note, jarring him from his trance.

When he looked up, Odessa was staring back at him, arms crossed and tapping her foot, but she didn't look mad. Her expression was simply flat.

"Sorry," he said, "I'm not really sure how to initiate these kinds of things. I'm out of practice. And I was never great at it to begin with."

Without a word, Odessa grabbed Tallis's hands and placed them on her exposed back. Her skin was warm and soft, and Tallis noticed himself tracing his fingers along the curve in her spine. She smiled softly back at him as she placed one hand on his chest and the other around the side of his neck. When he didn't initiate any kind of movement, she moved closer to him, her chest pressed against him as she started grinding to the beat.

Tallis questioned it for a moment. This wasn't the dancing he remembered from school, but he didn't mind it. He tried to push away the temptation to check out a glittery light fixture across the room. As his focus began to wane for a moment, Odessa leaned in closer, her head over his shoulder and her lips grazing his neck. His attention was back on her.

She ran her fingers up through his hair and he let out a sigh. He could feel her soft laugh on his neck. As she drew herself away from his collar, he took a hand from her back and set it on her cheek, pulling her in for a kiss, knowing he'd chicken out if he waited even a second longer.

The two of them melted together as she kissed him back. When they finally pulled apart and Tallis opened his eyes, Odessa glowed neon pink, as if her veins had been injected with pure light.

"Woah," Tallis said, letting her go and taking a step back.

"Ahh!" She bounced up and down, applauding. "I always love the look on your face when it hits you!"

Tallis looked for the double ring light above them, but it had been replaced by a grandiose chandelier, radiating tiny rainbows onto the floor. Instead of small screens, the floor now appeared to be made of quartz. His eyes continued to wander to look at the people around them, all of them alight like Odessa, but each their own color. Tallis held out his own arm, his veins glowing a rich aqua.

"Wanna see something cool?" Odessa asked.

"I think I already do," Tallis replied breathily, taking a 360 look at the club.

"No, look!" She turned around to show him her bare back. Her tattoo now looked like it was etched in green glow paint.

"This is wild!" Tallis ran his fingers through his hair as he took it all in.

"Wanna keep dancing?" she proposed, spinning back to face him.

He nodded back at her, his eyes tracing her veins as she stepped into his space again.

Tallis and Odessa held each other close, swaying with the music. Their light seemed to blur together into a bright purple as they danced, and he couldn't take his eyes off it the entire time.

Time seemed infinite, as if it wasn't part of their universe. The night rode on, and it was only when the REM began to wear off that they finally pulled apart again.

"Come back to my place," Odessa said. It wasn't a question or a request.

Tallis agreed by following her as she made her way back out the way they came. He wasn't sure if he should expect night or day when they stepped back out into open air. As it turns out, there was still a little left of the night.

Odessa led the way to the subway, and when it arrived, the two boarded without having said a word since leaving the club.

They fell back into the subway seats, even though their destination was only one sector away. When the station display lit up with the number three, they willed themselves to stand again.

"It's not far," she said, lacing her fingers between Tallis's and guiding him the opposite direction from Illusion.

They walked down the dark, damp street for a few blocks, making a couple turns before she stopped in front of a white concrete tower. The two walked up the narrow stairs to the front door.

"S'cuse me," she said, grabbing his hips and maneuvering him out of the way so she could get to the door. "There's a scanner."

She leaned down to look closely at the retina scanner, which let out a sharp chirp, followed by a thunk in the door.

Tallis reached over and pulled the heavy door open, moving out of her way again. "After you," he said.

She stepped inside and he followed as she walked up to an elevator, tapping the button with a manicured finger.

The elevator chimed and the metal doors slid open to greet Tallis and Odessa. Inside, she pressed another button— this one painted with a little number nineteen.

"Nineteen floors in your apartment?" Tallis noted. "That's honestly impressive for Sector 3."

Odessa smiled with her mouth, but it didn't travel to her eyes.

"I'm glad you didn't wanna go back to my place tonight. I haven't had a chance to clean. Laundry day is way overdue."

She still didn't reply, but instead continued her flat smile as she looked him over, only stopping when the elevator did.

The doors slid open again, revealing a short hallway with velvety red floors and cream walls. She motioned for him with a finger before she unlocked apartment 1903.

She pushed the door open slowly, walking in before Tallis. He followed just a step behind. Once inside, he wasn't even convinced they were in Odessa's apartment yet. With a twelve-foot ceiling, a see-through fireplace, and a floor-to-ceiling window spanning the entire living room wall, Odessa's apartment looked like the cover of a luxury living magazine.

He stepped slowly and delicately into the room, as if his mere presence could break the mini crystal chandelier or stain her plush white couch and fur rug.

"Want some wine?" she asked, stepping into a connected kitchen with huge quartz countertops.

Tallis didn't reply. Instead, he was tiptoeing to the window, overlooking part of Neuvale. The city lights seemed to pulse like a heartbeat, and Tallis started to question whether the effects of REM had worn off yet.

Odessa appeared beside him, holding out a glass of red wine.

"Thanks," he said, accepting it and taking a sip. "Is there REM in this?"

She shook her head. "I haven't put any in mine yet either. I wasn't going to put any in yours anyways. Not unless you want some. I don't give people REM without their knowledge."

"I appreciate that."

She nodded, turning to look over the city with him.

"How do you do that?" she asked.

"Do what?"

She motioned to the city and pointed back to him as if he were supposed to understand.

"I'm sorry," he said, "I still don't get it."

"I can tell by your face that you think the city is beautiful. You think everything is beautiful. All the time. How do you do that?"

"I mean, it's not really a conscious thing, I guess."

"When I look out my window, at first, I see the lights—they're pretty enough, sure. But then I think about all the people in the city. All the liars and the pigs. All the trash on the streets—I also mean that literally. And it's all so loud."

"I love to think about all the people in there though. Tons of them, and each one has their own story, their own life. You could pick any one of them from the crowd, and you'll never find another one like *that* one."

Odessa said nothing. Instead, she pulled out another small vial, pouring it into her wine and sipping while she continued staring out the window.

"I don't mean to pry," Tallis said, breaking the silence. She turned to look at him. "But do you use that stuff *all* the time?"

"Don't act like it's a big deal!" She took a sip, the corners of her lips turned up in a little smile. "I like it. What can I say? It just makes things… better."

"But you don't like to just see things as they are sometimes?"

"Sure I do!"

Tallis raised an eyebrow at her.

"Ugh," she scoffed. "If you saw half the stuff I see on a day-to-day basis, you'd be the same way. Some people enjoy smoking, some enjoy eating junk food, some enjoy alcohol. The thing is, all those things can kill you if you overdo it. I'm fine. If anything, this is the better vice."

Tallis refrained from arguing anymore, and Odessa turned back to face the window again.

By the time she was halfway done with her wine, she grabbed Tallis's hand and tugged.

"I wanna show you around!"

"I thought you'd never ask."

She giggled and led him into the kitchen, displaying it with a flourish of her arms.

"Ta-daaa!"

Tallis puckered his lips and snapped his fingers like a refined gentleman. Odessa laughed as she turned to open her gigantic fridge, pulling out two string cheeses.

"It's only one step away from being a charcuterie board, ya know," she said as she handed him one and unpeeled her own, stringing off a little of the cheese and dangling it into her mouth.

She continued the tour, next stopping in her bedroom, which bragged a similarly large window and a cushy bed with a pure white comforter.

"This apartment is insane," Tallis said, his head rolling around as he took in every detail.

"Thank you! Once I really got my footing at Illusion, I started getting regulars. You can thank Jerry, Noah, and Logan for this place!"

"Wow. Thanks, Jerry, Noah, and Logan."

She smiled, locking eyes with Tallis as she threw herself backwards on the bed. Her hair fanned out like a halo around her head, and she batted her big blue eyes at him. She patted the space beside her, and Tallis obliged, leaning back and letting himself fall.

He turned his head to look at her, and she locked eyes with him, holding the gaze for a minute before leaning in and kissing him.

"You know the best part about seeing beauty in

everything around you?" he asked, resting a finger on her jawline.

She bit her lip and smiled, her eyes wild.

"The moment when you finally find *the* most beautiful thing."

Tallis woke up to bright sunlight cresting over the city outside Odessa's bedroom window. He rolled over, away from the light and toward Odessa, who was still peacefully sleeping beside him.

He pushed back her hair and kissed her on the forehead before letting his feet hang over the side of the bed for a moment, eventually getting the energy to stand. After a few stretches and admiring the golden glow over Neuvale, he walked toward the kitchen, his bare feet patting against the cold floor.

It took him a moment to find a pan, but once he did, he pulled some eggs from Odessa's fridge, cracking them into the hot pan. Her fruit bowl was full of apples and avocados, so he pulled a couple of each, washing them and slicing them up. The toaster was left plugged in on the counter, so he found her bread and toasted a few pieces, setting avocado slices on one and apple slices on another. As for the eggs, he dumped some in the empty space on the plate, sprinkling a little pepper over it. It wasn't gourmet, but it also wasn't his kitchen. Not that Tallis typically prepared plated meals at his own place either.

Just as he was walking back toward her bedroom, Odessa stepped into the living room in nothing but her wrinkled white t-shirt and simple black underwear. Her hair was a teased nest of a bun on top of her head, wobbling with each groggy step she took in her march to the couch. She sat back, propping her bare feet on her coffee table as she wiped the night's sleep from the corners of her eyes.

Tallis stood in front of her, holding out a plate and fork. When she finally opened her eyes fully and noticed him, she jumped and put a hand to her chest.

"You scared the shit out of me!"

"Sorry. I thought you saw me coming."

"Nope," she said, shaking her head, her bun bobbing.

"I made breakfast," Tallis said, calling attention to the plate in his hands. "It's gonna get cold."

"Thanks," she said, taking the plate and setting it on the coffee table. "I've got coffee and juice, too, if you want."

Tallis returned to the kitchen to brew a pot of coffee, calling out to Odessa when it was finished.

"Do you have any syrups or anything?" he asked.

"No. I usually just drink it black. I've got some sugar, but that's about it."

He reluctantly stirred some sugar into his mug, taking a sip and recoiling at the bitterness, adding more sugar.

"I've gotta get going soon," Odessa said as she finished the last bite of eggs. "I've got errands to run before work. Thanks for breakfast! Ten out of ten service. Waiter was pretty cute, too." She winked.

Tallis couldn't hide his grin, even when he tried to mask

it by casually sipping his coffee.

Odessa stripped off the t-shirt on her way to the bedroom, disappearing for a moment, returning in sweats, a different t-shirt, and tennis shoes, a toothbrush flopping out of her mouth as she tried to collect dirty dishes while brushing.

"Don't worry about the dishes—I've got them. Just get ready," Tallis said, looking her up and down. "I thought you had to go to work?"

"I've got a wardrobe at work. I'm not wearing that stuff to the stores." At the last word, a little toothpaste dribbled down her chin and she groaned, wiping it up and rushing back to the bathroom.

Tallis finished washing the dishes right as Odessa returned, hair combed out and makeup applied.

"You look nice," he said as she hurried around the room, searching for her purse.

She looked over at him, not stopping her search. "Gotta pay for this place somehow."

When she found her bag, she scooped it up and made her way to the door. Tallis got the hint and put his shoes on before joining her.

"I hate to kick you out so soon, but I meant to be out the door earlier than this."

"Totally understand," he said. And he meant it.

She leaned over and gave him a peck so quick he questioned if they even made contact. At that, they were both out the door and she zipped off down the hallway.

"I had fun!" Tallis tried to call after her, and he wasn't sure if she even heard.

He made his way out of her apartment and out to the

street. Odessa had already disappeared. Tallis didn't realize how cold she kept her apartment until he was outside, his skin tingling with the warmth of the sun and the heat radiating off hot asphalt.

The warmth felt nice, and Tallis was already in a fantastic mood. He took his time as he strolled to the subway station.

He looked at his watch, sending her a quick text while he waited on the subway to arrive.

Thanks for last night. It was exciting, and fun, and I really needed that.

She replied back moments later. *Me too! You're so much better than the other jerks I've dated. You're much softer than those macho meatheads.*

Tallis read over her message a few times, the word "softer" stabbing like a hot knife each time. Did she not think he was capable of being tough? Brave? "Soft" didn't sound like someone who took risks. It sounded like someone who would work a desk job for the rest of his life while the "macho meatheads" adventured through the city as CAs.

The entire subway ride home, Tallis couldn't get her text out of his mind. He bickered with himself in his head—one moment telling himself that she didn't think he was capable of getting the promotion, that he wouldn't be able to make her feel safe and protected like other men, that he was more of a pet than a partner. The next moment, he'd try to convince himself there was no way she could've meant that much by her message. But no matter how hard he tried to convince himself, the first voice would always win.

What did you mean by your last message? He finally texted her.

What? I just meant you're able to hold a conversation that's not about sports or your latest gym regimen. It's refreshing.

Oh. That's it?

WTF did you think it meant? LOL

I thought maybe you meant I was weak or something.

You jump to conclusions too much. Maybe if you didn't spend so much time in your head.

I wish you'd stop saying that. His cheeks burned as he hit the send button.

I'm just saying it like it is. Get over it.

"Get over it" stung like a slap to his face. At that, he lowered his wrist and decided he needed to take a break from her messages and step back for a little while. He didn't want to say anything to make things worse, and knowing Odessa, she would just bite back harder.

Once he reached his apartment, he unlocked his door, pushing it open and freezing in the doorway.

"Oh my God."

Lolli was on the floor, shaking, surrounded by puddles of vomit. Her fur was wet from the mess, and she began to lurch before adding another puddle, this one with some pink liquid.

Tallis shouted, diving after her and inspecting her. She stared back at him with her small black eyes, her usually fluffy face now matted. She pawed helplessly at her mouth as she drooled.

"What do I do?" Tallis panicked, looking around the room as if there'd be someone with answers. "What do I do?"

He started hyperventilating, looking back down at Lolli as she shivered.

"Hang on, Lolli," he whispered.

He tapped his watch, found Odessa's name, and almost hit the call button, but something about it didn't feel right. He backed out of her contact information, pulling up Xavier's instead and pressing it.

"Please pick up!" he begged, his eyes darting between his watch and his beloved pet.

Eventually, there was a voice on the other end.

"You finally ready to say you're sorry?" Xavier asked, a tinge of sarcasm in his words.

"Please help me!" Tallis cried.

"Woah, bro, you okay?"

"No!"

"Wh—"

"Come here… now! It's an emergency. It's Lolli. I don't know what to do. I came home and she's throwing up and I think maybe there's blood in some of the throw up? I don't know. She's shaking. I'm scared, Xavier. Please!"

"Okay, I'm on my way, but you need to get her to a vet!"

"I don't know where the nearest one is!"

"Hang on, I'm looking it up now." There was a short pause. "There's one near the pet store in your sector. Corner of Willborough and Marks. Do you think you can get her there?"

"I think so. I can try." He looked down at Lolli, who had a wet paw on his knee as he stayed knelt beside her.

"I'll meet you there, okay? Just try to stay calm and get her there as quick as you can. I'm sure she'll be fine, but you gotta work fast with animals. How long has she been like that?"

"I don't know. I just came home to her like that!" He

started to search for her carrying crate, figuring it would be better than her riding on his shoulder.

"I mean, it's a Saturday morning, so you can't have been gone long. So, whatever this is, you caught it quick, so I'm sure she'll be fine."

"I've been gone since last night."

"Last night?"

Tallis found Lolli's crate, laying out a towel inside and delicately scooping his pet up, placing her in the carrier.

"I've gotta go! I've got her in her carrier and I'm headed out now."

He grabbed the carrier by the handle and supported the bottom with his other hand before rushing out the door.

"I'll meet you there as quick as I can."

Xavier hung up and Tallis hurried out of his apartment building and down the street, opposite the direction of the subway. He was familiar with the general area of the small pet store and veterinarian's office, but he didn't frequent it. Fortunately, it wasn't far, and he could remember how to get there.

As he ran, he kept glancing down at Lolli, who had hurled in her crate, soaking her towel.

"I'm so sorry! I'm so sorry!" he kept whimpering, forcing back tears.

She glanced up at him, and he read it as a look of betrayal.

When he reached the vet's office, he threw the door open and bolted to the front desk, wailing "help!" as he did.

The receptionist's eyes grew big, and she jumped back in her seat in shock.

"I don't know what's wrong with her but she's shaking

and won't stop puking and I think there's maybe blood—please help!"

The woman took off through the door beside her desk, reappearing a few moments later with a woman in a white coat.

Tallis reexplained everything and handed Lolli off to the vet, his stomach and eyes burning as he did. The vet didn't say much as she took Lolli through the door again, leaving Tallis and the receptionist in the lobby.

He started pacing, sniffling and running his hands through his hair, leaving it tufted on top of his head. Each minute ached and the crushing weight in his chest made him feel like he was drowning.

An eternity later, Xavier ran through the doors, scanning the room and zeroing in on Tallis.

"Where have you been?" Tallis wailed at him before he could utter a word.

"I came as fast as I could! I literally left right after we hung up." He stopped himself, changing the subject. "Is she back there now?"

Tallis nodded, sniffed, and cleared his throat.

"Hey, man," he hugged Tallis. "I'm sure everything will be fine. She's with the experts now. They know what they're doing."

Another nod.

Xavier guided Tallis to one of the waiting room benches.

"No sense in pacing. You're just stressing *everyone* out." Xavier chuckled uncomfortably.

"Sorry."

"You're fine, man."

Just as they sat down, the receptionist approached Tallis with a clipboard and pen.

"Sir," she said, handing the items to him. "I need you to sign the emergency treatment forms. They basically say you agree to whatever procedures the doctor deems necessary, that you don't hold us liable, and that you understand the charges are your responsibility. We do offer payment plans, if needed."

Tallis took the clipboard, skimming over the legalese before signing and dating at the bottom. He handed it back to her but held onto the corner for a second. "Do they know what's going on?" he asked. When the receptionist shook her head, he released.

A while passed in silence, only broken by the occasional newcomer checking their pet in at the front desk. Eventually, Xavier spoke up.

"I'm sorry about what I said."

Tallis had his face in his hands, his elbows on his knees. He pulled his face away, looking at Xavier and raising an eyebrow.

"The whole thing about that stripper. I was a dick."

"Fact."

Xavier scoffed. "I was just trying to watch out for you. I put myself where I didn't belong, and I was out of line. I just didn't want you getting hurt."

"I can look out for myself."

"I know—I know. I just mean… you're just… you're a *trusting* person, and I didn't want that to bite you in the ass."

"You think I'm naïve."

Xavier crossed his arms and slouched back in his chair.

"I get it. You're not the only one. It kinda sucks. I'm not stupid."

"No one thinks you're stupid, Tal."

"Hah."

"You're trusting. You see the best right away instead of assuming the worst. Do you know how many people wish they could be like that?"

"No one in their right mind. No one takes you seriously if you're like me."

"*I* take you seriously."

"You *didn't*."

"And I said I'm sorry."

Tallis let out a huffy sigh.

"What else do I have to do to make it right?" Xavier asked.

"I invited her to your wedding. As my date."

Xavier paused, breathing in slow. "That's great. I'm glad you found a date. I look forward to meeting her."

"No, you don't. That was a nice try, though."

"I just have healthy suspicions."

"And you're entitled to those but keep them to yourself."

A woman in a white coat walked through the lab doors and into the lobby, and Tallis felt his heart drop as he involuntarily stood. When he got a better look, he noticed it was a different veterinarian. He whined and sat back down, letting his face fall into his hands again.

"So," Xavier tried, "are you guys pretty serious?"

Tallis shrugged, not lifting his gaze. "I guess."

"I'm happy you found someone that makes you happy. That's really all that matters to me. You've been the best friend I could've asked for. For years. And you deserve the best. I know that's cliche as shit, but I mean it. I want to be able to go to your wedding and celebrate you and your happiness one day. I think that would be freaking awesome."

Tallis sat back again, nodding.

Then, the silence returned. A while later, Lolli's vet walked through the doors. Tallis shot out of his seat and she approached him, her brow furrowed and eyes looking sunken.

"Is she okay?" he shouted before she was even in front of him.

She waited until she was closer before responding. "She's stable right now—"

"What happened?" he interrupted.

"We were able to determine that your raccoon ingested a foreign object and it had gotten stuck in her stomach. We put her under and removed it safely, but she's resting right now."

"A foreign object? What does that mean?" he leaned forward, massaging his hands nervously.

"By the looks of it, she chewed off part of some sort of charger—for a laptop or phone or something. And she swallowed it."

"She's never chewed on cords or anything though! How does that even happen?"

"I'm not sure what to tell you, sir. Sometimes pets— especially raccoons—can be troublemakers. Just make sure you have adequate and appropriate toys for her and keep her on a regular feeding schedule. Sometimes animals get desperate when they're hungry, and domestic animals don't always make the best decisions on what is and is *not* food."

Tallis thanked the doctor repeatedly for saving Lolli. She

directed him to the receptionist to sign some more papers, and she disappeared back behind the door to check on Lolli.

At the front desk, the receptionist had Tallis sign some paperwork to confirm he was taking Lolli home and would follow any further treatment plans. She took Tallis's payment and paperwork, and instructed him to take a seat for a little bit longer.

"See?" Xavier said, patting Tallis on the shoulder as he returned to his seat. "I told you she'd be okay! You made the right move bringing her in."

"It's my fault she even had to come here."

"What do you mean? She chewed up a cord. It happens."

"No, it doesn't. Lolli doesn't chew cords— I swear. Never."

"That doesn't make it your fault! She got curious and chewed something she shouldn't have. Stop blaming yourself, man."

"She was chewing because she was hungry. She ate it because I never came home to feed her."

17

A short while later, one of the vet techs stepped into the lobby with Lolli in her carrier, which had been wiped down and cushioned with a new towel. Lolli was lying down, burying her face under her little paws.

Tallis almost lost the tears he was holding back when he saw how helpless she looked, and the guilt hit with a vengeance.

"Let's go home, Lolli," he said, taking the carrier gently, thanking the vet tech.

Xavier followed him out and walked with him to the apartment.

"Are you gonna be okay on your own?" Xavier asked him.

"I think so. The vet said the surgery went really well and they didn't have to make too big of an incision, so hopefully she recovers quickly. She's supposed to take it easy for a couple weeks, and I've gotta make sure she doesn't move around too much. I'm just going to put her favorite shows on the TV and sit with her."

"That sounds like a good idea. Call me if you need anything, okay?"

"Thanks."

Tallis took Lolli upstairs and into the apartment, delicately setting the carrier on the floor. He opened the little cage door on the front and squatted down to look inside at eye level.

"Hey, Lolli," he said softly, his voice cracking.

She didn't lift her paws from her face.

"I'm so sorry," he said. "Words don't do it justice, but I'd understand if you never forgive me. For what it's worth, I'll never do that to you again. I promise."

She sighed and wiggled in place a little, but still didn't budge.

"I know it's no excuse, but I really did lose track of time. I didn't think it through. I've never done anything like that. It's not something I normally would have ever done. I won't make that mistake again."

She still didn't acknowledge him, or the fact that she was free to leave her carrier.

"I'm going to put the detective shows on for you, okay? And I'll set out the really soft blanket you like. The grey one. It's gonna be so cozy."

He stood, disappearing into the bedroom for a moment to grab the blanket. When he realized Lolli was unattended, he panicked, running back to the doorway and peering his head around the corner to check on her. At this point, she was poking her head out of the carrier, swaying as she stood.

"Are you still dizzy? They said you were on some heavy-duty drugs. Poor thing. Let me help."

He threw the blanket across the couch and trotted over to Lolli, kneeling beside her. Tallis held out a hand on either side of her to steady her. With each tentative step she took, he scooted just enough to give her space, keeping his hands beside her to keep her from toppling over.

"I'm sorry," he said, "but I'm not picking you up. Normally, I'd love to just bring you right to the couch, but I don't want to hurt you."

When Lolli reached the couch, Tallis realized she wasn't going to be able to jump.

"Ah!" he said. "Wait!"

He pulled the blanket off the couch, folding it a couple times and laying it out on the floor in front of the couch, patting it with a hand to beckon her over.

She continued her slow pace until she made it to the blanket, half falling as she laid down.

"There we go! Good job! Isn't that better?"

He turned his attention to the TV, calling out a command to turn to the channel with Lolli's shows.

"How about this one?" He looked at her. She was dozing off. Tallis felt happy for a moment, watching her peacefully sleep, until he noticed her little arm, shaved from where the vet had to insert an IV. The guilt immediately crushed the sweet moment, sending him spiraling back into a sniveling mess.

"I'm so sorry," he started again.

As he looked around the apartment for the first time, he realized Lolli had gotten into more than just a cord. The corner of the couch looked as if she had clawed or chewed at it, and it appeared as if she had knocked several decorative things off a nearby table in her search for food. Tallis stared at the things on the floor while running his finger along the damage on his couch, his stomach burning.

The rest of the day was much of the same. Every time Lolli moved, sighed, or did anything more than simply exist, Tallis felt the need to apologize all over again.

At one point, Tallis tried calling Odessa, but she didn't answer. Instead, she texted him back.

What do you need? Busy.

Lolli needed emergency surgery. Been keeping her company but just wanted to call and chat.

Sorry. Hope she feels better soon.

To say Tallis was disappointed would be an understatement. Her words felt disingenuous, and it stung. He wasn't trying to glean shallow attention from a tragedy, but he felt like she should've shown some degree of concern. Frustrated, he turned his watch off entirely, undoing the strap and chucking it across the room.

The rest of the weekend, Tallis sat with Lolli on the floor. When he finally fell asleep, he laid beside her on the blanket, waking up to check on her every time he heard her make even the slightest noise.

When Sunday night rolled around, he realized he'd have to leave Lolli home alone when he went to work. He stood for the first time in hours, his legs tingly and off-balance as he walked to his computer to email Ms. Iris to ask for special permission throughout the week to come home and check on Lolli.

Ms. Iris emailed back faster than expected with a simple "That's fine."

He emailed her his thanks before shutting his computer back down and returning to Lolli's side. In his brief absence, she had wiggled her way off the blanket and halfway across the living room. When she saw his face upon his return, she stopped moving and kept looking up at him.

"Come here," he said softly, trying to guide her back to the blanket.

By Monday morning, Tallis still hadn't gotten a proper night's sleep, and he kept arguing with himself on whether or not he should even show up to work. Ms. Iris would've been understanding, but would it hurt his chance at the CA job?

With hardly any time to spare, he finally decided to get up and get ready for work. After all, he already had permission to go home and check in on Lolli throughout the day.

Once he grudgingly changed out of his crumb-covered lounge clothes, smeared some mousse through his hair, and brushed away the morning breath, he triple-checked that Lolli had some soft food, a bowl of water, and everything else she could need within her large crate. He felt horrible locking her in there while he was away, but anything else would risk her tearing her stitches.

"Just for a little while," he promised her as he set her gently in the crate. "I'll be back in a bit to check on you. And once you're all better, hopefully we won't have to keep using the crate."

He couldn't help but stand in his doorway, looking in on Lolli in her crate. She sat in the far corner of it, nibbling at her paw lazily. Unfortunately, he couldn't stay there forever, so he finally stepped outside and shut the door behind him.

Tallis was in his own mind—arguably more than usual—the entire way to work. It was only when he was about to open the doors of Opulence that he realized he left Ms. Iris's coffee on the sidewalk a few blocks back after setting it down to tie his shoe. He turned back the way he came, sprinting to save time.

When he reached the abandoned coffee cup, still on the sidewalk, he scooped it up and opened the lid. Someone had stuck a cigarette butt inside, and ash was floating all over the top of the coffee.

"Ugh."

He gave up. If Ms. Iris still wanted a coffee, he'd be more than happy to go get her a new one, but he wasn't going to be late getting to the office when there was a promotion at stake.

Only a moment past time, he walked through the elevator doors and over to Ms. Iris's office. As usual, she held out her hand without looking up or acknowledging him.

"I don't think you're going to want this one," Tallis admitted.

She looked up, the corners of her lips turning down and her eyes narrowing.

"I set it down for a minute to tie my shoe, and someone stuck a cigarette in it." He may have left out the detail about forgetting the cup on the sidewalk, but at least he wasn't lying.

He opened the lid and showed her the evidence.

"The nerve of some people!"

"You're telling me."

She took the cup, looked closer at the butt, and threw the entire cup of coffee in her trash can.

"Run and get me a new one," she said, handing him a stack of folders. "None of these are urgent, but keeping my sanity *is.*"

"Yes, ma'am."

Tallis dropped the pile off at his desk before turning to leave again. He was focused in his own mind about the task at hand. Once his elevator opened back up to the lobby of Opulence, he bolted out the doors as they slid open, ramming into a young man who was waiting for a ride up. The man's folder spilled out onto the ground, sending papers sliding across the slick tile floor.

"Sorry," Tallis said, helping the man collect his pages. He picked one up, noticing the familiar format of a resume. He held it out to the stranger. "Interviewing for a job today?"

"I sure am!" he beamed, taking the copy of his own resume. "It's my second interview for the open CA role."

Tallis's teeth clenched as he automatically started scanning over the man. He was well-dressed, his face alight with excitement, as reflected by his dimples and wide eyes.

"That's exciting. How'd your first one go?" Tallis asked, carefully observing the man.

"It went well, I'm assuming!" He chuckled and it was damn contagious. Tallis couldn't help but smile. "Well enough they're voluntarily speaking to me again!"

"That's awesome," Tallis said, softly smiling. "What kind of stuff do you do?"

"Wow, is this my interview right here?" He laughed

again, his perfect white teeth shone bright under the obnoxious fluorescents.

Tallis let out a forced chuckle. "Sorry. Was just curious! I'm sure you'll do great. Good luck!"

"Thanks, friend!" He tapped at his papers to shift them nicely back into his portfolio before pressing the button to the elevator, which greeted him with open doors only a moment later.

On his way to Bru, Tallis started to analyze himself. Was he that warm and friendly? Did people feel that happy when they talked to him? Tallis didn't feel like he was the kind of person people would want to be friends with, but that stranger seemed like the kind of guy you'd just want to go get beers with. Even if you didn't like beer.

It started drizzling outside on his way. He kept a quick pace, reminding himself not to get distracted by the reflective droplets of rain spattering against glass and concrete. After all, it rained at least once a week in Neuvale. It shouldn't feel special to him anymore, but for some reason, it had been his favorite thing about the city as long as he could remember.

For a few moments, he was proud of himself for staying focused, but as soon as a fat green frog bounced across the busy sidewalk, he stopped in his tracks to watch. It wasn't until someone nearly stepped on the critter that he snapped into action, darting down to pick up the frog and relocate it to the base of a flowerbed.

As he neared the coffee shop, he reached the pink puddle outside Buzz's Electrosuite. He stopped, watching the raindrops as they each shattered the glassy surface. It felt beautiful, but Tallis struggled to see the excitement in it today. It felt flat. Where was the glitter and glow? He attributed that dullness to the stressful and restless weekend he had, shaking it off and walking into the coffee shop.

He ordered Ms. Iris's new coffee, deciding to get himself a treat while he was there. When they called his name, he took the coffees and made his way back to the office, pausing to take a second look at the puddle, now bigger from the ongoing rain.

⸻ ⟨O⟩ ⸻

"Much better!" Ms. Iris said, taking a sip of her coffee. "And perfect timing, too. I've got another candidate about to start their interview. Didn't need to fall asleep during that." She stood from her desk and waddled off to the elevator without another word.

Tallis sat at his desk, setting his coffee down and flipping open the first folder from his stack. He skimmed over the information, trying to work up the motivation to open the program he needed for data entry, but couldn't bring himself to even try. With a big sigh, he leaned back in his seat and ran his hands through his hair. Tallis sipped at his hot coffee and continued staring at his blank screen, imagining the young man from outside the elevator. He probably started the interview with a great joke. The whole room would laugh, and just like that, they're all rooting for him. Just one flash of his bright white smile, and everyone would be pulled in. His face had CA written all over it.

Then, he imagined breaking the news to Lolli, Xavier, Vanessa, and Odessa that he didn't get the job. He pictured each of their faces and reactions. Lolli would probably just look at him with her cute little eyes. She'd probably be happy if he didn't get it—after all, the hours are more demanding. Xavier and Vanessa would apologize and insist they go out for drinks. Xavier would then make jokes about all the hiring managers the entire evening. Odessa… he wasn't sure about her. He almost got the feeling she wouldn't be surprised if he didn't get the job. Then again, he wasn't so sure he expected anything different himself.

It was only when the CAs came strolling into the office conference room that he finally snapped out of it and started logging information from the folders. As the CAs sat around the big table chitchatting, he peered over the top of his computer, as if it would help him eavesdrop.

"Have they picked anyone yet?" one of them asked.

"You know they haven't. Ms. Iris would tell us first, and she hasn't said anything. Stop asking every day!"

"I'm just ready to introduce myself to the poor sap that has to put up with *you* for the foreseeable future!"

"Jokes on you! Ms. Iris said *you'd* be leading their training!"

"She didn't!"

"Did!"

The bickering continued for a while before another one of the CAs spoke up.

"She's never late for meetings. Where is she?"

"She had an interview with one of the candidates this morning. It's probably running a bit long."

"Maybe it's whoever they've picked! Maybe she planned it before the meeting so she could bring them in to meet the team."

"I mean, it would make sense, but she still hasn't said anything."

"Guess we'll have to see!"

Tallis felt his heart racing as a pit formed in his stomach. Maybe they *did* pick that elevator guy. He wouldn't doubt it.

The next fifteen or so minutes dragged on. Tallis tried to focus on his work, but he couldn't help but repeatedly look over his screens to see if the team was meeting Elevator Guy yet. It was only when Ms. Iris finally showed up to the meeting—alone—that he finally felt like he could take a full breath.

She closed the door behind her after catching Tallis's nosey eye above his screen. He guiltily sunk into his seat and refocused himself on the task at hand.

Around lunchtime, Tallis decided to take a break to go check on Lolli. He notified Ms. Iris, who simply replied with a single nod of acknowledgement. Taking that as a yes, he left Opulence and returned to his apartment.

Lolli was resting in the corner of her crate, curled up on her blanket with one of her plush toys under her head and paws as if it were a tiny pillow. When she heard him at the door, she opened her eyes but couldn't be bothered to lift her head from its cozy spot.

"Hey, girl," he greeted, approaching her crate and opening it. "Wanna have lunch together?"

She looked back at him, shifting in place, unsure of whether it was worth getting up.

"I know, you're not used to me being home for lunch. But I wanted to make sure you're okay."

She blinked back at him.

"I've got applesauce."

She perked up, recognizing that word.

"I thought so." Tallis smiled, turning to the kitchen.

He opened his big jar of applesauce and poured a little into a bowl, setting it right next to Lolli before going back to make his own lunch.

When he finished making his turkey sandwich, he sat on the floor next to the crate, watching Lolli give her applesauce a good taste-test.

"I don't think I'm going to get the job," he admitted to her—the first time he had acknowledged it out loud. "There're just too many people out there who are a better fit."

She stopped eating, looking back at him with applesauce in the fur on her chin.

"I'm boring," he said, leaning forward to wipe her face. "I don't wanna be. I don't know how not to be. They don't want someone like me on the team. Someone like me is meant to process the papers and stay behind the scenes. Or maybe I'm meant to do something else, but I'm just not cut out to be a CA."

Lolli dipped her fingers in the applesauce, licking them while watching Tallis.

"But that means I'll still have the schedule you're used to. So, I guess that's good. And I already know how to do the job. It's low stress. Being a CA would be stressful. So, I guess I have that to be thankful for."

Just then, his watch buzzed. He turned his wrist to look, reading a message from Odessa.

I found a dress for the wedding. How do you feel about a green tie?

He typed back: *First of all, I have to wear whatever color they pick for me. Second… What kind of green we talking? Forest? Olive? Chartreuse?*

WTF is chartreuse?

Isn't it a bright green?

No clue. My dress is I guess like an emerald green. I'll send a pic.

A moment later, up popped Odessa's selfie in a low-cut, satin green dress.

That color really compliments your eyes. He messaged. *I like it!*

My eyes are BLUE.

A moment later, another text from Odessa. *No, I don't know what KIND of blue.*

He giggled at his watch, typing back: *So what if they're blue? Green can't compliment blue?*

That's not how color works LOL

He finished his lunch with Lolli, gave her a good scratch behind the ears, and locked her back in her kennel so he could get back to the office.

On his way, he stopped, taking in the city skyline. It felt different. Things felt grey and dull. He looked up at the sky, expecting rain clouds, but the sun was shining instead.

Weather is weird today. He messaged Odessa.

She replied with a question mark.

It's kinda dismal out. Looks like rain. I thought that was supposed to stop after early this morning?

It's sunny…?

Just kinda dark out.

No more than usual.

He stepped into the subway, watching rough textures of underground zip past the windows. The subway stopped at Sector 12, and he stepped out, making his way toward Opulence.

Before reaching for the door, he pulled up Xavier's contact on his watch, tapping out a text to him next.

Weather seem weird to you today?

He waited on a reply, looking up at the tops of the buildings, which seemed even more lifeless than his home sector.

I mean, I guess it's a bit warmer than usual. Why?

It doesn't seem dark outside?

Not a bit. It's hella sunny out! Gorgeous day to lounge by the pool. And that's exactly where I plan on planting my ass after work!

Is it supposed to rain today?

You tell me. You have access to modern technology, too. But no. Sunny all day.

Tallis started to wonder if maybe it was something wrong with his vision. After all, his time was always spent in front of computer screens. He wondered if perhaps his mom was right that it would one day damage his eyes. He scrunched his eyes shut, fluttered them open, scrunched them, fluttered them, and tried to take another look. Did it get darker?

Uneasy, he entered Opulence and trotted to the elevator after having spent too much time away from his desk as-is. He wondered if the long breaks were like the nail on the coffin of his chances at a promotion. Shaking off the thoughts, he sat back at his desk, grabbing at the next folder.

Can I see you later? Tallis messaged Odessa that evening on his way home from work.

Sure! Where?

Sector 3.

:)

They agreed to meet after dinner, and for Tallis, that was a plate of canned carrots and a frozen Salisbury steak meal.

After he ate, he changed into something a bit nicer and brushed the bits of steak from his teeth.

"Don't worry," he told Lolli. "I'm not spending the night. I won't be gone but a few hours."

He set some soft food and a bowl of water in her kennel and secured the latch before leaving. She pressed her face against the thin metal bars, wrapping her fingers around them and staring back at him.

He felt a tug in his chest as he looked back at her from the doorway.

"Ughhh… don't give me that look." His shoulders slumped and he stepped back into the apartment, crouching in front of her and reaching his fingers in the cage to pet her.

"I'm just going to see Odessa for a little while—"

Chomp.

Lolli bit down suddenly on Tallis's finger, her face crumpled up as she glared at him, finger between her sharp teeth.

"Ow! Let go!" He shook his hand until she released his finger, which had a couple tooth holes pierced through the skin. "What was that for?"

Lolli slumped down into her cage, letting her little hands fall from the bars. She turned her back to him, laying in the corner.

Holding his finger in his other hand, Tallis stood, clearing his throat before speaking again.

"I'll be back soon. I mean it this time. I know you don't

trust me, and I don't blame you. But I promise." He stepped into the bathroom, washing off his finger and wrapping a bandage around it. Back in the living room, he looked at Lolli again. "I'll see about getting you a treat while I'm out. Would you like that? Would that make it better?"

She kept her back to him.

"I'm going to make it up to you. I'm never going to hurt you like that again."

Still, she ignored him.

He felt bad leaving, but he was going to be late if he didn't leave that moment. Shutting the door carefully behind him, he left for the subway.

“Not working tonight?” Tallis asked as he greeted Odessa outside the subway with a quick kiss.

“Nope. One of the girls came in with some nasty rash and they sent her home. They’re disinfecting all the poles and reaching out to her clients to make sure they get checked out.”

Tallis shuddered. “What a mess.”

She shrugged. “It’s not the first time.”

He recoiled as she reached for his hand.

“Stop that! I’m not dirty!”

“How do you know you didn’t touch anything she touched?”

“Her and I are on different schedules! They called us all before I ever went in. I’m *clean!*”

“Famous last words.” Tallis grinned, intertwining their fingers.

She rolled her eyes. “Where to?” she asked as they climbed out of the subway station.

“Dream Depot,” he answered. “If you don’t mind.”

Her face lit up and she let out a joyous little squeal. "Yay! I'm so glad you like it!"

"I just wanna try making my own combination again. Things have felt kind of… off… today. I don't know how to explain it. Figure maybe something fun could get my mind off of it. Like hitting a reset button."

She shrugged. "Worth a try!"

They walked down the streets of Sector 3, with its litter and lights, stopping at the alley that housed Dream Depot.

"Is there anything in particular you wanna try this time?" she asked, stepping inside as he held the door open for her.

"Not really. To be honest, I don't remember all the options. It was a bit overwhelming." He chuckled faintly.

The dark store aisles greeted their curiosity, and the colorful tubes along each aisle lured them in with their intoxicating glow. They pulled their empty vials from the front of the shop before walking down the costuming aisle.

Tallis took his time reading some of the labels in front of the yellow tubes. He stopped when he spotted one that said "Royalty."

"Have you tried this one?" he asked her, pointing to the label.

She scoffed, flipping her hair behind her shoulder. "I've tried just about all of these, if we're gonna be honest."

"I'm not sure if I'm impressed or concerned," he said with a grin.

"Why not both?" She smiled.

"Would you recommend this one?"

"It's not my favorite," she said, "but it's definitely a cool one."

He decided to try it, filling his vial to the first line with the liquid. When they walked down the setting aisle, he found a blue tube, also labeled "Royalty."

Without a word, he filled his vial to the next line.

"Royalty costuming *and* setting?" Odessa noted.

"Like a good outfit, it should match," Tallis said, "right?"

"I mean, not necessarily. It's fun to mix and match!"

"Just trying something different."

"To each their own." She smiled, setting a hand on his back for a moment before skipping off down the aisle to make her selection.

As they finished up in the store, Odessa was so excited that Tallis had even decided to come to Dream Depot that she offered to pay for both vials.

"Thanks," he said as she paid.

"Happy to do it! I'm just excited you like it too."

"Why?" he asked, holding the door open for her again as they entered the dark alley. "I mean, I'm glad you're happy, but that's a weird thing to be excited about."

"How is it weird? People get excited when their significant others show interest in their passions! It's normal. You'd be weird if you *didn't* get excited about something like that."

"Fair point. It would be cool if you were interested in photography or writing or something. I write, so even if you were interested in reading my stuff, I mean… that would be cool, too."

"I *am* interested in that stuff," she said with a slight whine.

"You've never once wanted to talk about any of that."

"You've never initiated it! Don't blame it on *me!*"

The two continued with their bickering until they reached the hookah bar, taking a seat at the corner table and setting up two separate hookahs next to each other. Tallis poured a bit of his vial and took a puff, slouching back in his seat.

"What's your biggest fear?" Odessa asked after a while of silence.

Tallis scoffed.

"What?" she asked.

"You're gonna laugh at me," he said.

"No, I won't!"

There was a pause.

"Sharks," he eventually said. "I haven't been to the beach since I was little. I watched one shark documentary and that was enough for me. It's not even that I'm afraid of getting eaten by a shark. I know that's unlikely. I guess it's more like… if something *that* big and scary can live in the ocean, who knows what else is down there. No thanks."

She giggled. "There's no way *that's* your biggest fear."

"You said you wouldn't laugh!"

"I know, I'm sorry." She composed herself. "That's a totally rational fear! I just don't believe that's really your biggest fear."

"Oh yeah?" Tallis smiled, raising his eyebrows. "If it's not valid as my biggest fear, then tell me *yours!*"

She stared at him for a moment without saying anything. Even her body language was silent as she judged his trustworthiness.

"I have two. I don't know if I can pick."

"Alright, so tell me both."

Another pause.

"I'm afraid of judgement."

"Like afterlife sort of stuff? Heaven or hell kind of thing?"

"I mean, sure. But even on a shallow level, I'm afraid of people judging me. I know I don't always make good choices. I know my career choice isn't the most admirable or respected. I know I can be a bit hot-headed. But I don't want any of that to define me. I don't want people to make assumptions about me."

"I respect that," Tallis said, reaching for her petite hand with its manicured nails.

"Being ignored sucks, but imagine that feeling times a thousand. That's how it feels to me when people judge me. It's as if they're saying, 'this is who you are, and I won't listen if you try to prove me wrong.'"

Tallis let her speak as he simply stroked the top of her hand with his thumb. He kept his eyes locked onto her face, even when she herself would break eye contact.

"And that's what I love about you," she said, facing him. "I can tell you aren't judging me. I could tell you I'm deathly afraid of kittens and you'd probably try to keep me away from pet stores and shelters forever instead of ever making fun of me. You don't even care that I strip for other men, do you?"

"I know you don't mean anything by it. It isn't like you're dating all your clients. You're just trying to work to earn a living. And you put up with a lot of crap doing it. I think it's admirable that you're still sane."

"Who said I am?" She winked.

"True," Tallis said with a chuckle.

They were quiet for a minute before Tallis spoke up again. "You never said your second one."

"Depression."

"That's an unusual one."

"I don't really think it is. It's what took my mom. I'm worried one day it'll get me, too."

"Are you depressed?" he asked as gently as he could.

"No, I don't think so. I mean, I have days that I'm unhappy, but I think everyone has those. But I firmly believe in doing everything you have to do to hang onto happiness. If you have to travel to feel alive, you should travel as much as you can. If you have to sleep around to feel loved, I'm not here to judge. If you have to take REM just to survive another shift at a shitty job, I say do it."

"I think that's a reasonable way to look at life. It takes a lot of self-discovery to figure that sort of thing out."

"Thank you for not looking at me like I'm nuts." She leaned over and kissed him before sitting back and taking another hit off her hookah.

"I don't think I've ever asked," Tallis said, "and I don't think I've come across this information at work yet… but how exactly does REM even work?"

"What do you mean?"

"Like, what's the science behind it? How are we able to alter the formula so specifically? How does it change what we see, but we're still able to interact with things that are truly real? Like… it just makes real things look… unreal. It's gotta be some really intense scientific process or something."

She laughed, a little cloud of vapor puffing out around her mouth with each chuckle. "Hell if I know!"

"You've been doing it a while, right? You haven't gotten curious?"

"To be honest, not really. No." She leaned back with a smile.

"At all? You don't even care to know how it works?"

"As long as it works, it works. That's all I care about."

"Huh."

"That was an awful judgy sound."

"Was it? It wasn't meant to be. I just figure if you're going to take a drug every waking moment of your life, maybe you'd want to know the science behind it."

"Excuse me?" she huffed. "'Every waking moment?' Do you know *why* I take REM? Haven't I told you enough?"

Tallis struggled to find words, afraid of using the wrong ones.

"If you had to walk through piss and vomit filled streets just to get home, if you were pawed all over and pushed around by perverts, if you had to live a day in my life and know you gave up your dream… and now you're stuck… if you had any idea what it was like," she said, pausing to wipe away a stray tear. "You wouldn't wanna see reality anymore either."

"I'm sorry, I—"

"Just shut up already" she grumbled, crossing her arms. Tallis sighed.

"Damn, Tal! What's with the attitude tonight?"

"What the hell are you even talking about? I asked one question and you took it the complete wrong way and ran with it."

"The attitude! The huffing, the sighing… the attitude! Why are you being such a little bitch tonight?"

"I just made a sound! I didn't mean anything by it. I just think it's weird you've never cared how this drug works after all the years you've been putting it in your body—even if you have a valid reason for it."

"Excuse me? Okay, well, one—mind your own damn business about my body and what I put in it. Two—*you* blew it out of proportion. So what? I don't care how it works. You were the one being whiny about it. Three—you've used it several times and you never once questioned it until now!"

Tallis groaned, putting his face in his hands, elbows resting on the table.

"I'm going home," Odessa said, standing and taking the remainder of her vial.

"Wait—"

Her pace was quick, and before Tallis could maneuver his way out of the corner booth seat with his vial, she was already out the door.

Tallis moaned to himself, running his fingers through his hair. No sense in staying at the bar by himself. At that point, he just wanted to go home. Dropping the rest of his REM into his jacket pocket, he paid the bartender for using the hookah, took one more huff, and made the walk back to the subway.

Alone inside the subway station, he heard a scratching and tearing sound coming from a lid-less trashcan. Curiosity got the best of him, and he eased himself over to peek down into it. Inside, three greasy rats rummaged through food scraps, gnawing and ripping at wrappers. He turned his attention back to the subway tracks, and instead of seeing the usual dark bricks and grimy subway tiles, the station looked like a grandiose castle interior. Elaborate tapestries donned the walls and instead of the typical LED lights of the station, there were golden candelabras affixed to the castle stone.

"Woah."

Tallis gawked at a lady as she walked down the steps in a regal gown and tightly curled hair. She glowered at him, hugging her purse in tight and standing at the wall opposite Tallis.

The subway pulled up looking like a chain of horse drawn carriages. Despite his failed date night, he couldn't help but smile to himself as he looked over the horses on his way into the subway car carriage.

Inside, each bench seat looked like a small throne. Tallis looked down at his feet, his pants and shoes looking rather regal as he took his spot at the back of the subway. The woman with her purse skirted around him and picked the furthest available seat, still not letting her guard down.

Back at his apartment—the outside of which looked like a stunning castle with shimmering stained-glass windows— he greeted Lolli and opened her crate door.

Lolli stayed hunched over in her corner, refusing to look at Tallis.

"See?" he said as he walked off to get her food. "I told you I wouldn't be gone long!"

When he returned with her meal, he squatted and set it down beside her. She still didn't budge. He tapped a fatty part of her back legs, and she swatted back at him.

"Geez. Sorry." He stood, leaving her alone.

He packed up a lunch for the next day at work, got himself a bowl of chips, and sat down to watch TV. By the time he got comfortable, the effects of the REM had already worn off. Tallis wondered if maybe he got a weak batch, until he remembered he hardly got to take any before his evening abruptly ended. He shouldn't have wasted so much REM, leaving it in the hookah. He was grateful he only poured half of it in at least.

Once he was a few minutes into some house-flipping show, he could hear Lolli begin to munch her food. He wanted to acknowledge her, go pet her, talk to her, but he didn't want her to stop eating just to continue pouting. Instead, he chose to stay quiet and continue watching his show for a bit.

In the show, a woman and her mother-in-law worked together to turn old houses into luxury homes. Tallis watched as the duo transformed some crumbling cottage into a modern home with big windows and a heated pool. For some reason, he just wasn't all that impressed with the show. Bored, he flipped channels before the homeowners could decide if they wanted to stay in their renovated home.

Eventually, Tallis settled for some mindless sitcom, dozing off on his couch. Luckily for him, his alarm clock was already programmed to go off for work the next day. It started chiming bright and early, and his eyelids fought with him to finally open and greet the day.

Tallis brushed his teeth, fed Lolli, got dressed, and grabbed his lunch. He noticed himself running through his morning routine in his head, as if he might forget a step. When he realized, he questioned it. Why bother running through the list if every morning it's the same?

He locked Lolli up in her crate, giving her a kiss on the head (which she reluctantly accepted) as he trotted out the door, sliding a light jacket on at the last second.

At Bru, he ordered Ms. Iris her usual and bought himself a caramel macchiato as a treat. He rationalized it as a "pick-me-up" for the depressing evening he had the day before.

While waiting on his order, he stuck his hands in his pockets, fumbling with a piece of lint before his finger brushed up against cool glass. He reached down deeper, feeling the vial of REM in his hand. His mind wandered to a daydream of him at work while under the influence of REM. It would be exciting, taboo, but totally safe. The rush of adrenaline at the thought was undeniable.

The barista called his name, and he stepped up to the counter to retrieve his drinks. Once at the door to leave, he stopped, turning and backtracking to the little counter with all the sugar, cream, and stir sticks. Tallis popped the lid off the caramel macchiato, checked over both his shoulders—as if it mattered— and poured the rest of his REM into the cup before he could change his mind.

He pressed the lid back on, pocketing the empty vial and grabbing both cups as he left. It wasn't until he reached the doors of Opulence that he finally got the nerve to take a sip of his coffee. It had a slightly salty taste, but the REM complemented the caramel, much to Tallis's surprise. After all, he had picked the black licorice flavoring this time around (admittedly, not his favorite).

A few slurps in, and he had nearly forgotten he spiked his coffee.

Upstairs, he greeted Ms. Iris in her office, handing her the other coffee.

"How are the second round of interviews going so far?" he asked, hoping his impatience would be masked as innocent curiosity and the casual exchange of niceties.

She peered over her computer, an eyebrow raised.

"They're still in progress, if that's what you want to know," she answered.

"Oh." Tallis scrambled for an excuse. "I didn't mean it like that. I just figured those have got to get exhausting. Just wanted to see how you were hanging in there."

She crossed her arms, drawing away from her computer.

"Likely story," she said, "but no matter. Only natural to want updates. Unfortunately, all I can say for now is that interviews are still in progress and that you'll be notified of the results once we have them."

"Yes, ma'am."

He turned to walk to his desk, but she called him back. When he faced her again, she was wearing a raggedy looking jester hat. She stood, revealing the rest of her outfit—complete with shoes with curled toes. The bells on her hat and toes jingled as she approached him, a stack of documents in hand. It took every shred of his willpower to not laugh.

"These came in last night. I don't love that they waited until last minute, but I need you to prioritize these today. The rest of your stack can wait."

She handed him the documents, which all looked like weathered scrolls.

He gawked at her and at the stack of scrolls in his hands as she went to sit back at her desk. When she sat and he was still staring, she locked eyes.

"Was something not clear?" she crossed her arms again.

"Ma'am?"

"What are you staring at? Get to work."

He shook himself, said "yes ma'am," and returned to his desk with the assignments.

Once situated at his desk, he realized the computer looked like a tapestry, draped over the stone wall of his cubicle. He squished his eyes shut for a moment, opening them to the exact same vision. His mouse and keyboard looked like they were made of gems, and he tentatively placed his fingers on them.

Tallis tapped a random gem on his keyboard, and the blank tapestry before him filled with color. It looked like his login screen but woven into fabric.

"Hot damn," he muttered to himself, a grin spreading from cheek to cheek as he typed in his password.

He unfurled one of the scrolls—a simple data log. He found the icon for the program he needed at the bottom of the tapestry, clicking it.

A couple hours passed, and the effects of the REM began to fade. It started with the tapestry, which faded more and more with each blink until Tallis was face to face with his old computer. The scrolls turned to a standard document stack, the grey cubicle walls boxed him in again, and with it all came a sense of disappointment.

Tallis peered into the little hole in the lid of his coffee cup, expecting to see the final cold drops of leftover coffee, but it was completely empty. With a sigh, he chucked it into the trash can under his desk and got back to processing paperwork.

Are you breaking up with me? A text from Odessa popped up on his watch while he was working on logging appearance release forms.

What? What gave you that idea? he messaged back.

He leaned back in his chair, staring at his watch and abandoning his work for a moment.

You yelled at me during a date, and when I left, you didn't even try reaching out to apologize or see if I was ok. Idk how else I should read something like that.

I didn't yell at you!

WTF are you gaslighting me?

What?

I'm not crazy! You yelled at me!

I definitely did not, but I'm sorry if I came off harsher than I intended. I was really confused about the whole situation.

Wow. So genuine.

I'm being serious.

All she sent back was an emoji rolling its eyes.

How can I make things up to you?

Admit you were an asshole.

He read the text and scoffed. Was she being serious? He tried to replay the evening in his mind over and over, and each time, he didn't yell at her. If anything, *she* attacked *him*.

Another text from Odessa: *That's what I thought.*

He reminded himself that it's just words. All he had to do was admit defeat and guilt over something he didn't do—just suck it up for the sake of their relationship.

I was an asshole. He hit the send button and sat back, waiting.

Was that so hard?

A few seconds later, another text from her. *I forgive you.*

He tried to refocus on work, but a few minutes later, she messaged again.

I'm really looking forward to the wedding!

Tallis's blood went cold before he realized she meant Xavier and Vanessa's wedding. Then he just felt stupid.

Me too!

Next weekend, right?

Yup. I'll come get you and we can ride together.

Sounds good!

But things didn't sound good. The longer Tallis thought about it, the more he realized maybe Xavier was right about her. He hated to even entertain the thought, and his heart immediately began a debate with his head. Eventually, his heart won.

The wedding date arrived with such speed it would put street racers to shame. Before he knew it, Tallis found himself buttoning up his suit and spraying on some fancy, unused cologne he bought a year ago under the excuse he'd use it for "a special occasion." His best friend's wedding felt like a special enough occasion.

Tallis kept obsessively checking the time. His hair was styled, teeth brushed, tie perfectly straight, and emergency tissue for Vanessa or Xavier in his pocket.

"Whaddya think?" he asked, looking at Lolli, who was relaxing on the couch.

She looked at him, blinking a few times.

"You like?" He reached out to her, and she reached her little arms back so he could scoop her up.

Tallis walked her into the kitchen, pulling out a couple treats for her and handing them to her while she sat carefully in his arms. She had healed a lot since her surgery, but he was still playing it safe with her.

"Can I trust you outside the crate today? I don't want

to keep you locked up all day while I'm gone. I'd rather you be cozy. I'll leave the TV on for you, leave you all kinds of goodies so you don't chew my cords." He kissed the top of her head. "On second thought, I'll keep the bedroom and bathroom doors closed, and I'll make sure everything tempting is put up. Not that I don't trust you, but just for my peace of mind."

He placed her gingerly back on the couch, flipping the TV to the channel with the true crime shows Lolli liked, giving her a little head scratch before taking a lap around the room to close doors and put up chew-worthy things.

When the time rolled around for him to leave to pick Odessa up in Sector 3, he made sure Lolli had plenty of food and water for the evening. He said goodbye to her, ran through a checklist in his head, and walked out the door.

He texted Odessa while he walked to the subway. *On my way.*

Yay! I'm almost ready, so I'll head to the station in a sec.

K.

Potassium.

What?

You said k.

???

K is for potassium on the periodic table of elements.

Before he could reply, she sent him a picture of the periodic table.

Lol smartass. He grinned at his phone as he sent his reply.

As he stepped onto the subway, he got her response: an emoji that was blowing a kiss.

Not wanting to risk wrinkling his suit, Tallis opted to stand and hold one of the subway poles, rather than sit. A young woman sat across from his spot, and she eyed him up and down, a tiny smirk twitching at the corner of her lips, aching to make a full appearance. Tallis looked over at her, and her face beamed red as she whipped her gaze away from him.

He noticed her act, just like he noticed the way her auburn hair was woven into an intricate braid. As she continued to look away, he let his eyes wander to the strange tattoo all down her arm. She looked back at him, her pale face immediately turning red again as she locked eyes with him.

"I'm just going to be upfront about this," she called over to him, tucking a loose hair back into her braid. "You're really hot."

She smiled at him, uncrossing and recrossing her legs.

Tallis couldn't help but to grin, rubbing at the back of his neck as he searched for words.

He settled on a bashful "thank you."

"Dressed up for something special?" she asked, standing up and using the handrail to walk carefully back to him as the subway zipped down its path.

"I'm going to my best friend's wedding."

"Congratulations to your friend! That's so exciting! Where's the wedding at?"

"Some venue in Sector 15. It's called The Weylinde. I haven't seen it yet—they did the rehearsal in their backyard instead."

"Sector 15? Hun, you're on the wrong subway! We're headed down, not up! What time do you have to be there?"

"It's alright, I've got time. I'm picking up my girlfriend first."

The girl's smile faltered, and she forced it back. "That's

so sweet! She's a lucky girl. What sector is she from?"

"Three," he said, expecting judgment on the girl's face.

"That's my stop, too! My parents have a little place in three and I'm going to stay with them for the weekend. It's got some good little restaurants. Do you go often?"

"Somewhat. I haven't really tried any of the restaurants there, but there's a little bar we like."

They continued chatting until the subway reached Sector 3, and the two stepped off together. Odessa stood at the far end of the station, leaning against the tiled wall with her arms crossed as she scrolled at a tiny watch screen. She looked up as the doors opened, meeting Tallis's eyes and beaming at him, her smile fading as she spotted the pretty girl exiting at the same time who seemed awful friendly with him.

"Who's this?" Odessa asked as she met Tallis halfway.

"I'm Christy!" the girl chirped, waving at Odessa.

"New friend," Tallis clarified. "We were both headed to the same sector and chatted to pass the time."

"He told me all about you!" Christy said.

Odessa smiled softly. "We've got to get going. It was nice meeting you." She tugged Tallis's arm, directing him toward the other subway.

Once inside, Tallis was able to take a moment to truly get a good look at Odessa in her green dress. It was more modest than he expected. The bottom of the dress was shorter in the front, stopping just above her knees, while the back tickled the floor. The waist of the dress was cinched in tight, the straps delicate, and the neckline loose.

"You look gorgeous," Tallis said, tracing his hand down her arm.

"Thank you!" She looked at him and smiled, using her hands to smooth out her dress. "It's not too much, right? Or too little? I'll be honest—I've never been to a wedding in Sector 15 and I'm a bit nervous."

"Neither have I, but I think you look perfect. You'll be just fine."

She wrapped her arm around his waist, keeping her other hand on the subway pole for balance as she leaned her head into his chest.

"You look really nice too, by the way," she said, lifting her head again. "Goes without saying though. You always look nice. Honestly, I might have found one of the only men in Neuvale who actually consistently dresses like he gives a shit about his appearance and I gotta say, that's sexy as hell."

Tallis chuckled and thanked her. The two continued to hold each other, watching the station numbers track upwards on the screen above the subway door. When it finally flashed the number fifteen, they released their grip on the pole and exited.

On the way out of the station, Tallis reached out an arm in offering for Odessa to balance, but she strutted confidently up the steps.

"Thank you," she said with a smile, "but I walk in heels for a living."

"Ah, I suppose you're right. Maybe you should be helping *me* up the stairs!"

She held out a hand in a dramatic gesture. "For your convenience, my dear sir!"

He took her hand and pretended to stumble drunkenly, leaning into her.

"You saved me from falling! My *hero!*" He swooned,

and she laughed, swatting him off of her.

They walked together, holding hands. Fortunately, they were strategically ahead of schedule, so Tallis made sure to take his time guiding her down the streets so they could admire the stunning marble and quartz of the sector.

"Holy shit." Odessa stopped, looking up at a towering glass statue of a man on a horse. "How do you think the artist made this?"

"It was probably made in a factory or something somewhere. Maybe laser cutters or something designed and programmed on a computer."

"You don't think an artist made it? That's a bit disappointing."

"An artist *did* make it. Even if it was designed on a computer. That's still art. I mean, look at it! The details are beautiful. Somebody thought to include even the design of the buttons on the man's coat. It's art, no matter how they made it."

"I suppose you're right!"

"Woah," Tallis said with a chuckle, "can I hear you say that again?"

"Say wh—oh! That you're right? Fat chance! That was the one time. I hope you savored it!"

Tallis laughed, and they continued on their way. He followed the directions Xavier gave him, making several turns down what appeared to be a luxury neighborhood until they reached an expansive white house with palm trees lining the entire circular driveway. The wooden sign out front read The Weylinde.

"This is their venue?" Odessa gaped at the ostentatious rose quartz fountain in the center of the driveway.

Soft piano music played all around the vicinity, and the water in the center of the fountain sprayed up rhythmically with the beat.

"I've gotta get inside to meet with the guys. You're welcome to wander around until the ceremony starts. I hate to leave you alone, but it's just supposed to be the groomsmen in that room."

"Totally understand!" She smiled. "Besides, I'm more than happy to wander around this place."

He gave her a quick peck before darting off into the white house, following the signs labeled "GROOM."

Guided by the signs, Tallis walked down high-ceiling hallways filled with tropical plants in giant ornate vases until he reached a door with "man cave" crudely written in pencil on a piece of copy paper taped to the door.

He nudged the door open and stepped inside, easing it shut again behind him.

"Tallis is here!" Chris yelled in the empty room.

Just then, Xavier appeared from another doorway on the other side of the room.

"Hey, man! Good to see you," Xavier said, hugging Tallis.

"I like your classy signage," Tallis joked, motioning back to the door.

"That would be Chris's handywork."

"Don't mock my impressive penmanship!"

"I wouldn't dare," Xavier said with a grin. He turned back to Tallis. "We've got beer in the mini fridge over there, some snacks through that door, and here's your tie."

He handed Tallis a pale blue tie and disappeared back through the other door.

After a moment of awkward silence while just standing in the room, Chris spoke up.

"You're a bit early. The other guys are still on their way. You want a beer or anything?"

"Why not. Thanks."

Chris stepped over to the mini fridge and pulled out a beer, tossing it over to Tallis.

"I heard about your new girlfriend," Chris said.

"Oh yeah?"

"Mmmhm."

More awkward silence, broken only by the hiss of an opened beer.

"I also heard you talk about her like the sun shines out her ass," Chris said.

"I wouldn't go so far as to say that."

"Oh?"

"I care about her, that's all."

"That's not all from what I hear."

"And what did you hear?"

"I heard you practically cast Xavier aside for this girl. Your best friend for some slut."

Tallis groaned. "I'm not going to indulge you in this argument."

"I already gave Vanessa the talk years ago that she should never hurt my brother. I'm not against giving that same speech to one of his friends, too."

"I don't need some speech."

"Sounds like you do."

Xavier stepped back into the room, and Chris and Tallis went quiet.

It only took a moment for Xavier to feel the tangible

tension in the air.

"Did I miss something?" he asked.

"Tallis was just saying how beautiful he thinks the venue is, and I was telling him to prepare to have his mind blown by the reception space!" Chris said.

"Hell yeah!" Xavier grinned. "Tallis, dude, you're going to love it! It's in their garden out back. The walls are tall hedges, we're going to have twinkle lights all strung up above, little lanterns at the tables, some sick ass specialty cocktails—honestly, the taste testing for that has been my favorite part of wedding planning."

"Sounds like a fairy tale," Tallis said, only half present.

"Tell Vanessa that," he said, "because that's *exactly* what she was going for. You'd make her day. Well, hopefully not as much as actually getting married will, but you know."

"I'm really excited for you guys." Tallis thumped Xavier on the back. "There isn't a more perfect couple out there, and it's about time we have a big celebration for you guys."

"You getting all sappy on me?" Xavier played.

Tallis shrugged, a smile twitching at the corner of his lip. "Trying not to."

"Actually," Xavier said, "can I talk to you alone for a sec?"

Chris stared at them, unmoving, until he realized Xavier meant for him to leave. Once they were alone, Xavier spoke again, his voice soft.

"I just wanted to say I really appreciate you coming today, man. I know we hit a bit of a rough patch, and I take the blame for that one. I wasn't supportive, and I was acting like a dick, and I just want you to know how much it means to me that you actually came today."

"You thought I wouldn't?" Tallis asked.

"I mean, I had my doubts. If I were you, I'm not so sure I would've showed up."

"We're best friends," Tallis said. "Just because we had a fight doesn't mean anything changes. I mean, yeah, you were a dick, but you un-dicked yourself by apologizing. We're cool."

"You sure?"

"Absolutely. Although your brother seems to think otherwise."

Xavier muttered something to himself. "I'll handle him. He started drinking way too early today, and I knew he was going to cause some shit. I warned him. Just ignore him, alright? He's just shit-talking."

Tallis nodded.

"How about a snack? We've got a lot of time to kill."

The other groomsmen arrived a little while later, and the photographer came in to take their pictures. Once they were done, the wedding planner—a short man with a perfectly twirled handlebar mustache—scurried in and ushered them all off to the ceremony site in the ballroom of the house.

Guests were already seated, but there was still the buzz and excited chatter before the ceremony. Odessa turned back in her seat, spotting Tallis and blowing him a kiss. He smiled and gave her a subtle wave, worried about drawing Chris or Xavier's attention to himself or his date.

"Tallis, remember, you're walking with Vanessa's cousin, Maggie," the wedding planner said, grabbing Tallis's shoulders and maneuvering him over beside Maggie, who had her hair in a tight bun and her eyes fixed forward on the ceremony aisle. He could tell this girl was taking her role as a bridesmaid seriously.

The planner made sure everyone was in place, except for Vanessa, who was hiding behind a set of double doors for the big reveal.

While he waited for the cue, Tallis let his eyes wander, taking in the indoor venue for the first time. The ceiling was a huge glass dome with lush green ivy vining across it. Floors and walls made of pristine marble made the room feel endless.

Lost in every detail of the room, Tallis's head kept spinning around with each new thing he found to look at, until Maggie elbowed him in the side.

The music had started, and the guest sounds hushed, all turning to look back at the bridal party.

"Thanks," Tallis said to her in a hushed voice.

She nodded, her eyes still locked on the aisle.

When it was their turn, Maggie linked one arm through Tallis's, the other gripping her modest bouquet. They walked in sync—after Tallis consciously adjusted his timing to match Maggie's—until they reached Xavier and the officiant at the altar. They parted to their respective sides, waiting for the bride to make her entrance.

The music changed to something far more orchestral, and everyone rose from their seats to face the main doors. The wedding planner and a woman Tallis recognized from the rehearsal opened the towering double doors. Behind them, Vanessa stood, draped in layers of flowing white. The tiara on top of her braided head glittered in the natural light, her dress shimmering with each step she took toward them.

"Should she be wearing white?" an elderly man in the

front row whispered not-so-softly to his wife, who smacked his shoulder and told him to mind his business.

Xavier's smile turned to a brief snarl as he glowered at the man, only to rapidly redirect himself to his blushing bride. Tallis felt a blend of emotions as he watched his best friends greet each other at the alter and profess their eternal love.

He felt joy. After all, Xavier and Vanessa were meant for each other. Tallis had never seen two people who meshed so perfectly, and they made each other better people.

He felt sorrow. One day (a long time from now, Tallis hoped), one or the other would have to say goodbye first. He couldn't imagine what it would feel like to lose your soulmate.

He felt confused. When he looked over at Odessa, did he have the same look on his face as Xavier did each time he looked at Vanessa? Was she someone he could see spending eternity with?

He felt jealous.

After the ceremony, all the guests were ushered outside to a vibrant but manicured garden space, shaded by a grand tent top. In the center of the space under the tent, there was a table for the newlyweds under a halo of red roses.

"You look stunning!" Tallis stood from his reception table to hug Vanessa as the happy couple made their rounds during dinner.

"You're too sweet!" Vanessa cooed, rocking from side to side in her bear hug. "We're so glad you're here! You're lucky Xavier has a brother or we'd have made you give a best man speech today. You'd probably be less embarrassing than Chris." She made sure to raise her voice and look Chris's direction, a smirk creeping onto her airbrushed face.

"I wasn't embarrassing! I just gave the world's greatest best man speech!" Chris shouted back, raising his wine glass.

"I'll give you credit, Chris," Vanessa said, "it was far more tasteful than I think any of us expected."

"Precisely! Thank you!" He laughed.

"Is this your lovely lady?" Xavier asked, turning his

attention to Odessa, who was sitting beside Tallis with a sweet smile on her face.

"This is her," Tallis said. "Odessa, meet Xavier and Vanessa. Xavier and Vanessa, Odessa."

"He told us you were beautiful, but my God!" Vanessa chimed in. "Odessa, girl, you are *gorgeous!*"

Odessa blushed and smiled. "You're too sweet, Vanessa. If anyone here is gorgeous, it's without a doubt you!"

Tallis felt a weight drop off his shoulders while he watched Odessa and Vanessa getting along so well, but the longer he watched, the more something just didn't sit right. All of a sudden, he was brought back to the time he was in a private room at Illusion, waiting for Odessa. He remembered how she put on a flirtatious and friendly attitude that he later found out was entirely fake. Once the memory crept in, he couldn't help but wonder if this was all an act too.

The couple finished exchanging pleasantries with the others at the table before skirting off to thank another table of guests for making an appearance.

Tallis turned back around to face the table. Odessa was adjusting her hair and humming to herself.

"What do you think of them?" he asked bluntly.

"Hmm?"

"Xavier and Vanessa."

"Oh!" She smiled. "They seem perfect together, from what I can tell! And Vanessa is a sweetheart!"

He turned his attention back to watching his friends walking over to greet another table. Beside him, Odessa had popped the lid off a little vial she pulled from her cleavage. She poured some of the REM into her wine and swirled her glass around.

"Want some?" she looked at him, still swirling her glass.

"Not today."

"You sure?"

"100%. It's my best friends' wedding. It's beautiful here. I really don't need to take that right now."

"Suit yourself!" She set the half-empty vial on the table, discreetly covering it with her napkin and taking a sip of her wine.

They sat together without another word exchanged until the servers set their meals down in front of them.

"They really went all out, didn't they?" Odessa said, poking at an edible flower adorning her side salad.

"They did," Tallis said mindlessly, stabbing at his salad and eating the flower without a second look.

"Wow," Odessa said.

"What?"

"Mr. Admirer of All Things Beautiful didn't even zone out on his salad flower. You feeling okay?"

"I'm fine. Just hungry, I guess."

"Mmh."

Odessa set her flower aside, eating the rest of the salad first.

About halfway through dinner, she excused herself to go to the bathroom, scurrying off. Their other tablemates had wandered off to chat with another table, leaving Tallis alone. He sat back in his seat, already full from the extravagant meal. As he waited, his eyes drifted over to the little vial peeping out from Odessa's napkin.

He leaned forward, plucking up the vial and giving it a wiggle, sloshing around its contents. In complete disregard for his mind, his hands began to undo the stopper, lifting it to his glass and pouring a little in. He realized just then what he was doing, and he stopped before he could empty it, resealing it and setting the vial back down.

Tallis sat back in his seat, wondering how he could be so stupid and selfish. After all, this was the biggest day in Xavier and Vanessa's life, and he wanted to be fully present in the reality and beauty of it all. The longer he sat, the more disgusted he began to feel with himself until he picked up his glass and walked it over to the nearest rose bush, tossing the contents to the roots.

"You good?" Odessa called over, clearly having just witnessed Tallis's internal crisis.

"Yeah, bug landed in my wine," he lied.

"Ew."

"Yeah."

"Did I miss dessert?" she asked.

"You were only gone like three minutes."

"A lot can happen in three minutes!"

"Not dessert."

"Have you ever seen me eat dessert? Three minutes is generous."

"Damn."

The two laughed and made their way back to the table. Just as they were about to sit back in their seats, the DJ called everyone's attention to the extravagant cake display at the other side of the reception space. The guests all rose, following Vanessa and Xavier to the cake.

The rest of the reception went off without a hitch. Vanessa and Xavier were the living definition of happiness, and everyone near them could instantly feel the warmth.

About an hour before the evening's dancing was set to end, the happy couple hopped into their limo and were whisked off to start their honeymoon, leaving the rest of the attendants to enjoy the party themselves.

Tallis and Odessa danced to nearly every song the DJ played, only stopping to rest their feet when he played group songs where everyone else seemed to know the choreographed dance except them. During one of their breaks, Odessa pulled her little vial of REM back out, tipping it back like a shot.

"Really?" Tallis asked in disbelief.

"What?"

"More?"

"Don't act like you're any better. I know you used some while I was in the bathroom."

"Actu—"

"—and you can't judge it like that anymore. You've tried it and you know it's not that bad."

"I'm n—"

"—if I recall, you were actually the one who proposed we go to Dream Depot last time!"

"I'm just sa—"

"—and now you're trying to make it seem like I have a problem? Screw you, Tallis!"

"Stop interrupting me!" he burst.

She went silent, her eyes wild. A couple other guests nearby gave them the side-eye as they eavesdropped on the drama.

"And now you have the balls to yell at *me?*" she said with a snarled lip. "Get lost."

She grabbed her previously discarded heels from under her seat, storming off.

"Odessa!" he called after her, getting up to chase her, but the stares and halted dancing of the other wedding guests stopped him in his tracks.

Tallis only felt the burn of their eyes dull as he, too, left the wedding.

Where'd you go? He texted Odessa.

He paced under the streetlights in front of the venue, staring at his watch for a reply. After a few minutes went by, he growled, throwing his wrist down and pacing faster. One more glance at his watch and he realized she wasn't going to reply, so he wasn't going to wait around.

When he returned to his apartment, he slammed the door shut behind him, rattling the frames on his walls. Lolli looked at him from the couch, her ears back and eyes wide.

"Dammit!" Tallis yelled, grabbing the nearest thing on his desk—an old book about photography techniques—and hurtling it toward the far wall. It collided with a smack, falling to the ground with dented cover corners.

Lolli hopped down from the couch and scampered over to him, looking up at him with concerned eyes and outstretched arms.

He let out a sound not too different from a disgruntled dog before sending another book soaring into the wall, and with that, Lolli shuffled away and sat behind the coffee table to wait out his tantrum.

When he ran out of books, he let out a huff, rubbing his hands over his face before walking off to the bathroom and slamming yet another door. The more rational part of his brain finally woke with the bang, telling him to take a long shower and calm down. He opened the bathroom door back up, chucking his watch out onto the floor before locking himself inside to shower.

He took his time in the shower, telling himself he wasn't allowed to get out until he could clear his mind enough to think of literally nothing. About an hour and four minutes later, he finally achieved his goal. He knew fully well his discipline and willpower were of no help, but rather the dwindling warm water of the shower.

After he put on some lounge clothes, he squatted down to pick his watch off the floor, seeing nothing but an empty inbox. He sighed, closed his eyes, took a deep breath, and opted to put his watch in his bedside drawer for the night.

When he went to go lay on the couch, Lolli timidly peeked out from around the corner, observing him. Seemingly convinced he was done throwing books, she hurried over to him, hopping up beside him on the couch and leaning into him.

"I missed you, too," he said, scratching her behind the ear. "I should've stayed back and partied with you."

She looked at him, her eyes sleepy.

"Me too."

A short while later, they both fell asleep.

Tallis didn't hear from Odessa for the next two weeks. He had to hand it to her—she was committed. Maybe not to their relationship, but committed, nonetheless.

In the final few days before she finally reached out to him, Tallis went to work just like every other day. This time, instead of greeting him with a stack of files, Ms. Iris stood and ushered him out of her office.

"Ma'am?" he asked, his heart beginning to race.

"This way," she said, leading him to the conference room, the door already closed.

"Did I do something?"

She just continued to lead him to the room, opening the door and urging him in before her. Staring back at him were the smiling faces of all the CAs.

Tallis's mouth gaped, and he stuttered, struggling to find words. "I got it?" he finally managed.

"No," Ms. Iris said, melting the joy completely off Tallis's face. "Not yet, at least."

"Oh. I don't understand though."

"We've narrowed it down to a few remaining candidates, and this is the next step. Welcome to your Spontaneous."

"What?"

"I'm going to leave you to it." She patted him on the back and stepped out of the room, shutting the door again.

He turned back to the CAs, who were still grinning at him.

"I don't have anything prepared," he said, "I didn't know about this part."

"That's why it's called a 'Spontaneous,'" one of the CAs said.

"Sit." Tiabelle, the CA who spoke with him before he applied for the position, motioned to an empty chair next to her.

He froze for a second before processing her command, his body flinching when he realized he was supposed to move and take a seat.

The CAs watched him for an aching moment before one of them finally spoke.

"Tell us a story. Something true. Something recent."

"About what?" he asked.

The CA shrugged. "Up to you."

Tallis hummed to himself for a second. "Ah. Well, has the hiring team filled you guys in on anything about me?"

"Pretend they haven't."

"Okay. Umm…" He cleared his throat, straightening his posture. "I'm dating a stripper. I'm pretty sure she's addicted to REM. My best friend warned me right off the bat she was bad news… but I brought her to his wedding. It was a couple weeks ago."

He proceeded to tell them about their argument, leaving out the part about his temptation to take REM, instead, he said he knocked the bottle over and spilled some.

A couple of the CAs jotted something down in their notepads before turning their attention back to him.

"Describe her to us," Tiabelle requested, "in one word."

Tallis sniffed, leaning back in his seat and looking briefly at the ceiling as if it were hiding his answer.

"Electric."

Again, they wrote in their notes.

"So, just like that, we're going to play a word association game. We're going to say a word or name, and you're going to give us one word. Whatever comes to mind."

Tallis nodded in compliance, crossing and uncrossing his legs, wringing his hands.

"*Opulence.*"

"Adventure," he answered.

"*Film.*"

"Story."

"*Work.*"

"Growth."

"*Photo.*"

"Immerse."

"*Words.*"

"Options."

"*Tallis.*"

He paused. "Unfinished."

The CAs were quiet as they recorded his responses. When they finished, they all looked back at him again.

"That's all we need," one of them said, "thank you!"

"That's it?"

"Mmmhmm," she hummed.

"O-okay?" He stood, glancing at them one more time just to be sure before leaving the room and closing the door.

Tallis sat at his desk for a moment before realizing he needed something to work on. He walked over to Ms. Iris's office, standing in her doorway.

"Ma'am?" he called to her when she still didn't notice him. "Are there any documents for me?"

She giggled. "'Are there any documents'… of course there are. There are always documents." She reached into her desk drawer, pulling out a fat folder and holding it out.

"Thank you," he said, stepping in to retrieve it.

"How'd it go?" she asked, not letting the folder go when he reached for it.

"Uh… I'm not sure, to be quite honest. I'm not really sure what they were looking for."

"Fair enough. Were you surprised?"

"Understatement."

She grinned. "When the hiring team decided to bring you into the next round, I was quick to volunteer to bring you into your Spontaneous. I knew you'd be a nervous little mess and I couldn't pass that up."

She released the folder.

"No offense," she added, "of course."

He nodded.

"You're close to the finish line, one way or another," she said.

"Thanks."

He returned to his desk with the folder, getting straight to work. After the adrenaline of his Spontaneous had faded, the day began to feel just as monotonous as any other. In a moment of weakness, he pulled up a photo of Odessa from the wedding.

In the photo, Odessa held her glass high in one hand, her other hand at her side with her arm bent, accentuating her curves. She stared him down through the still, her eyes intense, but her close-mouthed smile soft yet concealing.

The smile that once intrigued him and set his mind ablaze now left him feeling nothing. He tried scrunching his eyes shut for a moment, clearing his mind, and opening them to the photo again, but nothing.

The day she finally messaged him—and she did message first, because Tallis had managed the self-discipline to resist saying anything since the wedding—Tallis had just gotten home from work for the weekend.

Can we talk? Is all it said.

Tallis read the message, his stomach flipping and making him feel sick. He hated that he couldn't tell if it was nerves.

He sat on the couch, the slump in the cushion waking Lolli. She turned to him, saw he was paying more attention to his watch than her, and proceeded to stretch up to nibble on the band.

Tallis's eyes flickered to look at her, and the glare gave her pause. He lowered his wrist.

"You're right," he said to her, "I don't need to answer her right now. She made me wait, so clearly she's in no rush."

Lolli listened intently (at least that's what Tallis told himself, but he knew she was just ready for a snack).

As Tallis sat, he kept glancing at his watch, expecting more messages from her. His mind felt hazy and cloudy, but the longer he sat, the more his mind wandered to the moment of their fight at the wedding. He wondered if it would even classify as a fight, considering he hardly got to defend himself. To Tallis, it would more accurately be classified as a bit of a verbal beating.

He walked over to the small window in his bedroom, looking out over part of his sector. The street seemed colorless and Tallis felt acid in his throat. The cloud in his head grew into a storm and he sunk to the floor.

He sat there, sulking for a moment with his head down in his arms, trying to remember the last time he truly felt like himself. The last time things felt bright. The most recent moment he could recall was when he used REM at work and things looked like the inside of a castle. Though it wasn't his favorite blend, he couldn't think of another time work had felt so fun.

Tallis stood, taking a deep breath to collect himself before walking back into the living room. He bypassed the couch and walked straight to the front door.

"See you in a bit," he said to Lolli, "I left you plenty of food. Please don't eat my stuff while I'm out."

He made his way to the subway, as if his steps were pre-programmed. The only time he stopped was to watch a particularly flashy hologram of an upcoming action movie. He wondered who thought it was a good idea to make a hologram of a man with a gun in the middle of a popular street, even if it was for an arguably more popular movie series.

Once the subway reached Sector 3, he stepped off and continued his robo-walk, passing by Illusion without even turning to look. He walked right by the hookah bar and kept going until he reached the familiar alleyway. The purple eye of Dream Depot watched him as his feet guided him straight through the door.

The colorful tubes of REM and the warmth of the shop greeted him like the smell of cookies at a grandmother's house (albeit, not Tallis's grandmas—neither ever baked for him). He stepped further inside; the barrel of recycled vials was magnetic. He fished out one vial, rolling it around between his thumb and forefinger. His face felt hot, and his heart pounded against his ribs. Simply being inside the shop made him feel like a hypocrite.

Tallis let the vial drop from his fingers and back into the barrel with a quiet clink before turning and walking away. When he stepped back out into the cool air, his nostrils were flooded by the smell of ozone and a hint of trash. His eyes and chest burned, but clearing his throat and running his hands over his face did little to cure his ailing. Perhaps REM wasn't so bad after all, and maybe he shouldn't have been so judgmental of Odessa. He took a deep breath, turned, and reentered the shop.

Back at the barrel, he retrieved another vial and was about to walk away when he thought to himself how it would be much more responsible to get several vials now, instead of having to come back whenever he wanted more REM.

He pulled out an extra two vials, thinking three ought to be enough. After all, it wasn't like he used the stuff every day, and he still didn't love the thought of continuing to use it anyways. He took the little vials and made his way to the costuming aisle, working his way up and down it, narrowing down his options as if he were comparing nutrition labels at the grocery stores.

He stopped at a label marked *Tropical*, filling one of his vials up to the first line. The next one he filled up with *Fashion Show*. The last: *Color*. As he was filling the final one, he noticed a smudge in the vial. When he lifted it to eye-level to take a closer look, he felt sure there was something off about the glass.

Tallis took the vials to the checkout counter, where the man at the register was busy poking around at his own watch.

"Find everything alright?" the man asked without looking up.

"I actually have a question," Tallis said, willing the man to look at him. Once he did, Tallis held up the strange vial. "There's something in this one."

"Are you wanting me to check which costuming you put in there?"

"Uh—no. Not that. I mean aside from the REM itself. There's something in the glass. It's hard to see until you bring it up to the light a bit." He moved the vial up, holding it in front of the man.

"That just looks like a scuff mark to me. Some of these vials are super old and should probably be thrown away, but it's totally fine. Just not as pretty as the others."

Not fully convinced, Tallis kept looking at the scratch in the vial up against the light.

"If you don't wanna use it, pour it out and get a new vial. I'll just have to charge you for the bit you dump out."

Tallis hesitated. "I'm sure it's fine," he said, "like you said, probably just a scratch."

He thanked the man and made his way to the settings aisle, keeping careful track of which vial was which so he could match settings to costuming. When he finished filling each vial completely, he returned to the counter, setting them down.

"Which colors do you want?" the cashier asked.

"Blue," Tallis handed him the tropical vial, "like the ocean."

Expressionless, the man turned to mix the colorant into the first vial of REM, handing it back to Tallis.

"Purple—it's a luxury color," he handed the man the fashion show mixture.

"And the last one?" the man held his hand out for the last one after adding the purple colorant to the second.

"Yellow," he handed him the one meant to make things more vibrant and colorful, "because it's the brightest color. And yellow is the color of optimism and I could use some of that right about now."

The man, unamused by Tallis's reasonings, dyed the final vial.

Tallis tapped to pay from his watch as the man bagged up the vials, handing them over the counter.

"Have a good one."

"You too," Tallis called back as he stepped back out into the dark, damp alleyway.

He walked halfway down the alley before stopping, looking behind him at the purple eye on the Dream Depot sign. Even the eye looked void of its usual color. He stopped where he was, leaning against the wet brick wall with a deep sigh as he looked into his shopping bag. His eyes stung, and a scratchy lump set up shop in his throat. The blue vial sat atop the other two, catching a glint of light from overhead. His hand plunged into the paper bag as if it had a mind of its own.

In one swift movement, he plucked the top from the vial and sucked down half of the aquamarine juice. He put the vial back in the bag and stood still, slumped over against the shop wall. A moment's pause, and then he let out an enraged yell, pounding his fist back on the bricks behind him. Things didn't feel real anymore—it seemed like he was living in a black and white movie and REM was the only thing with color.

His heart threw itself repeatedly against his ribcage. He didn't want to take REM anymore, but he couldn't stop himself.

She still hadn't messaged him anything else since her last text, but Tallis replied:

Now?

His hands rattled every time his watch buzzed with some meaningless notification. When the buzz was finally the one he wanted, he broke out in an immediate sweat.

Where? she asked.

Are you home?

Yes.

10 minutes.

He peeled himself from the wall, brushing away mud before taking off down the street toward Odessa's apartment. When he reached the white concrete tower he remembered from their night together, he paused at the bottom of the steps.

Here.

Coming.

Just as he looked up from reading her response, the white concrete tower had transformed into an almost comically tall bungalow. The ground beneath it was now crystalline water full of tropical fish and colorful shells.

"Woah," he let out breathily, turning to look at the

rest of the street, which now resembled Odessa's faux-bungalow apartment.

Just then, the door swung open, Odessa standing in the doorway in nothing but a grass skirt and a pair of shells. It took Tallis a moment to look past the costuming and realize how bloodshot her eyes were.

His smile quickly faded to concern as he darted forward to hold her.

"I'm sorry," he said, without realizing why.

She pressed her ear to his chest as he held her head in close, stroking her blonde hair, stopping each time he reached a tiny snarl.

"Do you wanna come in?" she asked, her voice quivering.

She led the way inside and into the elevator. If nothing else reminded Tallis that his eyes were deceiving him, it was the straw and seaweed elevator that, under normal physics, would never function.

Her once magazine-quality luxury apartment now looked like the lobby of a tropical resort, complete with a bowl of fruit on the coffee table, a bamboo bartop, and tiki torch lamps.

"I've missed having you here," she said, taking a seat.

"I've only been over once."

"So?" she said. "It's felt lonely ever since."

"I figured you didn't want to talk to me."

"You figured wrong."

"Why didn't you message me, then?"

"I was hoping you'd apologize first."

Tallis was taken aback, but he kept it to himself, pausing and choosing his words carefully.

"I should have. I'm sorry." He didn't have to say what he was sorry for. If anything, he was sorry he even bothered to open his mouth about her taking REM at the wedding.

"I know," she said, her smile sweet, the fire of a tiki torch flickering in her eyes. "Sit."

She motioned beside her, and Tallis accepted. The closer he got, the more he got pulled into her warmth. Was it her or was it just the REM? He couldn't tell the difference.

"I'm sorry, too," she said, nuzzling up against him, "I shouldn't have been so obvious about the REM. I know not everyone agrees with it, and I know it was a classy affair. I should've been more discrete. I hope you're not too embarrassed by me."

"I'm not embarrassed by you at all!"

"Are you sure? I'm a college drop-out stripper who took drugs at your best friend's wedding. It's like a cheesy comedy or a really sappy drama movie or something."

"You're not an embarrassment," Tallis repeated, pulling her in closer.

She looked up at him, her eyes wide, wet, and bluer than Tallis felt like he had seen in a long time. It was refreshing to see such a beautiful color.

"I'm not sure I believe you," she said.

"If anything, I admire your ability to live the life that you want. You aren't afraid of anything—you know how to be wild and exciting and free. I'd do well to take a page from your book!"

That one worked. She started to smile, and she patted at her tears with a beach towel on the back of the couch—Tallis assumed it must've actually been a blanket.

"It's getting late," she said, looking down at his watch. "Stay the night?"

"I shouldn't, I've gotta get home."

"Why? I've got everything you need here!" She perked up, sitting on her knees on the couch, bouncing as she waited for him to change his mind.

"I shouldn't leave Lolli home alone."

"Did you feed her this time?"

"She's got a full bowl of food."

"Then what's the big deal? You spend eight hours or more at work every day anyways, so it isn't like you're with her all the time. What's one night?"

"I…"

She bounced faster, her seashells hanging on for dear life.

"Alright," he submitted.

"Yay!" she cheered, getting up and scurrying to the kitchen to pour them both some wine, her grass skirt shifting with each step. Tallis stared, willing it to shift a little more.

The next morning, Tallis woke up to an empty bed. He eased himself up, stretching and groaning the whole way until he was vertical.

"You okay in there?" He could hear Odessa call from the kitchen. "That's an awful lot of groaning in there! It couldn't have been that bad!"

"Just stretching," he hollered back, shuffling out of the bedroom and joining Odessa in the kitchen. The effects of the REM had clearly worn off, replacing the aesthetic of a tropical resort with Odessa's sterile white apartment.

"Coffee?" She held out a small white mug of black coffee.

"Is there any sugar in it?"

She shook her head. "Out."

He grimaced at the liquid in the mug, dreading its bitter taste but craving the caffeine. He took his mug of bitter to the couch, taking a seat and allowing himself to zone out on the view from her window.

"You're lucky you have me," Odessa said, her voice chipper, almost grating as she plopped down beside him. Her own coffee threatened to slosh out of the mug.

Without turning to look at her, he simply sat and listened, knowing she had more to say.

"I mean, after all, I might just make the world's best cup of coffee," she said, eyeing his untouched mug.

Tallis just kept staring out the window, the city looking nearly void of color. He wondered if it had gotten worse overnight. When he didn't respond or look at Odessa, she let out a dainty cough and spoke again.

"I was worried you'd find someone else while I wasn't talking to you," she admitted, "I mean, you're hot, you're smart and creative… you're a sweetheart. Any girl would go nuts for that."

He finally turned to face her. Odessa had set her coffee down and was sitting with her legs crossed under her. She rubbed at the back of her neck for a second and continued.

"But then I thought about it some more. You spend entirely too much time in your head. Girls like attention. They want a guy who lives in the moment, not in a cloud of thoughts all the time. That's why you're lucky to have me—I'm able to look past things like that! I see the good traits you have and I love those!"

When she could see the hurt on his face, her smile faded and she scooted closer to him.

"Hey," she said, "look… I'm actually really proud of you. You've been getting a lot better about that zoning out stuff. I mean, it's bound to happen sometimes—I get that. But you're changing for the better!"

"I need to go home," is all he said, standing from the couch, leaving his mug on the table and walking straight to the door.

"Wait… what?" She spun around on the couch to watch him; her face scrunched.

"I'm going home."

"Why?"

"I need to go feed Lolli," he lied, his eyes burning as he refused to look at her, instead, standing at her door while holding the knob.

When she didn't say anything else, he turned the knob and disappeared out the door.

Tallis missed color.

The trip back to his apartment felt flat, and he felt numb. Part of him acknowledged that Odessa's words stung. The other part wondered if his mind really was a burden to people, and if perhaps she was right that no one else would bother to put up with him. Maybe he really was lucky that he had her.

How's Lolli? She messaged him, just a few moments after he stepped into his apartment.

He sent her a picture of Lolli, who had fallen asleep on the couch with a gnawed-on piece of carrot tucked under her chest—presumably a snack for later.

Love her! she replied.

Lolli made a quiet snarling noise as her leg began twitching in her sleep. She accidentally knocked her nibbled carrot to the floor, to which she jolted awake. Her furry face scanned side to side, searching for her treat.

"You dropped this," Tallis said, walking over and plucking the carrot from the floor, holding it out to her.

She grabbed it with her little paws, looking up at him as if he was the hero who found a child's lost dolly. She hugged her carrot close, still watching him.

"I told you I'd be home. Sorry it was longer than I meant to be gone. I regret it."

He sat down beside her, scooping her up and setting her on his lap. She tried to scramble down and he stopped her for a moment before letting her go.

"Sorry," he said to her as she sat on the floor, bathing her ear as if cooties were real.

After sitting for a moment, he perked up.

"Wanna get some fresh air?" he asked her. "I know it's been a while. I think we could both use it."

Clueless, she just kept sitting on the floor, holding her lint-covered carrot. After a moment, she shoved the dirty carrot in her mouth, her eyes crossing as she looked at it sticking out between her teeth.

Tallis changed into something more comfortable and grabbed his camera before filling his pocket with goodies for Lolli. He squatted down and held out a hand to her.

"Up?"

She understood this word, and climbed her way up his arm, perching herself on his shoulder. He looked over at her, eyeing the carrot still in her mouth.

"Can we leave that gross thing here? What if I put it somewhere safe? Right here on your spot on the couch, okay?" He coerced the carrot out of her mouth and set it down before the two left the apartment.

At the park, he tried to find a pretty backdrop to take pictures of Lolli like the last time. He remembered feeling like himself when he was here before. Things felt colorful and alive then, as if each day was a new adventure instead of a dull routine. He wondered if maybe he was just coming down with the world's slowest flu.

"Stay," he said, setting Lolli down in a little patch of dandelions.

He snapped a couple pictures and felt like the yellow should've been brighter. There was no way this spot wasn't perfect for a picture—why didn't things look right?

Lolli began to nibble on one of the flowers while he critiqued his photographs. When he noticed, he scooped her back up, pulling the flower from her mouth.

"I don't know if raccoons are supposed to eat those," he said softly. "Sorry. Better to play it safe!"

She quickly swallowed a stray petal that had stuck to her mouth, locking eyes with him the entire time.

"You're lucky you're cute."

She sneezed, another petal shooting out her nose.

"See? If I sneezed up part of a flower, it would just be gross. You do it, and it's still so damn cute. Everyone should adopt a pet raccoon—who couldn't benefit from having a furball like you in their home?"

Lolli reached for his camera strap and started gnawing.

"Okay, *that's* not so cute. Knock it off." He laughed, gently removing the strap from her sharp teeth. "Sit still, I want to get a picture of you for Xavier and Vanessa to remind them what they're missing out on during their honeymoon."

He handed Lolli a treat, snapping a few quick pictures while she contently munched on it.

"How about we stop on the way home and get something extra special?"

She looked at him, only understanding the word "home." Toddling off to a nearby tree, she hurried up to the first branch like a kid whining that they didn't want to go to bed.

"Come on, I want to get you a treat." He reached up for her. "*Treat.*"

Her ears perked up, and after analyzing him for a moment, she stretched her arms out, grasping for him. When her paws contacted his arm, she clung on and allowed him to set her on his shoulder once more.

"I wanna take you to my favorite coffee shop," Tallis explained as he walked to the subway, Lolli bobbing along on his shoulder.

On the subway, a couple of teenage girls cooed over Lolli from the other side of the cart.

"Your raccoon is really cute!" one of them mustered the courage to shout.

Tallis smiled like a proud dad. "Would you girls like to pet her?"

His question was met with thrilled squeals as the girls nearly trampled each other on their way to Tallis.

"How old is he?" one asked.

"Is it a girl or boy?" another asked.

"What's her name?"

"Does she do any tricks?"

Tallis began to worry that Lolli would feel overwhelmed with the excessive attention and noise, considering most of her life was spent cozied up on a couch with her crime shows. Surprisingly, she was eating it up. With each scratch behind the ear or under the chin, she wiggled her way closer to the girls' hands, allowing her eyes to close.

"I think she likes you guys," Tallis said, stunned by how calm she was.

"What's her name?" one of the girls asked again.

"Her name is Lolli. I'm taking her to a coffee shop to get her a special treat."

"Raccoons drink coffee?" one of the girls asked, tilting her head and scrunching her face at him.

"Lora!" the girl beside her smacked her shoulder. "That's stupid. Raccoons don't drink coffee."

"I bet they could! Look it up!"

The friend rolled her eyes.

"I'm just hoping to get her some whipped cream," Tallis said, "the coffee's just for me. Even if she can drink coffee, she doesn't need caffeine. She's a bit of a troublemaker and I can't imagine what she would do if I caffeinated her."

The girls giggled and the subway came to a stop at Sector 12.

"Say goodbye, Lolli," Tallis looked at his pet, who at this point was so relaxed she had a bead of drool on her chin.

"Aww!" the girls pouted as Tallis took Lolli and exited the subway.

The nice weather had turned to a bit of a drizzle. Every few drops of rain that landed on Lolli's fur warranted a dramatic shake, each time flicking water all over the side of Tallis's face.

Shortly before reaching Bru, Tallis slowed to eye the pink puddle outside Buzz's Electrosuite. He knelt down and motioned to the puddle.

"Look," he said to Lolli, flicking at the surface of the water, sending ripples of pink across its surface.

She leaned down to get a better look, eventually spotting

her own reflection in it once the water settled. Excited, she leaned forward more and more until she lost her grip on Tallis's shoulder, falling into the puddle with a smash. Tallis gasped at first, having tried to catch her, but upon seeing her reaction, he sat there on the sidewalk laughing. Instead of being bothered by the puddle, Lolli stood in the middle of it, picking up one foot at a time, watching the way the water's surface changed as she put it back down.

"Do you like the puddle?" Tallis asked her, beaming. "I've always thought it was pretty the way it catches the light."

He watched her for a moment, beginning to feel an ache in his chest. The puddle felt dim, almost dingy. It was just street water with a little bit of pink reflecting in it. He supposed it was still pretty, but it didn't have the same bright shine to it that he could've sworn it used to have.

Tallis looked up at the sign for Buzz's Electrosuite, wondering if perhaps their neon sign was simply growing dark and dying out, but it seemed normal. He looked back down at the puddle. Lolli had decided to sit in the middle, still staring down at the reflection.

"Silly girl," he said, picking her up, water dripping from her drenched fur, "let's get you dried off and warm. Then I'll get your treat. Sound good?"

Inside Bru, Tallis stepped up to the counter, sopping wet raccoon in his hands. The barista looked mortified as she stared back at him, forgetting her typical customer greeting.

"Do you have a spare towel or anything? Or paper towels?" Tallis asked. "She fell in a puddle."

"Uh—we have hand dryers in the bathrooms," she said with a strange tone, as if asking a question.

"Thank you." Tallis walked toward the back with Lolli,

water droplets plummeting to the hard floor the entire way.

Inside the restroom, he spotted the hand dryer and looked at Lolli in his outstretched hands.

"You're going to hate me," he said, her expression completely clueless as he held her under the dryer and pressed the button.

The dryer whirred to life, fluffing out her wet fur as she flattened her ears as if to block out the sound of the rushing air.

While drying her tail off, the bathroom door opened and an older gentleman walked in. His eyes immediately fixated on Lolli, then on Tallis. Without a word, he turned around and left the bathroom.

"Sorry!" Tallis called out at the closed door.

When Lolli was most of the way dried off, he allowed the dryer to shut down, his ears still ringing even in the newfound silence of the bathroom.

"That's a little better, isn't it?" He handed Lolli a carrot from his pocket after he set her back on his shoulder.

Back in the main shop itself, he approached the girl at the counter once more.

"Can I get a mocha latte for me, and a little cup of whipped cream for her?"

When his order was ready, he stepped back to the counter, grabbing the two cups and carrying them over to one of the small tables at the far end of the coffee shop. He set Lolli on a chair, holding out the cup of whipped cream in front of her.

"All yours," he said, scooting the cup closer to her.

She looked down at it and back up at Tallis before sticking her paw right into the whipped cream. Confused, she held her cream-covered paw up to eye level.

"You eat it," Tallis tried to explain.

Clearly not understanding, she held her paw out in front of Tallis's face as if to say, "do something."

He pointed at the cup. "Treat."

When she still didn't test it out, he scooped up a finger full of whipped cream and blotted it on her nose. She went cross-eyed trying to look at it before licking blindly at her nose. Once she got a taste, the message clicked, and she plucked up the cup between both her front paws, stuffing her face and licking frantically until the entire thing was clean. When she pulled her face out, her whiskers and nose were completely covered in cream.

Tallis flicked his camera on, snapping a few close-ups of his messy pet before helping wipe off her face and paw.

———◆—‹◉›—◆———

When they returned to the apartment, Tallis sat at his computer to video call Xavier and Vanessa. While the call rang, he uploaded his photos of Lolli from the day and sent a few of his favorites to the couple.

"Hey, man, what's up?" Xavier answered, the video at an unflattering low angle of his chin as he sat up in bed.

"Just calling to see how you guys are doing on the world's longest honeymoon. I won't keep you long," Tallis said.

"Man, I'm so glad we saved all that paid time off until now! It's fa—"

"Tallis!" Vanessa squealed from out of frame. "These pictures of Lolli are *everything*! She is the most *pure* creature I have *ever* seen. How do you get anything done with such a cute baby around all the time?"

"Who's to say I *do* get anything done?"

Vanessa popped into frame, sitting in bed next to Xavier and leaning against him, the smile on her face never faltering.

"We're having a ton of fun!" Vanessa said. "I couldn't have asked for a better trip!"

"I'm so glad to hear that," Tallis said.

"We've been glass-bottom kayaking, parasailing, and snorkeling with beautiful tropical fish. It's amazing here!" she continued.

"The drinks here are the bomb," said Xavier.

"You *would* focus on the drinks!" Vanessa nudged.

"Have one for me, will ya?"

"You got it, brother," Xavier said with a nod.

"Love you both—have a great rest of your honeymoon," Tallis said before hanging up.

The apartment felt empty and quiet with the absence of his friends' voices all of a sudden, even though they were only on a screen. He sat back in his chair, imagining them on all their adventures during their trip. The joy he felt for his friends was genuine, but he couldn't ignore the sting of jealousy as he let envy creep in like a toxin. The more he tried to push the feeling aside, the worse it dug in.

He began to question what he had done to feel so alone. So unhappy. So hopeless. He was happy for his friends, but he envied their bliss. They didn't seem to have to think about their relationship. It was effortless. Tallis didn't know why he felt exhausted just thinking about his relationship with Odessa. He cared about her and loved the excitement of dating her, but something was missing, and it wasn't just the color.

24

Unable to sleep, he got up earlier than usual for work on Monday morning. After wasting over an hour staring at a cobweb on his ceiling fan, he decided he may as well get ready to face the day.

Unfortunately, the day truly had it out for Tallis.

Because he had some spare time, Tallis decided to put in extra effort and make a genuine breakfast for himself. When he went to put mousse in his hair while leaving his breakfast cooking, he came back to a disaster. Lolli was sitting beside the stove, munching on the fried egg in her hands while the bacon began to burn.

"Get down!" Tallis called at her. "And stop stealing my breakfast! I'll feed you in a minute. Chill!"

He removed the rest of the egg from her hands, throwing it into the sink before picking her up and setting her by her empty food bowl. She looked at the bowl for a half second before her gaze shot back to him.

"I'm working on it!" he defended, filling her bowl.

She started to scoop handfuls of her food while he was

pouring, dunking it in her water to soften it.

"Weirdo," Tallis teased, smiling endearingly at her. "Although I guess it's not all that different from cereal. So… bon appetite, I guess."

He scraped together the edible bits of his ruined breakfast, picking aimlessly at it. What once would have still felt like a special treat to him now just tasted charred.

Eventually giving up on his breakfast, he retreated to his closet, using the display to select an outfit that he felt would at least convince others that he had his life together—a white button-up, thin black tie, and simple black slacks.

"I'm headed to work," he said to Lolli as he prepared to step out the door. "Be good. Kiss?"

He leaned down to meet her place on the couch. She leaned up a little, her nose sniffling—likely curious about his breakfast breath. Her nose tapped Tallis's lips, and he made a kissing noise at her.

"Love you, Lolli," he called as the door closed behind him.

As usual, Tallis stopped at Bru to pick up Ms. Iris's coffee. Bru was nearly empty, which was unusual for that time of day, but Tallis had been lucky before. When it was his turn in line, the barista greeted him with a genuine smile.

"I remember you!" she said, her ponytail swinging as she leaned forward. "How's your raccoon doing?"

It took Tallis a moment to realize this was the same barista as the one from his weekend adventures with Lolli.

"She's good, thanks. Wasn't happy about the hand dryer, but she handled it alright. I think she forgot all about it when I gave her the whipped cream."

"Aww. She looked so sad when she was all wet! Glad her day got better."

"Thanks." He paused. "Wanna see a cute picture of her with the whipped cream all over her face?"

The barista's face lit up. "Is that even a question? Of course I do!"

Tallis smiled back, pulling up a photo on his watch and holding it out for her to see. When she leaned over to get a better look, Tallis got a whiff of her cotton candy perfume and allowed himself to take a deeper inhale before she pulled back again.

"She's so cute! You should submit that picture to some kind of pet product company or something. Or whatever store you got her from! That's a fantastic picture—you could probably make money off of it. If you wanted to!"

"That's really sweet of you, thank you."

"I'm serious! You've got a real talent. Anyone who can get that good of a picture of an animal already has my utmost respect. I've got a cat. He doesn't sit still long enough for a good picture."

Tallis blushed and rubbed the back of his neck.

"I really appreciate it," he said.

"So, what can I get you?" she asked, her eyes sparkling under the dim light over the register.

"Medium iced coffee with two pumps of lavender and a splash of cream." It was almost like a pre-programmed response.

"I didn't peg you for a lavender guy!" she tapped the order into the register.

"It's not for me," Tallis said. "It's for my boss."

"You don't want anything for yourself?" she asked.

He was surprised she didn't seem to judge him for being a coffee-getter.

"No, I'm okay. Thank you."

She crossed her arms and looked him up and down.

"Look, there's no one in line behind you. No one is waiting, so I've got some time to kill. If I make you my own special recipe, would you try it?" she asked. "My treat."

"You really don't have to do that."

"Not to brag, but I tend to be a pretty good people reader, and I can tell you need this. Plus, it's not technically free. In exchange, you have to be honest with me about how it tastes. I'm trying to get this drink on the menu, but I need to know I'm not the only one who thinks it's good."

"Alright. I'll give it a go."

She beamed and seemed to hop in place.

"Yay! One Avalyn, coming right up!"

"Avalyn?" he asked.

Her face flushed pink. "It's my name. Yes, I named it after myself. I swear I'm not that vain. I was just really excited and proud when I came up with it. It'll be my legacy!" She put her fists on her hips like a superhero in a billowing cape.

Tallis smiled. "It's a cool name. I like it."

"Thank you! What's yours?"

"Tallis," he said, reaching out a hand to shake hers. She accepted, grinning.

"So that'll be all for you?"

"Guess so."

He tapped his watch to pay for Ms. Iris's coffee, as Avalyn turned her back to him, grabbing a cup and filling it with different syrups and creams.

"Have you worked here long?" Tallis asked. "I feel like

I've never seen you before."

"I just started. I used to work at a coffee shop in Sector 10. I wanted a change of scenery, so I found this place, applied, and got the job a few days later!"

"Well, congrats," Tallis said. "I'm sure you'll love it here. I've been going to this coffee shop every day for a long time. It's only gotten better and better."

She looked over her shoulder at him and smiled.

A few moments later, she returned to the counter with two cups in hand.

"This one's your boss's," she motioned to one cup, "and this is yours!"

"What's in it?"

She grinned, tapping her fingertips together like a stereotypical villain.

"Not even a clue?"

"Nope. Try it!"

He picked the cup up, putting it to his lips and looking at her over the rim of his cup before turning it back and sipping.

She waited, bouncing subtly on her toes behind the counter.

"Is that almond?" he asked, smacking his lips together a few times. "And cinnamon?"

"Nutmeg!"

"And there's something extra sweet in there. But just a hint. I can't tell what it is, but it's really good!" He went back for another taste.

"It's a latte with almond, nutmeg, and a little caramel drizzle!"

"This is fantastic. It tastes like a hug from a grandma or something."

She giggled. "I like that name better than naming it after me. That's it. It's officially The Grandma Hug. This can be your claim to fame—you just named my first famous coffee."

"First?"

"I'm not stopping at one drink! I've gotta invent other flavors. Before you know it, The Grandma Hug will be a national hit."

Tallis pretended to flip long hair over his shoulder. "No autographs, please. I'll need to send my assistant to get my coffees from now on."

"Hey, you never know! One day, you won't be getting coffee for your boss anymore. Before you know it, someone will be getting *your* coffee."

He scoffed.

"I'm serious!"

Just then, his watch buzzed with a message from Ms. Iris.

Where are you?

He instantly broke out in a cold sweat.

"I hate to leave so abruptly, but I really have to get to work. I'm so sorry!"

Tallis snatched up both the coffees and bolted for the door, shouting an "I hope to see you around!" back at Avalyn, who just gave a dainty wave from her position at the counter.

When he reached Opulence, hands full, he jammed his elbow into the elevator button repeatedly as if it would summon the pod any faster.

While waiting for the elevator to reach the ground floor, two other workers approached, standing in wait as they chatted.

"I heard they finally picked the new CA," one person, a lanky woman with frizzy blue hair, said while mindlessly scrolling her watch.

Tallis nearly dropped both coffees, his entire body flinching at their words. He turned to face the two.

"Did you just say they decided on a CA?" he asked, telling himself he didn't hear right the first time.

She looked up at him in unmasked disgust for his eavesdropping. He realized it but brushed it off. After all, did it really count as eavesdropping if she said it loud and clear right next to him?

"Sorry," he said. "I was one of the finalists for the position. I hadn't heard anything since the last part of the interview process."

"Then you probably didn't get the position," she said, glaring at him before looking back down at her watch.

Tallis's stomach and heart felt like they were in a contest to see who could do the most flips. He coughed a few times reflexively to try to steady his heartbeat as he grew dizzy.

"Ew," the woman looked over at him again, taking a few dramatic sidesteps away from him. Her companion mirrored her.

An eternity later, the elevator finally dinged as it reached their level, sliding the doors open to welcome them inside.

"You go first," she said with a shooing motion. "I don't want to catch whatever you've got. I have a vacation coming up."

"I'm not sick."

"That's okay." She widened her eyes but furrowed her brow, repeating the shoo.

Tallis stepped into the elevator and hit the button for his floor, making uncomfortable eye contact with Blue Hair while he waited for the doors to close again.

Once the elevator arrived on his floor, he shot out the double doors, making a beeline straight for Ms. Iris's office. He held her coffee out, the ice sloshing against the walls of the cup with a rattle.

"Sorry I'm late," he said without letting himself catch his breath.

As she took the coffee from him, he realized he could be doing this same thing for the rest of his life. The panic of her disapproval and his lateness turned into indifference.

"We've got a strict deadline to meet on the Lowrance Co. project. I need this stuff inputted by end of day today. No exceptions."

"Yes, ma'am." He took the hefty stack of documents from her, turning and trudging to his desk.

He sat, immediately slumping over, head in his hands. The stack of documents mocked him from beside his monitor. He thought to himself that he better swallow his pride and get used to the idea that he'd be getting someone else's coffee and processing data and documents until old age prevented him from being of any further use to the company. Tallis certainly wasn't making enough to ever retire.

The more he sat and stewed in his own self-pity, the more his mind began to wander to his friends. Xavier and Vanessa lived extravagant lives, made fantastic money, and had more vacation time than they knew what to do with.

Even if he was doing the same kind of work, at least he could have an interesting lifestyle outside of work, if only he made that much money or had that much free time. Unfortunately, he was fully convinced he would never make the money, have the spare time, or work the thrilling career. He would be happy with just one out of the three. The thought of never achieving any of them pulled on him like pure gravity.

He couldn't get himself to flip open the first folder in the stack. The thought of even reaching for it summoned a lump in his throat. Eventually, eyes burning, he willed himself to grab the folder and whip the front open as if it would bite him if he touched it too long.

Lunchtime rolled around, and he had hardly progressed through his stack. He looked over at Ms. Iris's office, and she was immersed in something on her computer. Tallis sat for a moment, watching and weighing whether going on a lunch break was worth risking her stopping him to ask for a progress report. Deciding he didn't want to hear a lecture, he refocused on his work, suppressing the hunger pangs brought about by a disappointing breakfast.

His watch buzzed and he looked down. It was Xavier.

Don't forget, we're coming home on Friday. Wanna get lunch or something? I've got some cool pics to show you!

Sure, was all Tallis managed to reply.

He began to daydream about food. His stomach grumbled and he adjusted himself in his seat as if that alone would silence it. In the moment, nothing sounded better than a beef melt from BBQuisine.

He fumbled through one of his seldom-opened desk drawers, digging around through old copies of irrelevant documents and long-forgotten office supplies, eventually fishing out a granola bar. He looked at the expiration date. It was a year expired, but he convinced himself it was fine— probably just stale.

Famished and craving a distraction, he tore into the bar, taking off an entire half in one bite. It was definitely stale, but edible. It would have to do.

Tallis stayed at work until it was close to dinnertime. He was just about finished with the last document in the stack as Ms. Iris was tidying up her office for the day. He sped through the last of the data, hitting the submit button just as she reached his desk.

She didn't say a word, but her raised eyebrow and crossed arms said it all.

"It's all been submitted," he said. A second later, he threw in a "Ma'am."

"Perfect. Now go home. It's been a long day. I don't know about you, but it felt like the Monday of all Mondays today."

"Absolutely," he said with an exhausted puff.

She began waddling toward the elevator, with Tallis trailing a few steps behind her—strategically far enough that he wouldn't feel obligated to hold a conversation with her. It was only when they were both stuck waiting on the elevator that he felt the pressure to say something.

"I—" He wanted to ask about the CA position. He wanted to ask for a name, demand why they didn't pick him, ask what was so wrong with him. Instead, he awkwardly cleared his throat, pretending he never meant to say anything at all.

"Do you need a lozenge?" she asked, reaching into her purse.

"No, ma'am. Thank you."

She removed her hand, staring forward as the elevator opened. He allowed her to step inside first and he reluctantly followed.

The ride to the ground floor was achingly silent. When it finally touched down, the two stepped out and exited Opulence.

"Get some sleep tonight, Tallis," Ms. Iris said, grabbing his forearm and preventing him from escaping. "You look half-dead. Can't have you inputting data if you're too tired to think straight. You'll end up screwing up an entire contract or something. *Rest.*"

He nodded.

She released his arm. "See you tomorrow."

It was on the word *tomorrow* that the realization truly set in that he was doomed to live a life documenting data from *other* peoples' adventures, never going on any of his own.

Ms. Iris left, and Tallis stood, frozen for a moment, processing. He took a deep, shaky breath before making his way home.

Dark clouds loomed overhead, only making the world feel more colorless than before. The city grew darker with each step he took, the first thick droplets of rain spattering against his arm as he neared Bru.

He debated stopping inside to see if Avalyn was still working. The rain was likely only going to get worse, so he could easily wait it out in the comfort of the coffee shop. He assumed her shift had ended by now, and the more he thought about it, the more he really didn't feel like being around other people anyways. Everyone else seemed to be buzzing with life but him.

Deciding against stopping, he kept a brisk pace as he walked down the too-familiar street. As usual, the pink puddle caught his attention, but only briefly. It looked bigger from the weekend's rain, and it was undoubtedly only going to continue to grow. He watched its surface as each raindrop sent pink ripples like tidal waves across it. Growing bored, he lifted his gaze. Tallis continued to the subway station and left the puddle behind.

The closer he got to home, the more he began to lock in on the idea that he only knew one way to feel a sense of excitement and adventure anymore, now that his one shot was ripped from beneath him.

Once he got home, he walked right past Lolli, who sat loyally by the door to greet him. He reached for the small vial of yellow liquid on his bedside table, looking it over and eyeing the smudge inside.

When he made this mixture of REM, he picked all the options labeled "color." He wasn't even sure what it would do with color. Part of him thought perhaps it would turn everything into strange colors—reds would be blues, pinks would be greens, and so on. Another part of him wondered if it would simply make the world around him feel colorful and bright again like he desperately missed. Either way, things couldn't feel more grey than they did at the moment.

He undid the stopper, pouring half of the mixture into a leftover glass of water from the night before. After a quick swirl of his wrist to disperse the golden yellow into the glass, he turned the water up, chugging the mixture.

Still holding the glass, he looked to his bedroom window.

At this point, the rain was streaming down in a constant flow, obscuring his view outside. He sighed, setting the glass down again. It had a little yellow residue pooled at the bottom, but he knew he mixed enough into the water, so he left it. He stepped out into the living room and sat next to Lolli on the couch.

"You watching this?" He motioned to the TV.

Lolli was half-asleep, lazily watching the show with sleepy eyes.

"I'll leave it on, then." He rested a hand on Lolli's side, his fingers gently stroking her thick fur.

For a moment, Tallis allowed himself to enjoy the simple peace before the dark thoughts began to slink back into his focus.

"Even if my love life is complicated, my professional life has plateaued, and my personal life would put just about anyone to sleep," Tallis said, looking over at Lolli beside him, "at least I've got someone who loves me no matter what."

He scratched behind her ear, and she stretched out, resting her head against his leg.

His watch buzzed with a message from Odessa.

What r u doing? :)

He read over it a couple times before deciding to disregard it for now, putting his attention back on the TV. Whatever crime show Lolli was watching this time told the story of an entire cheerleading squad who mysteriously disappeared in some creepy hotel.

Unable to focus on the show, he stood and walked to his computer, pulling up his files and deciding to try to organize them just to keep his hands and mind busy while he waited for the REM to make him feel better again. He knew it wasn't technically medicine, but something about it felt mentally healing to him. It was starting to make sense why Odessa always took it.

He made a few new folders, sorting some of his short stories by genre and date. The room seemed to grow darker, and he blamed it on the storm overhead, a crash of thunder confirming his theory.

Flicking his desk lamp on seemed to make almost no difference, as all the light in his apartment dimmed. Aggravated, he walked over to another lamp—one with a heavy, solid glass base that he kept beside the couch. He flipped the switch, flooding the room with warm light, only for it to begin to grow even darker until the lights in the room gave off only a faint and foggy glow.

"What the hell." Tallis grumbled, looking for another light source. When he turned back around toward the rest of the living room, he nearly jumped out of his skin.

He couldn't see the walls. It was as if he plummeted into a dark expanse—he couldn't see more than a couple feet ahead of him, and what little he could see was black. He turned back to look at the couch and the lamp, only spotting darkened blurry patches where furniture used to be.

Tallis scrunched his eyes shut. When he opened them again, nothing had changed. Everything was still endlessly dark, with nothing more than strange, blurred shapes around him. He squeezed his eyes shut again, covering them with his palms as if he could force sanity back into his head.

Open.

Shut.

Open.

Shut.

Open. No difference.

His heart began to race as he spun in all directions, craving something familiar. When he lost all sense of orientation, he began to feel queasy. Unable to make out any defined shapes in the room certainly didn't help matters.

He carefully lowered himself to the floor. If nothing else, he was just grateful to feel even that much.

After a couple deep, shaky breaths with closed eyes, he crossed his arms over his knees, allowing himself to rest his forehead against them. Cradled in his self-formed cocoon, he sat there, trying to regulate his breathing and will away the nausea and dizziness.

When the sickened pit in his stomach finally began to subside, he reluctantly but hopefully raised his gaze above his arms. While he was still surrounded by the same eerie darkness, there was something different staring back at him now. Almost instantly, his head began to spin again, and his stomach did tricks as his eyes locked onto a slick, black creature huddled a few feet away.

The creature was almost demon-like, with four spindly legs, glowing yellow eyes, and a wide mouth full of pins for teeth. It shuffled backwards, pressing itself into one of the darkened blurs before him. The way its limbs moved seemed unnatural, and it refused to blink.

Tallis tried backing up slowly, hoping the demon didn't see him. It crept forward with each step back he took, its unblinking eyes locked onto his. As it got closer, he was able to better see its body. Its entire abdomen was nothing but a sleek, black skeleton. An empty ribcage.

He stopped, staring the creature down and holding his hands up as if it would understand he meant no harm. If anything, he wished it would do the same in return.

It inched toward him and his lungs refused air as he froze in place. When it was only about a foot away, he felt every muscle in his body seize. The demon stretched a taloned foot out to him, clinging onto his pant legs and pulling itself up, never breaking eye contact.

At this point, Tallis's entire body was vibrating, and he couldn't hold back a muted whimper as the creature neared his chest. Now that it was up close, he could see its head was just a tar-black skull with eyes and a full set of teeth. He panicked as he could feel its sharp claws through his shirt. If it wanted to hurt or kill him, it would have a better chance closer to his chest or neck. He couldn't let it up any further.

Tallis let out a horrific screech, willing his hands to grasp the demon and fling it from his body, sending it across the floor. He spun on his heel and tried to flee, but instead propelled himself into one of the shapeless blurs.

He tumbled over it, sending something crashing to the floor as he banged his head and elbow on the way down. Moaning in dazed pain, he propped himself into a seated position and rubbed at the top of his head. While he was getting his bearings and assessing any bodily damage, he could hear the skittering of the demon's nails against the floor.

All of a sudden, the clicking sounds stopped. Then, there was a soft thump as its sleek black body appeared, seeming to rest on top of the blurred shape he had just toppled over.

Tallis pawed all around the empty darkness around him for something — anything — he could use to protect himself. His heart sank when his hands kept coming up empty.

The demon began to lower itself down the blurred obstacle, creeping toward him with growing intensity, its crawl unnatural. He scrambled backwards, his hand landing on something solid. As the demon ran toward him, he lunged out with the blurry object in hand. When he swung, the object crashed into the demon's skull with a heavy thud.

Without so much as a single twitch, the creature fell sideways, limp on the floor.

Shocked with himself, he leaned forward, hovering over the sleek skeletal demon. As it lay there completely still, thick liquid began to ooze from its black skull. The longer he stared at it and the further out the liquid began to seep, the more deeply unsettled he felt. After all, skeletons don't bleed.

Overwhelmed by fear, he scrambled to his feet, backing up slowly, his eyes still on the motionless demon. He let out another whimper as he kept backing up, only moving to either side when he felt himself bump into more blurred obstacles.

Eventually, he spotted what looked like a black door. He threw it open, slamming it shut behind him, ensuring it stayed in place by pushing his back up against it.

Tallis sunk down to the floor, crumpling like a ragdoll. He covered his eyes with his hands, preferring the self-made darkness to the forced darkness around him.

Focusing on his breathing, he stayed glued to his spot, praying for it to all stop.

His watch buzzed, and he screamed, forgetting it even existed.

It was difficult to make out the screen, but with enough squinting, he was able to read a message from Odessa.

Are you mad at me?

He messaged back one word: *HELP.*

Instantly, she replied. *Are you ok???*

Even the thought of her didn't bring him any comfort. He felt utterly trapped in his own personal hell with no foreseeable way out. He wondered how he ever got here, and the longer he questioned where he went wrong, the heavier his heart felt until the grief and regret spilled from his eyes.

While Tallis's dark night was the worst of his life, the reality of the next morning brought no relief.

He woke up dehydrated, his dry eyes stinging in the harsh morning sun. Initially pissed off by the bright light, Tallis covered his face. It was only when he realized it meant the darkness was over that he nearly leapt to his feet.

The view from the bedroom window was crystal clear now that the night's storm was over. He looked out over the soaked street, just grateful to see it at all. When he turned back around, he noticed his shut bedroom door.

He paused, staring at the door. He remembered going through a door last night and closing it behind him. It wasn't until then that he realized he was in his apartment the whole time. To him, it truly felt like he took an overnight trip to hell, only to get spat back up because it wasn't his time.

Pieces of the puzzle began to click in his mind. He walked over to his bedside table, plucking up the half-empty vial of REM with two fingers, holding it up to the light from the window.

The smudge in the glass stared back at him, and everything made sense. What initially felt like relief at solving the mystery of his night quickly metamorphosized into panic. Tallis's entire body went cold when he realized what he had done.

Unwilling to believe it, he floated to his bedroom door, his hand resting on the knob for a moment before turning it and stepping into the living room.

He crept toward the couch, first spotting the bloody base of the lamp on the floor, then her body.

"No, no," Tallis muttered, his fingers shoved over his mouth.

He stood there, staring.

"Please, no."

His eyes were on fire, and the bile began to rise in his throat. He sprinted for the bathroom, only getting his face in the toilet seconds before emptying himself into it.

When his body decided he had enough, he leaned backwards, sobbing uncontrollably.

He knew he'd have to go back out there. There was nothing he could do to make this go away.

After giving himself a minute, he stood shakily to his feet, using the wall to steady himself. He took a deep breath and forced himself back into the living room.

His throat burned and his eyes blurred with tears, making it hard to see. He almost wondered if it would've been better to stay in the endless darkness forever, never able to see more than shapeless blurs.

He knelt beside Lolli and found himself unable to look at her head without feeling sick all over again. He raised one hand, partially blocking his view as he stroked her cold fur with his other hand.

"I'm so sorry," he managed to blubber. "I'm sorry." The last word came out as a wail.

He sat back against the base of the couch, giving into the tears again, but nothing came.

"You didn't deserve this. Any of this. I'm so sorry. I didn't realize. I'm so sorry!"

His watch buzzed, but he ignored it, too busy wondering what he could've done differently—ultimately only concluding that he never should've taken the REM to begin with.

When his watch buzzed a second time, he huffed and raised his wrist to eye level. He had about thirty messages from Odessa since his last one to her.

Where are you?

Are you safe?

CALL ME.

If you don't text me back, my anxiety is going to tell me you're dead. Answer me!

He kept reading the messages, eventually reaching the most recent one: *I don't know why you think it's funny to send a message like that and not respond. I hope you're proud of yourself.*

With a sigh, he typed up a short reply.

Bad REM.

She replied almost right away. *Like, the bottle was tainted?*

Yup.

Damn. Never a good time. You good now?

No.

Did you hurt yourself or something?

Or something.

Tallis?

Now's not a good time.

I know it sucked. They always do. But that kind of thing isn't that common, so I wouldn't get too hung up on it.

It was worse than you think.

Trust me, I've had my fair share of those. Once they're done though, they're done. No big deal. Just suck in the moment. Like getting a shot or something.

That was the worst night of my life.

Don't you think you're being a little dramatic?

His face was on fire. The longer he sat there, the worse it got until he launched up from his spot on the floor, storming off to his bedroom. His eyes locked in on the half bottle of REM, which he plucked from the table and threw against his wall without a second thought. He screamed, tearing through his apartment until he found the third bottle of REM, chucking the tiny vial at the same target, purple liquid splattering against the white paint. He felt a twinge of relief with each throw, but he wasn't done yet.

Back in the living room, he spotted the glass base lamp, an animalistic sound rising from deep in his throat as he practically ran, snatching it up and whipping it against the floor. Thick glass chunks scattered against the floor with a wall-shaking crash. He could hear his downstairs neighbors knocking on their ceiling—presumably with a broomstick. Enraged, he flipped the floor the bird before kicking over his coatrack and yelling again.

He lifted his watch to eye level, his hands shaking as he typed out a message to Odessa.

This is all your fault. Before he could send it, he deleted it. He knew he had free will this whole time. He couldn't blame all of this on her.

Tallis lowered his wrist, pacing back and forth until he raised it again to type something else.

You never liked me for who I am. Or who I was. I can't do this anymore. We're done.

He stared at the message for a moment, his finger hovering over the send button. After taking a deep breath, he sent it off, staring at the screen as the message popped into their conversation, awaiting reply. For a moment, he felt relieved. At least, until her reply came through.

You're funny. You're the one with confidence issues. If it weren't for me showing you how to loosen up a little, you probably never would've gotten that interview.

It took every ounce of his restraint to resist messaging her back. Instead, he felt the anger boil up and topple over. He stomped back off to his bedroom again, violently slamming the door behind him and letting himself fall back onto the bed. In the brief moment of silence, the only thing he could hear was his own ragged breathing and rapid heartbeat. Suddenly, his wrist buzzed. He looked, expecting to see another complaint from Odessa, but instead reading a message from Ms. Iris.

Are you going to make a habit of this?

He realized the time, and rather than feeling panicked like he normally would have, he felt numb. He was incredibly late for work, but there was no way he was going to be able to compose himself enough for it today.

Family emergency. Sorry I didn't text first. Need to take care of personal things. Can I take a few days?

You've got until Friday morning. Hope everything is OK.

Thank you.

He opened his bedroom door slowly, looking over at Lolli.

"How am I supposed to do this?" he asked.

He wanted to call Xavier, but he didn't want to explain how any of this happened. The fact that she was a gift from Xavier and Vanessa would only make things worse. Just as he had decided it would be best to deal with things on his own, his watch chimed. It was as if his friends could tell he needed them.

How are you doing? Vanessa texted.

Good. Why? Don't worry about me—enjoy your honeymoon! He read over his text a few times, wondering if the exclamation mark was overkill, but he really didn't want his friends worrying about him.

You seemed a bit off when we video chatted the other day. Xavier noticed it too. Figured I'd check in on ya.

I'm good. Thank you, though.

Stop lying.

Really, Tallis insisted.

Tallis, I've known you long enough to tell when you're being a big, fat liar. Like right now. You're easier to read than you think. This only ends when you tell me what's up.

Tallis took a deep breath and let it all out in a big, shaky sigh before typing up his reply.

Lolli's dead.

There was a painful pause as he waited for her response. Before she sent anything, Tallis sent a second message.

It was my fault, Vanessa. I messed up bad.

A minute later, she finally replied, and it was far softer than he expected. He wasn't even sure why he expected anything different of her. *Oh, sweetheart. I'm so sorry. Do you wanna talk about it?*

I don't know. Not really, but I feel like I should.

Whatever you think is best. We're here for you.

He took a moment to compose himself, rubbing at his stinging eyes and clearing his throat. Instead of typing up a full explanation, he used his watch's voice record feature to send his friends the story of how he tried REM and felt like he was losing himself more and more every day. He told them about how everything felt grey and he just wanted the color back. At the end, he recounted his previous night, even though it took him a few tries to get through the recording without breaking down. Through it all, he never mentioned Odessa's role—he took full responsibility.

Giving himself up to tears again, he waited for Vanessa's reply, even though a part of him didn't care anymore what anyone thought—nobody could have hated him as much as he hated himself in that moment.

Eventually, his watch buzzed.

I'm really proud of you.

He read her reply a few times, wondering if the voice recording wasn't clear and perhaps she misheard something.

She clarified with: *That must have been really hard to talk about, and really hard to go through alone. Xavier and I should have realized something was wrong but we just got so wrapped up in the wedding. I'm sorry we weren't there for you. But it sounds like you're turning things around now, and we're going to make sure we're there for you this time.*

His lip began to quiver, and he bit it as he read her message. Suddenly, if even for just a moment, he didn't feel so alone.

Tallis returned to the living room, sitting on the floor in front of the couch again and looking back at Lolli's blanket on the couch behind him, tugging it to the floor. There was a light thud as something hit the ground. He lifted the blanket, spotting Lolli's gnawed-on, lint-covered piece of carrot.

He bit his lips again as they quivered, trying to hold back. He spread the blanket on the floor, smoothing the wrinkles and creases, picking off fuzz and crumbs until it felt worthy.

Looking up to the ceiling as if searching for an escape route, Tallis reached over for Lolli. He delicately scooped her up and set her in the center of her blanket, placing her carrot between her little paws.

He folded the blanket slowly and deliberately, covering and wrapping her like a fragile gift. There was still a scarlet stain on the floor where she once lay. Tallis sat beside the stain, Lolli wrapped in blankets and cradled in his arms.

As bad as he wished he could hold her forever, he knew it wasn't an option. But he wasn't ready to say goodbye yet. He lost track of time, sitting there and holding her, bouncing between self-hatred and self-pity.

"I'm so sorry," Tallis said, his vision blurred with tears as he looked down at the blanket bundle in his arms. With another shaky sigh, he stood and walked out his front door with her.

Nowhere felt as perfect of a resting place for Lolli as the park. Unfortunately, Tallis didn't own a shovel. Living in an apartment never gave him much reason to. He knew his apartment maintenance man lived in a ground-floor apartment within his building, and Tallis had seen him planting shrubs by the entrance in the past, so he knew the man must own a shovel.

Blanket bundle in the crook of his left arm, he stretched his right out to knock on the door labeled with the large white letters MAINTENANCE.

"Submit your workorders online!" a gruff voice called back.

"It's not a workorder," Tallis shouted back.

"Go away!"

"Can I please just borrow a shovel?"

"What the hell don't you understand about 'go away?'"

"Please!" Tallis called. "My pet passed. I'd like to bury her. Please, sir."

Silence. Defeated, Tallis turned to leave, determined to find another way to give her a proper burial. Just as he was about to reach the end of the hall, he heard a door open behind him.

"Here."

He turned, and the man was holding out a shovel.

"Thank you," Tallis said, walking back and taking the shovel in his spare hand.

The man nodded. "Just leave it outside my door when you're done."

"Yes, sir."

Tallis retreated down the hall and out the front door, making his way to the park. He was grateful it was the middle of a workday, and he hadn't really passed anybody on his way there.

After wandering around the park looking for a place that felt right, he stopped at a walkway lined with flowers.

Each bed of flowers was different and beautiful in its own way, and Tallis was having trouble deciding which he felt Lolli would have liked best. Indecisiveness eating him alive, he stopped and set the shovel down, balancing the blanket bundle in the crook of one arm while he raised his watch up. He tapped the screen and held it to his mouth, speaking softly. "What are some different flowers symbolic of?"

His watch chimed before spouting off a few varieties and their meanings. Several flowers down the list, it said, "Daisies are symbolic of innocence."

"Perfect," Tallis whispered, looking down at Lolli. He picked his shovel back up and continued down the flowery path, only stopping when he reached a small patch of daisies.

"How's this?" he softly asked the bundle of blanket. His eyes began to burn, so he cleared his hoarse throat as if it would help.

He set her down beside the bed of daisies and positioned himself to dig. Foot on the top of the blade, he pushed his weight down and heard the earth part.

Tallis dug the flowers up, careful not to damage the shallow roots as he set the flowers aside to dig deeper beneath. When he finally had a deep enough hole, he traded the shovel for Lolli wrapped in her blanket.

"I'm going to do better," he said, looking at the bundle in his hands as he knelt down, setting her in the hole. "I promise."

He took a moment before reaching for the shovel and standing again. With each scoop of dirt, he sniffled and stopped to wipe his eyes and nose, which had turned red and begun to chafe.

At last, he topped the grave with the unharmed flowers,

carefully setting them back into the dirt and patting it level. He stood back. It was definitely obvious someone or something had messed with the dirt, but the average passerby would never question it.

He was about to leave before he realized her grave was lacking a marker. He looked around the park, searching for something sturdy, eventually finding a large, flat rock. Now, he just needed something to write on it with.

Over near the park's playground, a mother sat with her young daughter, a blonde girl in pigtails with a coloring book and markers. The mother was intently watching a second blonde child, who was climbing up the slide and giggling.

"Good morning," Tallis said, approaching the mother and daughter.

The mother narrowed her eyes at Tallis, her gaze flickering toward the shovel in his one hand and large flat rock in the other. Her arm shot across her daughter defensively.

"I'm sorry!" Tallis backed up a couple steps. "I didn't mean to worry you. I just wanted to know if I could borrow one of your daughter's markers for a second."

"Absolutely not!" she nearly snarled.

"I understand. Thank you for your time."

"You can borrow my marker!" the little girl chimed, wiggling her brown marker in the air at him.

Tallis looked at the mother expectantly.

"Put the shovel and rock down," she commanded.

"Yes, ma'am." He set both down.

She took the marker from her daughter, getting up and standing in front of the little girl as she handed it to Tallis.

"Thank you," he said, taking the marker and squatting beside his rock on the ground.

He popped the cap off and wrote out Lolli's name in big, neat print across the top. He sealed the marker back up, stood, and handed it over to the mother.

Her brow furrowing further as she eyed the rock, she took the marker back and continued standing in front of her daughter, waiting for Tallis to leave.

He took the shovel and rock and went back toward Lolli's grave. Fortunately, to him, it was easily recognizable. He took the grave marker and set it in the patch of daisies, standing to look it over for a minute.

"I can't thank you enough for everything you were for me. You were the friend I needed through some hard times, and I'll never forget it," he said, head held low. "I'll never forgive myself for this. I shouldn't. But I'll make sure it wasn't in vain. I'll do better. I'll be better. I'm sorry I couldn't see what I was doing until it was too late. I should have never tried REM. I should've never pursued Odessa, or pushed Xavier away, or forgotten about you when you needed me. You always seemed to see the best in me. You were so innocent and pure and didn't deserve this. No matter what was going on outside the apartment, you were always there, ready to cozy up and watch TV with me. Thank you. I hope, wherever you are, there are all the carrots and apples you could ever want. You deserve it."

Tallis stood for a moment, looking down at the flowers, sniffling loudly and wiping the bottom of his nose with the back of his hand. He kept watching the grave, as if the guilt would wash away, or as if she would miraculously burst from the ground. He missed the weight of her on his shoulder, but it was time to say goodbye.

He turned, taking the shovel and leaving her beneath the daisies.

The next few days, Tallis hardly did more than feed himself. He tried to find escape in watching TV, but he couldn't bring himself to sit in Lolli's spot on the couch. Sitting next to it only reminded him of how alone he was. He missed the way she would nuzzle up against him, nibble on her snacks, and watch her true crime shows.

Until Thursday evening, he hadn't heard from anybody, aside from one message from Xavier reminding him about their lunch together tomorrow. It was enough to make him realize he'd also have to face work again. He knew it was only a matter of time. He wasn't ready to get back to the lifelong monotony, but he had to pay the bills somehow. If nothing else, he figured he may as well just live at his desk—there was nothing for him at home anymore.

While he was brushing his teeth instead of eating dinner, his watch buzzed. He looked down at it. It was Ms. Iris.

Check your email.

He rolled his eyes. She couldn't even wait until he came in Friday morning to send him stuff about work. He finished brushing his teeth and trudged over to his computer, reluctantly logging into his email. At the top of his inbox was an email titled: *Tomorrow*.

"Great," Tallis said with a groan. "She's already sending me a to-do list."

He clicked the email. As the words populated the screen, the first one his eyes locked onto was the word "congratulations."

"What?" he asked aloud, blinking rapidly and leaning forward, squinting.

> *Dear Mr. Tallis,*
>
> *We are pleased to tell you we've selected you as Opulence Incorporated's newest Creative Anchor. Congratulations!*
>
> *Next week is your first official week as a CA, however, tomorrow we need you to fill out some paperwork for HR and begin your orientation. Please bring a copy of your birth certificate and social security card.*
>
> *Once again, congratulations!*
>
> *Sincerely,*
> *Opulence Incorporated Hiring Team*

Tallis read the email over and over again, repeating the word "how" out loud as he processed.

Is this real? he messaged Ms. Iris.

Her reply simply said: *Congratulations, Tallis. Well deserved.*

A few minutes later, he got another message from her: *Guess I've gotta start getting my own coffee, huh?*

From his desk, he turned to face the couch, excited to tell Lolli the good news. As the reality set in that he never could, the beaming smile on his face faded.

Later in the evening, Tallis messaged Vanessa and Xavier to let them know about his promotion. Instead of texting him back, they called him. When he picked up, he was met by Vanessa's squeals and Xavier yelling, "Congrats, bro!" in the background. It was nice to have their support, and for a moment, he felt like he could feed off their joy. As soon as the call ended, his apartment felt like a tomb again.

Tallis had trouble sleeping that night. Ever since the bad vial of REM, he didn't feel at peace in the dark, so he left several lights on throughout the apartment. Unfortunately, that much light didn't permit much sleep.

At one point that night, he got so restless just sitting and staring at the ceiling that he got up and walked to his closet to pick out his outfit for the morning—something he rarely did in the past.

After piecing together a respectable and classy combination of clothes, he still wasn't feeling any sleepier. He went to the kitchen, chopping up an apple as a workday snack, setting it aside. Holding a slice in his hand, he looked over toward Lolli's bowl, feeling a sense of emptiness. He stood in the kitchen, fidgeting with a strand of his hair as he pondered other things he could do to pass the sleepless night.

He went into the bathroom, pulling out his toothbrush, toothpaste, deodorant, hair mousse, and razor, laying it all out on the sink in the order he would use them in the morning. Aggravated, he grumbled and marched back to his bed. He still wasn't truly tired, but he knew he needed the sleep.

After another failed attempt at sleeping in his bed, he wandered out to the living room, falling back onto the couch. He curled up in Lolli's old spot, his eyes focusing on a stray bit of fur stuck to the cushion. A tear rolled down his cheek as he lay there, eventually drifting asleep.

His alarm woke him abruptly and he fell off the couch in a startled flail. It felt like he had only just fallen asleep. He whined, going back to his bedroom to shut the alarm off.

When he went to the bathroom to start getting ready for work, he was reminded of his nighttime antics. He scoffed at his own ridiculousness, looking down at his toothbrush and other toiletries just sitting in a neat line on the sink.

The entire time he got ready for work, he closely monitored the time on his watch, terrified of being late for his first day as a CA. He still had one stop he wanted to make before work.

He slipped into his work outfit—which he had also found the time to iron overnight—and tied his shoes.

On his way out the door, he looked back into the apartment, missing the times he used to say goodbye to Lolli without having to mean forever.

This was the first time Tallis had left his apartment since burying Lolli. The sun tingled his skin with unfamiliar warmth. He looked up, the sky looking a little bluer than he remembered.

He took his time on his way to Bru. Thanks to his sleepless night, he was out the door earlier than expected. When he finally reached the cozy little coffee shop, he was reminded that he was doing it for himself this time. His smile tugged at the corners of his mouth as he pushed the doors open, the familiar sweetness flooding over him.

"Tallis!" a sweet voice chirped from behind the counter as soon as he stepped inside.

"Good morning," he called over with an awkward wave from the back of the short line.

The few people in front of him each ordered their coffees, and he eventually made his way to the front.

"I was wondering if I had scared you off!" Avalyn said. "The Grandma Hug is a big hit! My boss approved it, and it's on the menu now. I've even heard people say they love the name, so congrats on that one!"

"That's fantastic!" Tallis said. "I'm so glad people like your drink. I mean, how could they not? It's amazing."

Her face turned bright red. "Thank you!"

"Can I tell you something?" he asked, checking to make sure no one was waiting in line behind him.

"Sure," she leaned forward, as if it were a big secret.

"I don't have to get my boss's coffee anymore. I got a promotion."

She squealed and clapped for him. "I told you! That was so fast, too!"

He chuckled. "Not really, but that's a whole other thing."

"That's so exciting though. And I'm honored you'd share the good news with me!"

"It just meant a lot to me the other day… the stuff you said. No one has been that nice to me in a while."

Her smile faded. "I'm sorry to hear that."

"It's alright. I just wanted to say thank you."

Her lips stretched into another sweet smile.

"So… what can I get *you?*"

"Hmm…" he pondered aloud. "That 'Grandma Hug' drink sounds awful special. I'll take one of those."

"Absolutely!" She spun on her heels, going straight to the coffee machines and syrups to make his drink.

When she returned, he tapped his watch to pay, thanking her for the drink.

"Good luck with your first day on the new job!" she said.

"Thanks! I'll see you around." He turned to leave, and she called out after him.

"Com'ere," she hollered, motioning to him.

He stepped back to the counter, eyebrow raised.

"Please forgive me if this is a bit forward," she said. "But… could I maybe get your number?"

Tallis couldn't control his grin. He let out a brief nervous laugh. "That's very sweet, but I've got a girlfriend."

"Oh," she said, sinking back. "I'm so sorry!"

"Don't worry about it," he said with a gentle smile and nod, turning to leave again.

As his hand touched the door, he paused, holding it in place. He turned back and walked to the counter yet another time.

"Do you have a pen?" he asked.

She looked confused, but she handed him one from behind the register. He reached for a napkin from a nearby table and scribbled down his number, handing it to her.

"I—" She read it a few times. "I thought you had a girlfriend?"

"I did," he said, pausing for a moment. "Things weren't really working out for us. We only recently broke up, and I guess I said no out of habit or something. Is that weird?"

She smiled softly, shaking her head.

He lifted his hand in a short goodbye wave, walking out the door this time.

Tallis wanted to make good on his promise to Lolli. He was going to do better, and this was the first step. For the first time in a long time, he didn't know what tomorrow would bring.

He took a left toward Buzz's Electrosuite, walking straight past the pink puddle without a glance.

AUTHOR'S NOTE

Thank you so much for taking the time to read my book! *Thieves of Joy* was such an exciting book to write, and I hope you enjoyed reading Tallis's story.

The story idea came to me when I was searching online for cyberpunk computer backgrounds (yes, I'm a nerd). One picture in particular stood out. It showed a city street with little shops, including one that said "Dream Emporium." The longer I looked at it, the more I wanted to dive into the world the artist created. I played with ideas in my mind about what that dream store would sell, and I ended up down a creative rabbit hole. That's where REM came from.

I know chapters 25 and 26 are heavy. If you've read it already, you know the part I'm talking about. Believe me, I tried to think of ways around it. I tried to think of alternatives, but nothing would accomplish the same end result. This isn't a story about adventure or love-- it's a story about a man losing his innocence.

If you've enjoyed this book, please take the time to leave a review online. It helps readers like you find my books, and it helps fight the imposter syndrome.

Thank you again-- readers like you make it worth all the late nights editing.

www.uberguberman.com/review

THE EOS DAWN SERIES

BY JEN GUBERMAN

"Outstanding. The story grabbed my attention right from the very start." - Goodreads

How far would you go for freedom?

EXPLORE THE NEW TERRITORY AT
UBERGUBERMAN.COM

@jengubermanauthor